ALSO BY ALAN S. COWELL

*Killing the Wizards: Wars of Power and Freedom
from Zaire to South Africa*

SCAFELL PIKE, THE HIGHEST MOUNTAIN IN ENGLAND
formerly "The Pikes" or "The Pikes of Scawfell"; "Scafell Pikes" on Ordnance Survey maps

A
WALKING
GUIDE

A NOVEL

Alan S. Cowell

SIMON & SCHUSTER
NEW YORK   LONDON   TORONTO   SYDNEY   SINGAPORE

SIMON & SCHUSTER
Rockefeller Center
1230 Avenue of the Americas
New York, NY 10020

SIMON & SCHUSTER and colophon are registered
trademarks of Simon & Schuster, Inc.

Designed by Kevin Hanek

Five illustrations from *The Southern Fells* by A. Wainwright
(Michael Joseph, 1992). Copyright © 1960, 2000 by Betty Wainwright.
Reproduced by permission of Penguin Books Ltd.

Manufactured in the United States of America

1   3   5   7   9   10   8   6   4   2

Library of Congress Cataloging-in-Publication Data
Cowell, Alan.
A walking guide : a novel / Alan S. Cowell.
p.   cm.
1. Amyotrophic lateral sclerosis—Patients—Fiction.
2. Triangles (Interpersonal relations)—Fiction. 3. War correspondents—Fiction.
4. Mountaineering—Fiction. 5. Mountaineers—Fiction. 6. England—Fiction. I. Title.
PR6103.O97W355 2003
813'.6—dc21   2003040098
ISBN 0-7432-4470-2

Acknowledgments

Thanks are best if kept brief and heartfelt—even at the risk of failing to give all credit where it is due. So here goes.

Two British neurologists, Nigel Leigh and Lionel Ginsberg, helped in a way that can't be quantified—unless miracles can be weighed and measured. Professor Leigh provided a diagnosis that changed my life, enabling me to contemplate writing a novel, and took time to read parts of the manuscript concerning his specialized field. Dr. Ginsberg and the wonderful staff of the King Edward Ward of the Royal Free Hospital in London kept me going and keep me going. I also turned to Dr Ginsberg's "Lecture Notes on Neurology" for guidance. Any errors are mine.

To Neil Dowie of the Keswick Mountain Rescue Team I offer apologies for bending his standard operating procedures to the requirements of fiction. I hope, though, that I have preserved the spirit of the remarkable, life-saving work performed by the Keswick team and others like it.

Thanks—again—are due to my indefatigably optimistic agent Michael Carlisle and his colleagues at Carlisle & Co., particularly Kathy Green. And at Simon & Schuster, Michael Korda did me the great honor of guiding this book as Gabriel Weiss oversaw its emergence into its final form.

I wrote this book while on assignment as a foreign correspondent for *The New York Times* in London, and I drew on reporting in the field for much of the backdrop to the story. I would need to thank so many people at *The New York Times* to make a comprehensive list of those who, over the years, have sent me to work in exciting places. So I'll confine myself here to offering my thanks to the publisher, Arthur O. Sulzberger, Jr., and to the editors past and present who offered support and understanding.

Above all, I want to thank my family—my wife, Susan Cullinan, for her inspiration and companionship, and daughters Sarah, Rebecca and Amanda for putting up with a double dose of absenteeism on my part as a news correspondent and would-be novelist. At least, though, we managed now and then to set foot together on the Lake District hills, and for that I am forever grateful.

For all my girls

A WALKING GUIDE

Prologue

...Summit close. Feel it, sense it. Fall didn't help. Slipped on boulders and my leg hurts. Bad leg, of course ...

... Sitting, see ice form on rocks. September, for Chrissakes. Know it's there, the summit—only have to get up and push on and I'll get there. Started from Camp Two—haa haa—at first light. Weather awful. Big wind coming up over the col. Horizontal sleet. Barely drag myself out of the sleeping bag. But soldier on. Right? What we do. Soldier on, take it on the chin. So out of the tent. Compass bearing from the map. Tricky, because I wasn't sure I'd camped in the right place. Weather indescribable. Freak storm. If I hadn't fallen, it would have knocked me over. But I fell. I did. Just when I needed my leg to work, it didn't. And it's cold.

... No one else around. But I wanted it that way. Solo bid. Dawn start. Summit alone. And there won't be anyone else around. Not up here. Not in weather like this. Color note: gray rock, encrusted with ice like salt deposits. No. Like crystals. Visibility zero. The cloud has descended like a blanket. No, scrub that. The cloud has fallen here and come to rest, wrapping my world in its frigid grayness. Even worse.

... in the middle of the boulder field. Ice Fall. Khumbu Glacier. Ice crystals look as if they have been here forever. But I have to move ... get frostbite. Or hypothermia. You slip away in a dream world, feel warm and happy and your eyes start to close. Want to sleep. Should sleep. In the cradle of the angels.

... more scared than I ever was. More scared than Beirut, Sarajevo, Grozny, Gaza ... in the war zones, you could hide in a cellar or a bunker or behind a wall. You could call in on the sat-phone and hear a voice, even if it was a

I

clerk at the comic back in New York. Home base. But there's nowhere to hide up here. No one to talk to. Wind always finds you. And cold.

The woman clicked off the small tape. She emptied its cassette onto the plush, red sofa in the hotel suite he had insisted on reserving before—what had he called it?—his expedition. It fell among the others, five of them annotated in smudged handwriting that had become almost illegible: location, date and time; curios amid the floral upholstery, the mock-antiques. She had spent the night with his tapes. How typical of him to mold their content to the image he wished to project as his testament. And how galling that his confession should sow the seeds of so much pain.

The woman called for coffee as soon as the kitchen staff arrived, introducing hints of life into the still hotel by the lake, like an ocean liner making ready to sail—a muted clatter of pots and pans, a half-heard telephone, doors hissing open and closed, voices kept theatrically low. She uncapped a small, gold-nibbed fountain pen and wrote a single sentence in a black notebook whose cover was held in place by a thong of elastic. She placed it among the tapes, next to a folded, smudged fax message.

Pulling back the heavy, lined drapes, she saw a sky whose rage had gone, cauterized by the same storms as had made the final tapes so indistinct. The locals said the storms were the worst in memory. Was that supposed to turn back the days since he had walked off alone into the mountains? Restore him to her? She mussed her hair in a vanity mirror. The whisky had deepened the dark stains under her eyes.

Outside, the lake mirrored the foothills—indigo water, emerald slopes, sky losing dawn's rose-glow to a hard azure. But there was nothing to stay for, least of all the view.

Chapter One

TORVER, ENGLAND. SEPTEMBER 2000

The night before the expedition Joe Shelby and Eva Kimberly spent the countdown hours in a comfortable hotel converted from a substantial country house—a place of some grandeur, with high-ceilinged, corniced rooms, heavy, chevroned drapes and gas fires built to resemble hearths of live, glowing coals. From afar its whitewashed gables rose in pristine splendor against the somber greens of the lakeside. From within, the tall sash windows offered an oblique view of water and mountain across tiered lawns guarded by pines, partially obscured by the floral curtains of a four-poster bed in hand-carved oak. They found its solid presence and hint of depravity somehow embarrassing, but neither of them said so.

Driving north he had ventured that they should, perhaps, overnight in the small tent he had purchased—with much attention to weight and ease of assembly—to acclimatize for his uncertain, solo pilgrimage to the high ground. But she demurred, saying the only kind of tent that interested her was the large type with polished floorboards and mosquito netting and en suite facilities, as deployed on the more discerning safaris in the African savanna, with retainers to bring shaving water or pink gin, as appropriate to the hour. And, in his condition, she said with what she hoped was a fond smile, the less time he spent in imitation of Mallory and Irvine the better, considering what happened to them.

Over drinks in a bar adorned with horse brasses and small, framed lithographs depicting the peaks and slate-roofed farmhouses of the district, he challenged her, saying maybe—and, mark you, no one to this day could prove otherwise—those two British mountaineers had actually reached their objective, the summit of Mount Everest, before they disappeared back in 1924, so victory had been theirs after all.

Death was quite a price to pay for a mountaintop, she persisted, and that silenced them both until he said, low and rapid and in one angry breath: but it's better than a paralyzed death in a sickbed, stuck with catheters and evacuation tubes and electronic monitors; better to be frozen to death on a mountain than immobilized by the terminal failure of your own body.

In the end of the light, they took a gentle, halting stroll—a limp for him, a slow-motion promenade for her—around the graveled pathways cutting through the grounds, down to the stony shore where a dark, chill wind coaxed shivers from sightless depths. Their breath steamed and not just from recent whisky. Up there, on the high ramparts of granite and fellside rising from the opposite shoreline, the cold would be more intense, and impossible to flee for a hotel lounge or a four-poster bed bathed in the luscious glow of a phony fire.

Later, in the small hours, with a crackle of autumn rain on the windows, cocooned in the four-poster, they reached for one another in the way of people seeking comfort through familiar sequences and levers of arousal. Both were on their best behavior. Behind the drawn curtains, neither wanted fights or ghosts to spoil the farewells. One phantom in particular stalked them both and they thought that, if they did not name her, then she would not appear to haunt them.

Now, under a low, damp sky pebble-dashed with cloud, they stood together at the point where they would part, he for the mountain, she, reluctantly, to wait.

His destination, Scafell Pike, was not, essentially, a big mountain, but it was England's highest—the best, most rugged, least forgiving that the land could offer at a coy 3,210 feet, littered with vertical crags and treacherous boulders and plain hard going. By the route he had devised in hours with maps and guides and memory, it lay two days hence—at his pace—beyond intermediate ranges of hills and passes where he would make camp. Drawn as a straight line, the distance from where he stood to the summit was a mere ten miles. But counting the twists and turns from start to finish, he would, if successful, cover over twenty miles, with 5,650 feet of steep ascents and 4,350 feet of tricky descents (where, as on Everest, accidents often happened) over uniformly unforgiving ground, vulnerable to rapid-fire changes in weather and temperature, where the rocky trails could turn to rivers of water or ribbons of frost. And, once at the summit, he would need to plod down to the valley of Borrowdale when his limbs were at their most fatigued. The descent would take him across the pass at Styhead, where the mountain rescue team kept its stretcher, prepositioned for upsets on the forbidding central massif of the Lake District, the hub from which the valleys radiated like spokes. Quite recently, an older man had gone missing in September and the rescue team had found his body in January on a rugged bluff of rock called Great End, one of the final markers on his own itinerary.

One last time, Joe Shelby went over the checklist—he liked checklists—that tallied his gear: tent, sleeping bag, specialized walking poles, an aluminum bottle filled clandestinely with whisky (water would come from the streams and tarns of his beloved English Lake District, whatever people said about nuclear irradiation from the Sellafield plant or lingering microbes from stricken sheep), GPS satellite navigation aid, ultra-lightweight stove with minimal fuel, dehydrated meals, halogen headlamp, old-fashioned oil-filled compass, laminated maps at 1:25,000 scale cut into manageable sections, spare socks, waterproof gaiters, gloves, toothbrush, bandages and liniment in case of slips or blisters. He balanced carefully on his good, right leg as he reached into the trunk of the car for his rucksack, hefting it with his better, right arm, maneuvering his dead left arm awkwardly. He had parked the car next to a field at a junction where a small road led north with a wooden signpost proclaiming: Walna Scar and Coniston Old Man. Another rusty signboard offering "Horseriding" had come loose from its metal anchorings and swung in the wind.

As he pulled on his waxed Austrian mountain boots, he recalled old army surplus footwear, with leaky uppers and laces prone to snapping—the boots he had worn, once, to assail the same mountains in the time before doubt and affliction when all things were possible and had proven to be so. Ambitions, conceived as he strode these mountains, had been fulfilled. From this small corner of rock and hill, his horizons had stretched to the broad vistas of Africa and the Middle East, Central Asia and the Indian subcontinent—his Great Game. He had served his apprenticeship in his chosen craft as a local reporter covering small courts and inquests and scandals, but had always known that far-flung events would lure him. As a junior reporter, consuming the national newspapers, he coveted the datelines with a fierce hunger—Cape Town and Hong Kong, Dili, Jerusalem; he craved initiation into the mysteries of gunfire at close quarters. On the television news he watched men and women no different from himself standing in front of the cameras, against backdrops of bombed buildings or blazing hospitals, superconfident in their flak jackets. He knew he could handle those places himself if only someone would pay his ticket and publish his articles. And he knew he could humble those familiar TV faces by taking one step

6

further, beyond the point where the satellite dish functioned and into the real maw of battle. When he thought those thoughts, his gut burned and his throat caught and, sensing his hunger, sponsors came forward to subsidize third-class tickets and fourth-class hotels in first-rate hellholes.

As an itinerant freelancer, owning little more than a laptop and a sleeping bag, he hitchhiked and bussed himself across Anatolia and the Levant and southern Africa, accumulating a sheaf of articles about unpleasant events in unsavory places that became his portfolio, established his credentials. Simply by traveling on the cheap he saw things the bigtime reporters did not see in their business class airplanes and chartered trucks. It gave him cachet but did not make him popular with his peers. He did not care: every modest triumph brought the goal of his raw ambition closer. Finally, through the intercession of an old-timer encountered in the Congo, a prestigious American weekly news magazine hired him full-time onto its staff, offering a salary and expenses, and sent him to chronicle gunfire in Gaza, earthquakes in Turkey, war in the Persian Gulf, mayhem in Crossroads and Rwanda and Kabul and Tashkent. He witnessed the pain of people who had come to learn that collateral damage was the military term for the sudden death of children, lovers, husband or wife or parents. He won the titles he craved—foreign correspondent, war correspondent—and the job took him to many places, far from any definition of home: he was an Englishman, writing for American readers from countries that wiser people on either side of the Atlantic would happily avoid. Once, he tallied his score like some men counted their sexual victories—eighty countries, eighty names from the map, but only three that had been visited without the need to write for the weekly magazine, which he referred to privately as the comic. (His sexual scorecard reflected lower numbers than his reputation suggested.) But those journeys now seemed irrelevant—episodes glimpsed through the filter of professional detachment. Here, on the approaches to Scafell Pike, with his limbs weakening, lay his true battle, to be fought on this home turf—the only place on earth where he could gauge whether anything of the teenager in leaky army surplus boots had survived to sustain the man in his fancy, Austrian footwear.

Above the village of Torver, where he made his farewells with Eva Kimberly, the great, gray battlement of Dow Crag rose above a skirt of scree three and one quarter miles to the north—his first objective at 2,555 feet. Beyond that he imagined his route unfolding through mysteriously named landmarks: Camp One at Wrynose Pass, Camp Two at Esk Hause, before the final push to the summit of Scafell Pike. Already, ahead of him, he could imagine the rocky, steep trails and the granite outcrops pulling tendrils of mist to pale smears of lichen; the dark mirror-stillness of the high tarns; the summits, marked by the protrusion of single cairns and the cumulative traces of countless bootprints, an army of spectral memories, some of them his own, from long ago.

✍

Eva Kimberly linked her arm through his bad, left arm, massaging the flaccid muscle that had once grappled Windsurfers, swung rackets, hauled a way up mountains, steered motorcycles along rutted trails. Now, the arm hung true as a plumb line, just as useful to his current intention.

"You don't have to go," she said.

"That's why I'm going."

"Not because it's there?" Even as she smiled, she shivered inside the black sheepskin coat they had bought together during a vacation in Rome. In the store just off the Piazza di Spagna, he joked about her susceptibility to the merest hint of a chill in the air, her phobia of what the Italians called a colpa d'aria, a malignant draught. But, she said, if you were born and raised near the equator as she had been as a native of

Africa, if your days had been framed by the rapid dawns and dusks of Africa, heralded by the pampering of servants with drinks—tea in the morning, sundowners in the evening—then you would, of course, be more sensitive to the rude, northern climate that had molded him.

"You could at least wait until your test results from the neurologist."

"They won't really make a difference. Let's not argue."

"I'm not arguing. All I'm saying is that, for all you know, it could suddenly get worse while you're up there."

"Then I'd better get going before it does get worse."

"Shouldn't I come with you?"

"We talked about that."

"And what about the weather? The forecast isn't great."

"It never is up here."

She disentangled her arm from his and lit a cigarette. The smoke curled blue in the early morning stillness. In his backpack, alongside his maps and miniature tape recorder, he had stashed tobacco and Rizla cigarette-rolling papers, wrapping them carefully in Ziploc plastic to keep his supplies dry. But while he still had the chance to simply flick a cigarette from a pack, without the complications of one-handed rolling, he would do so. Before he could protest his own ability to do so, she lit one for him and handed it to him.

Her curled, rust-red hair nestled on the black, furry collar of the heavy coat, an affirmation of light in the northern gloom. Even now, in September, with the season's changing, the horizons were closing, the hours receding, shrinking into a perpetual gloaming. When the European winter came, the African summer beckoned and, on this chill morning, she felt the pull away from his mountains to her savanna, her beaches, the sour smell of Africa and woodsmoke, the upstairs-downstairs counterpoint of mortar and pestle in the servants' compound and high-altitude tennis balls on the rolled, clay court. Together they called London home, defining it as their apartment overlooking the Bill Brandt lampposts and rolling greenery of Primrose Hill in London. But home, really, was far to the south, in a continent that did not really offer a home to people of her kind anymore. Home for a generation or two, but home for all that, in the sense that home is an anchor, a set of familiar references, a place where the surprises are all expected.

Joe Shelby had once boasted he had no home beyond the fitful, feckless world of the wandering expatriate remote from the burdensome ties of taxes and voters' rolls and fixed coordinates. "I'm their shit-holes man," he said to explain why he seemed to be constantly heading for the airport with his flak jacket in his carry-on bag, his laptop over his shoulder. "I go to the places no one else wants to go."

Only after she burned her own bridges, abandoned her own, true home to follow him, had she discovered that—for all the exotic stamps in his passport—home, in reality, was such an alien place of rock and rain as this. That, she thought, would explain the penchant for shitholes.

"Have you got everything?" Wasn't this what western women traditionally asked? Have you got your sandwiches and thermos, dear, your newspaper and season ticket for the train?—questions just as applicable to sons as husbands, to quaintly forgetful menfolk in general, to relationships, unlike theirs, based on promises and routines.

"Like what?"

"Oh, you know. Loo paper. Matches. Salt. Condoms. Whatever."

"Condoms?"

"Just in case. You might meet somebody."

"Jesus."

"It was supposed to be a joke. Never mind. You're nervous, aren't you?"

"Let's not fight."

"No. Let's not fight."

It was time now to make a start. The route seemed unfamiliar, yet, not too many years back—yesterday in his memories—this had been his stomping ground. The walk to Dow Crag was merely the warm-up, the preliminary to the grapple with unyielding granite on rock-climbing routes pioneered years ago. Eliminate A. Gordon and Craig's. Down-to-earth names for climbs ranked at a middling level of severity that nonetheless brought the fierce joy of conquest and survival. Now, the walk itself was the challenge—the meandering start through the first band of woodland and the old mine workings, then crossing the Walna Scar Road and on to the tiny, dark lake called Goat's Water before the rocky scramble to the foot of the crag. There he would veer sharply left to South Rake—the rock climbers' easy way down—to strive for the summit ridge and the first peak, first of the expedition, first in years, first since his strength had begun to ebb inexplicably a bare six months ago, leaving him with a useless arm and a trailing leg.

Almost overnight, his mobility had been curtailed. Like the Kafka figure who awakes as a carapaced beetle, he had collided with the first tremblings of disability. Running, even jogging, tennis or squash—all that was now denied. Movement required a focused mental effort, hardly the best qualification for the scrapes and close calls that drew him to his job. He needed two hands to shave or clean his teeth. In hotel rooms, he wrote his articles with his bad arm balanced precariously on crossed legs, hunched like Quasimodo. Or he simply wrote one-handed, the worst punishment of all, stemming the flow of thoughts behind a crude barrage of physical inability. He had no idea what had cursed him in this way, still less why he had been selected for malediction or by whom. The ailment was anonymous, capricious, attacking like a guer-rilla fighter with ambushes and concealed mines, armed with the ele-ment of cruel surprise and the advantage of unpredictability. He had no way of knowing when or where the next attack would come, the next worsening. He knew only that it would come and he prayed it would hold off for three more days to allow him a chance for one last triumph, alone in this inhospitable terrain where the seasons played tricks and there were no shortcuts.

The only common ground among the physicians was this: had it been cancer or AIDS or a more familiar condition, there might have been an element of explanation or prediction; but his condition was less charted, moving mysteriously in the secret, hidden places of the nervous system. It could be X, they said, it could be Y. It had not yet fully revealed its symptoms and its cause might never be known. But he had no wish to go gently into the twilight of disability, or into that good night he had seen so often engulfing others in the sprawled indignity of sudden death from cross fire or massacre or battle. He had no wish to become one of those plucky souls in wheelchairs, beyond movement or speech but stubbornly insisting on remaining alive when, really, they had no further use for themselves and had become a burden on everyone else.

In the planning for his expedition, he had studied ordnance survey maps and detailed guides, finding them efficient but inadequate. What he was really looking for was a walking guide that showed a way backward, not forward, to the center of the mystery, to the point of wholeness where past and present were reconciled. Before it was too late, above all, Joe Shelby wanted a haven where all his dreams—fulfilled and unfulfilled—might dock and be tethered as one.

She interrupted the reverie.

"Was it open?" She knew he had asked the priest at the austere, granite church of St. Luke's for a private blessing on the morning of his start. She imagined that an appropriate donation to the church roof fund would have been made.

"The chapel? Yes."

"Then you're squared away with the almighty, at least. It's only three days. And I'll see you at the other end with a big hug and a bottle of champagne."

"You know it's only . . ."

"Please don't say it's only one last trot . . ."

"Around the paddock. But it was your idea, you know."

"I know," she said, reaching into her coat for a handkerchief to dab at the corner of her eye. "It's only the wind."

From a pocket of his shirt he withdrew a small, gift-wrapped package.

"You can open it, if you want."

She eased off the silver paper to reveal a black notebook held closed with a built-in thong of elastic.

"It's supposed to be modeled on the kind Hemingway used. It's Italian. I thought you might like it. Just in case."

"In case? In case what?"

He shrugged and smiled, put his good arm around her for a final, brusque embrace and turned, leaving her to contemplate his offering: was she now to chronicle her thoughts, match them to his? Could he do nothing without the support of words on paper that could enshrine falsehood just as easily as they bore testament?

The track led between gray, drystone walls made of chunks of rock and slate laid painstakingly alongside and on top of one another, without cement, solid structures held together by the artfulness of their construction. The walls themselves encased fields which the sheep of the district had been trained over generations to regard as home, however far they roamed on the mountainside above. Local farmers called this instinct hefting and she understood that people, too, were tethered by invisible forces that drew them back to a geographic point they might stray from but never escape.

He would not turn to wave, but she followed his movements nonetheless, her hands pushed deep into her coat pockets, a cigarette smoldering by her foot where she had dropped it for the final embrace. If she pretended, she could see in him something of what he had been— the slender height of his body, the unkempt shock of straw-colored hair. But the retractable aluminum walking poles, the clumsy swing of his left leg denied all pretense, and her recall of what Joe Shelby had been— what she had been—returned with all its sharp corners and rough edges, without the secret harmony that held the drystone wall in place.

Chapter Two

How do people meet? And what, anyhow, is this notion of "meeting"? At dinner parties, when all else fails, people ask: and where did you two meet? And what kind of answer do they expect? Oh, you know, I just gave him a quick blow job while his wife's back was turned and we sort of took it from there? A conversation stopper indeed. A head turner. An imposer of sudden silence. Of course people did not say that. "Meeting" is a sanitized term, with the deception built in, assumed, not evoked. Of course, they "met" only after the divorce was finalized and the kids had gotten used to the idea and the spoils and friends had been reallocated. Of course, they did not "meet" in separate hotel rooms paid for in cash and with false names in the register. Of course, they "met" and bluebirds sang. Deception, especially, must be camouflaged, for that is its nature, couched in its own traitor's tongue, as if it never took place at all.

On the shoreline at Naivasha, on the lawns of thick, springy kikuyu grass stretching down to the water, Eva Kimberly is standing next to Jeremy Davenport. It is this moment of togetherness—an informal reception line of two, a dynastic couple—that she will come to associate with the question of when people meet, how they meet, how they define their meeting. She is thinking: when did *they* meet, she and Jeremy Davenport? Was it when, as toddlers, they shared a bathtub? Was it when they played tennis and rode gymkhana ponies together because their parents owned neighboring ranches and socialized? Or did they only really "meet" when consummation overtook them in her late teens, when she finally succumbed to Jeremy Davenport's wayward campaign that seemed to have meandered through many preliminary skirmishes before arriving at the citadel of her virginity?

But they have met. They are a couple. Jeremy runs photo safaris for wealthy, usually American clients who delight in his post-Hemingway blend of canvas and champagne, candles and hot showers in the bush. The men love his stories and lore of the savanna. The women love his white hunter looks and tanned calf muscles. Eva has a primary school and preventive medicine clinic in the Rift Valley which she finances by selling Masai and Samburu artifacts along with other Africana in a boutique at the capital's most expensive hotel. One day, clearly, they will marry. They have met and will remain met.

Until this day at Naivasha.

The venue is her father's garden party in the grounds of a lakeside hotel which, every year, he hires in its entirety for the weekend, both to stage the event and to provide accommodation for guests who traveled hundreds, even thousands, of miles in four-wheel-drive cars and private airplanes to attend—and for other guests, and there were always some, who found it simply too trying to make their way home after hours of sunlit libation. Among a certain segment of her society, invitations were coveted, guarded jealously. For this was a tribal rite, a reaffirmation of a certain way of doing things, of being, a throwback—in reality—to an era of luxury and predictability whose memory would not easily be relinquished. People had been known to fly in from London and Cape Town and New York for the event.

From the earliest, golden memories of childhood, Eva Kimberly had never ceased to enjoy the day with its grand buffet and spit-roast of lamb and suckling pig, its champagne and strawberries, its sequences of toasts and speeches. She recalled herself as a young girl, dressed in her newest, prettiest clothes that came still wrapped in packages from London, dodging between the burly adults, the ministers and ranchers and hunters, craning for a glimpse of her parents—always at one another's side, regal and amusing and feted by everyone. And, since the death of her mother in a safari accident, she had become its principal organizer, anxious—for her father's sake as much as her own—to balance any new blood on the guest list against the codes and protocols built up over the decades that had made the event such a high point in the social calendar.

The Kimberlys called the gathering their family birthday, commemorating the day—almost a century earlier—when the first of the Kimberlys, Josiah, stepped from the puffing train at Nairobi and breathed the sweet air of the African uplands. With his commission and credibility newly minted in the campaigns further south, Josiah Kimberly had set out to make his mark, farming and hunting, in the heyday of colonial settlement. Only in the most secret of family conclaves, over very late whiskies and far beyond the hearing of eavesdroppers, was it acknowledged that Josiah Kimberly had been anything less than an officer and gentleman, that his sojourn on the diamond and gold fields "down south" had been marked by anything less than probity. But, whatever those lapses, hinted at but never explained, Josiah Kimberly had founded a dynasty that had both contributed to and survived the land's many torments. The Kimberlys traced their history through the highest councils of colonial administration and through the booms and busts of coffee plantations and safari concessions, beach developments and the shoals of sleeping partnerships with government ministers who turned out to rank among the corrupt of the earth. There had, of course, been the bad apples, the black sheep, the dark horses—Kimberlys cited in the malicious gossip of the pink gin set at the Muthaiga Club, or mentioned in the closed police archive of the Delves Broughton murder case, or ranked among the sybarites of the Happy Valley people, whose Djinn Palace stood on the same shores of this same lake as her father had chosen for his annual celebration. But, overall, the Kimberlys had preserved the impression of aristocracy, a post-colonial elite, the kind of people who bred polo ponies and knew where they stood, with deference, in this remote continent.

An only child, Eva Kimberly was the last scion and the first to know for certain that her tribe's tenure was coming to an end, that the welcome had been overstayed. Her ancestors had frolicked—indifferent, it almost seemed, to any offense they might have given—but her generation had become the dynasty's conscience, the payback. The African families who sent their festering sick to her clinic in the Rift Valley and their shoeless children to her school were her new family. Where the whites and the Kimberlys ended, the Masai and Samburu began—infuriating, needy, proud, ungrateful, the burden previous generations had ignored. The garden party was the last rekindling of the old days, when the banner of a distant crown fluttered over the colony. Settler farmers in pressed safari suits mingled with onetime white hunters and African government ministers, local chiefs and elders of the Masai, Asian traders, expatriate engineers.

Washed up on this shoreline came the rogues and flotsam too, accorded a place at the annual table out of habit and pity, tied to Africa because other parts of the globe made too many demands on their frailties—minor aristocrats whose family jewels had long since been squandered, people with secrets and sins they covered under geography's cloak, far from the place of commission. Others, like her father, Neville, were the stalwarts, the tribal elders who had steered their people from the colonial era into a modus vivendi with a newer order, putting their shoulders to the independence wheel in the belief that skin color alone did not define the right to call Africa home.

. . .

Eva Kimberly is standing with Jeremy Davenport, surveying the motley. She has been in the Rift Valley, among her adopted tribe, and is wearing a floral, shin-length cotton dress, very retro, to hide the bites of many insects on her long, horse-and-tennis-muscled thighs. The bites have come from sleeping in huts that resemble collapsed chocolate cakes covered in gray thatch. Jeremy, as is his wont, is wearing a tailored, light-olive and meticulously pressed safari suit with a short-sleeved jacket, long trousers and brushed, tan suede shoes. He is a caricature, she a leading lady. Anywhere else you would think they were heading for a fancy-dress party or a movie set. But they are not out of place among the crimson Masai robes and polished spears, the turquoise saris of the Asian women and the gaudy yellow and black kangas of the ministers' wives with their towering headdresses. There is even the occasional gray morning suit—as if this were Buckingham Palace.

For the first time, Eva's father has permitted her and Jeremy a share of the guest list—a ritual passing on, a broad hint to them that his longevity can no longer be taken for granted, that, perhaps, he has suddenly realized he is mortal and all this will soon be theirs so they had best make their marital disposals. She has invited a sprinkling of aid workers—young Scandinavians and Germans in sandals who ooze guilt toward one people of one color and quite arbitrary indignation toward people of their own hue, usually, in their case, a painful, raucous pink rather than white or tan. She has chosen, also, some of the people from her business, and some of the younger people she knows in Nairobi among the diplomatic corps. She has invited the most senior of the elders from her Rift Valley projects, but none of the patients or lesser workers, whose eyes would bulge at the sight of this plenty, this munificence, this excess, whose lives would henceforth be corroded with envy and resentment.

Jeremy's choices are the people who arrive late, in open jeeps, already tipsy, parking their bush chariots alongside the more staid ranks of Volvo estates and Land Cruisers and, still, a dusty Rolls Royce or two. He hints that he may have invited another couple he bumped into at a bar at Karen and may have put his foot in it because they are not quite top drawer—a war reporter and his photographette, his moll, fresh in from Rwanda. She is slightly angry only because of the way he mentions the female, the moll, in that dismissive, can't-stand-the-sight-of-her voice men use when they are trying to disguise the hots.

They arrived on rented motorcycles, bandannas around their heads. They wore jeans and bush shirts, and sleeveless vests with multiple pockets, offering no compromise with the dress code of the day— national or tribal. They saw Jeremy and waved, but did not offer themselves for introduction to Eva Kimberly. Jeremy Davenport had depicted them as a couple, but she could see the definition was loose, as in those relationships where the bonding has worn away, like an old building that has seen too many bad times and can barely weather another storm. Joe Shelby and Faria Duclos arrived together, but did not speak to one another. When they entered the great crowd around the barbecue pits and the long trestle tables groaning with vats of Pimms and tubs of ice-cold Tusker beer, they did not reach for one another the way some couples do in a new and strange environment, turning to one another to get their bearings, set their social compass. They had no plan in common. They had no need of each other's comfort. And if she could see that, so, too, could Jeremy Davenport. Was this, she often asked herself later, the point at which they "met," she and Joe Shelby?

Of the two new arrivals, Faria Duclos turned most heads—an impossibly skinny, hollow-cheeked woman with wild, jet-black hair, who looked like an icon of the sixties and the Rolling Stones. She carried a worn

Leica camera in a scuffed leather pouch on her belt, and seemed indifferent to most things beyond the images she saw in the range finder. Joe Shelby was the more gregarious, athletic and lithe, carrying with him a roguish scent of danger that drew men and women alike into the orbit he spun around his anecdotes and war stories. Watching them circulate—he talking, laughing, making people laugh with him, she photographing people who had not requested that intimacy—Eva Kimberly thought of classroom physics where she had learned the explosive impact of particles fired into fissionable material.

"Who on earth invited the circus?" Eva Kimberly murmured to Jeremy Davenport.

"Guilty as charged," he said. "Trying to get them interested in a wildlife conservation story."

"Who? Captain Wilderness or Mata Hari?"

Among the Naivasha set, nobody volunteered a liking for reporters with their intrusiveness, their questions, their penchant for articles comparing the white tribe in its most recent incarnation to the decadents of a bygone generation who thrived on cocaine and promiscuity. Journalists were busybodies, trouble causers, outsiders who failed to understand the delicate balances of white life in Africa, the ties that bound farm owners to their staff, their servants, the almost feudal innocence of this mutual dependence. Journalists saw the world in stark, literally black-and-white terms of master and slave, exploiter and exploited. They snuffled for secrets like truffle dogs. And, my God, the White Highlands of Kenya had plenty of secrets, though none that should ever be permitted to surface in the overseas press, in the scandal sheets of London and New York.

For all that, the strangers could never be completely repulsed or ignored. The tribe craved news from beyond the perimeter fence, and the arrival of Joe Shelby and Faria Duclos stirred the curiosity and whetted the appetite for word of what went on, beyond the bougainvillea hedges and the gymkhanas and the scuttlebutt. Over the alfresco lunch around the barbecue, women clustered to Joe Shelby, deploying well-practiced arts of flattery with their inquiries about Rwanda—what he had seen, what he had felt, among the massacred, the wounded, the soldiers with uneasy fingers on bloodstained machetes, cocked rifles. Playing the expected part, he responded with tales of horror that confirmed Africa's natural order of savagery and induced luxurious shudders of relief: it had not been here, at least, it had not been among their people that the murderous blades had reaped their grim harvest.

None of them took umbrage, either, at the photographer who moved among them, taking celluloid imprints of their souls, as if this confirmed their importance, dusted their ritual with the glitter of celebrity. And Joe Shelby told a good story, with skilled ease, heightening the hazards while deprecating his own part in their chronicling. Had he been afraid? "I laugh in the face of danger." It was a remark he attributed to an American colleague, but the inference was that he, too, rejected fear.

He was, they all said later, a true war correspondent, an adventurer, "the real thing." Yet, with an accent that fell somewhere in the mid-Atlantic, with cadences of southern Africa and middle England, over-laid with Americanisms, who would have guessed then that home was somewhere at the end of a rocky track in Cumbria?

The African light seemed to pick out every spiky leaf on the acacia trees by the lake. Eva Kimberly remembered the pod of gray-pink hippopotami with their barking chorus carrying easily across the lake, the marabou storks that circled the gathering like vultures awaiting their turn at the kill, the kites that hovered above, utterly still, and the mocking, hardy-har call of the ungainly, comedy-act birds called hornbills. She remembered the unblemished azure skies and she remembered her resentment at the outsiders' intrusion, her flush of annoyance that they would take her to be some kind of colonial stereotype. Standing alongside Jeremy under the scarlet blooms and deep shade of a flame tree, in a broad-brimmed straw hat and her long, Edwardian dress, nibbling a Pimms, she must have resembled a player on the set of *White Mischief,* as if she were just one more Kenyan popsy, an ornamental lotus-eater. And that was certainly not the case, as she had quickly pointed out when Jeremy Davenport introduced them. Meeting Joe Shelby's vaguely impudent stare, she listed her achievements—her fund-raising boutique in one of Nairobi's five-star watering holes, her work in preventive medicine and vocational training—almost as if she were presenting her C.V. to a prospective employer.

There had been an altercation, somewhere in the throng, near the drinks marquee, an indistinct confrontation apparently involving Faria Duclos and one of the Masai elders.

"Better sort it out," Jeremy Davenport said, glancing at Joe Shelby with one eyebrow raised—a staged, quizzical look that she knew well. "I invited her, after all."

"Faria can look after herself," Joe Shelby said, taking another pull on a bottle of cold Tusker beer. How odd it seemed to her later that Jeremy Davenport had been the one to introduce her to him, and to abandon her like this, in the shade of a flame tree.

"You seem very sure of her," she said and, to her surprise, he laughed with the merest edge of bitterness.

"The one thing about Faria is that you can never be sure of her. As soon as you think you can, she does something to make sure you aren't. We go way back."

"And you? Can she be sure of you?"

"She never asked."

The altercation with the Masai elder, it seemed, erupted after the French photographer woman had made some remark about what, if anything, the old man wore beneath his red robe. Or was the mystery as closely held as the Scots with their kilts? The question had, apparently, been put with some humor. The elder had taken umbrage. The woman had tried to take his photograph and he had raised his carved stick toward her. Jeremy Davenport intervened, stepping between them, speaking to the elder in his own language, in the respectful cadences due a senior representative of his people. He returned with the spindle-thin Frenchwoman giggling and hanging on his arm. "'E save me from the savages," she said, bursting into laughter. Her eyes, Eva Kimberly noticed, were bloodshot, as were Joe Shelby's and she assumed they had sampled the local marijuana that was sold quite openly—ready-rolled into cigarettes—in the Nairobi marketplace. Why else would she laugh so much? What was so hilarious about upsetting a respected elder, a man of wisdom and dignity? Joe Shelby said nothing. Jeremy Davenport shifted uncomfortably.

"Oops. Sorree," the woman said, exaggerating her heavy French accent to fill the awkward silence, hamming it up as if she enjoyed Eva Kimberly's embarrassment. "I make a fuck-up. Non?"

Yes was the answer to that. Yes, she made a fuck-up. She made a fuck-up at the Kimberly annual gathering and she continued making fuck-ups wherever she went. She arrived at the Muthaiga Club and smoked marijuana, quite openly, on the terrace. She photographed the presidential guard with its rifles and reflective shades, and was duly arrested, forcing the French ambassador to intervene for her release in what the French newspapers called a diplomatic incident. She leaped from her car in the Nairobi game park and approached a pride of lion on foot, against all the rules, beating a retreat only when a young male lion began padding toward her.

"She's crazy," Joe Shelby said at Naivasha. "In fact, she's even crazier than usual."

"I rather think," said Eva Kimberly, "that there's a method to her madness, and it's directed at you."

As the party wound down, well into the darkness, and the guests departed with a handshake and a congratulatory nod to Eva Kimberly and her father, Joe Shelby said he would quite like to interview her and Jeremy Davenport said: well, that's a new word for it. Jeremy Davenport said he was hoping to persuade the French photographer woman to do a feature on his safari business for worldwide syndication. But, still, you could not yet say that Eva Kimberly and Joe Shelby had met in that sense of the word.

❧

The intrusion of the two journalists might simply have become a memory, a fleeting, comic interlude that Eva Kimberly would recall with wry amusement once time had softened her irritation.

She and Jeremy were anyhow due to retreat for a vacation at the Kimberly beach house at Jadini, on the Indian Ocean coast. And, had the two strangers simply left town, then Eva and Jeremy would have returned from the coast to find life reset in familiar rhythms. But, for reasons Eva never quite understood, the journalists' distant, faceless editors ordered that they stay on in Nairobi for a while and the two of them seemed to be on everyone's guest list, a novelty attraction, an amusing diversion from the usual fare of expatriate chitchat and veiled, resentful commentary on the corruption of the presidential elite. She caught glimpses of them at cocktail parties and buffet dinners on the lawns of diplomatic residences. She saw one or the other of them in the Member's Enclosure at the Ngong racetrack. She heard secondhand stories of furious, public rows between them, apparently involving retaliatory accusations of cowardice and insanity. They were, Joe Shelby told her, in a holding pattern, awaiting a possible new assignment further south where yet one more crisis seemed to be brewing. "They'll only want it if it's boom-boom," Joe Shelby said. "The comic likes boom-

boom." She became aware that her encounters with Joe Shelby were not really coincidences: with his lover less and less in evidence, Joe Shelby seemed to be seeking her out. He dropped by her boutique, feigning surprise at meeting her, although her staff told her he had visited several times and asked when she would be available. He cornered her at receptions, monopolizing her conversation. His suggestion of an interview turned out to be no more than a pretext for morning coffee and an invitation to dinner. He barely bothered to open his notebook, still less take notes. Her friends reported that he asked many questions about her, about Jeremy and their relationship. She found the attention unsettling, all the more so when she awoke one morning at Jeremy's home in Karen, on the outskirts of town, to find herself wondering whether Joe Shelby would arrange another casual encounter, and hoping he would. Once, in the early hours, she stopped herself from using his name as she embraced her fiancé's slender, naked flank. She found she was expecting Joe Shelby to cross her path at some stage every day. But she had not been expecting it when Jeremy Davenport sprang the news that he would be away for a couple of days on safari. With Faria Duclos.

"Finally interested the photographer in the safari business," he said, as if volunteering for punishment. "She wants to update her wildlife portfolio."

"Well, that's certainly a new word for it."

~

JADINI, KENYA. SEPTEMBER 1999

The afternoon breeze, stiffening as it blew onshore, clattered among the palms above her chosen place in the coral sand. The beach started where the low wall around the Kimberly mansion ended. Behind her, the house was quiet, its blue shutters closed. Every detail of its dazzling white stucco, its red-tiled roof, was familiar. This was the house her father had built before it became fashionable to maintain a place at the coast, on the very front line between Africa and ocean. This was the place she had spent thirty Christmases and most of her birthdays and New Years. Why go anywhere else? Why follow the trails to Mauritius or the Caribbean or Marbella when you had your own, personal three acres of paradise, with all-year staff and fishermen who came to the door each morning offering a catch still fresh from the ocean; where the wizened, shrunken retainers who now called you madam had once carried you as an infant on their broad, strong backs, wrapped in a kanga cloth. Eva Kimberly had taken her first steps in this house, uttered her first words of Swahili and English. It was as much part of her as she was bound to it.

She sloughed off her faded, favorite kikoyi in stripes of ocher and lemon, and laid it flat on the sand. At her feet, the beach—dazzlingly bright—stretched down deserted to the water. Gone were the days when hordes of German tourists would jog up and down in regimented, aerobic bands: with crime and malpractice corroding her native land, mass tourism was little more than a memory. Even at the family beach house, guards were required around the clock and no one ventured far outside after dark.

Under the wide brim of a straw sun hat, Eva Kimberly narrowed her eyes to peer out towards the reef where the Indian Ocean pounded on the barrier of coral reef in a line of fierce white breakers. At her side, she laid out her minimalist beach equipment—lotion, cigarettes, novel—but she had no incentive to read about the adventures of others when her own life seemed to be spinning, throwing off fantastic sparks. Since Naivasha, it was as if a hidden treasure had been prised open in her imagination—dare she say, in her heart?—just enough to offer glimpses, but no more than that, of alternatives, possibilities.

The two outsiders seemed to have spread themselves around town, invited themselves to lunches and dinners—the toast and talk of Nairobi. Well and good. They would come. They would go. The outsiders always moved on, returned to their safe little worlds, where societies had been trammeled into uniformity, where life straddled the median line, remote from the poles of elation and terror that framed Africa. They would go on, like bees, sucking the nectar of one blossom before abandoning it; or like vultures, watching for the kill then feeding off it. Joe Shelby had told her he lived in Rome and was about to move to London. She tried to imagine what that might be like, how it might be to drive home without scanning the rearview mirror for assailants, without the sentries at the gate and the Rottweilers loose among the frangipani. On vacations in Europe or the United States, she was sometimes struck by the pointless bustle, the breathless pace, the quickened, strident voices. Just standing in the maelstrom of JFK or Heathrow, you saw people with more value in the shoes on their feet or the coats on their backs than her people in the Rift Valley might earn in a year or a lifetime. But, once she had overcome her reservations, once she had unpacked her bags in a hotel room or apartment, she secretly relished the idea of not sleeping behind the locked steel of a rape-cage, of living without a handgun in the bedside drawer, far from the Sisyphean struggle against corruption, theft, indifference—the elements that composed Africa's great, fatalistic chronicles of threadbare survival. She encountered them in miniature at her school and clinic. But how could outsiders ever understand the despair when the antibiotics were stolen, when the nurse had no transport to attend the sick, when the officials wanted their cut before approving the importation of the most basic medicines? How could she explain that it came as no real surprise when one of her ambulances was ambushed by marauding Turkana tribesmen? Or that the funerals for those killed in the ambush might themselves become arenas of retribution? In western, modern lands, gratification seemed to come instantly, without the arduous negotiation that accompanied the smallest transaction among her people. Yet, how rarely would a life in London or New York be illuminated by the brilliant smile of a child rising in health after a bout of malaria, or of a mother's survival after a difficult birth, or the capricious appearance of a man with a spear, come to offer some modest gift for a brother's cure? But how much of your soul did you need to invest for those rare, sparkling moments?

A bright orange and red sail had appeared, scudding just inside the reef where the gusting, strengthening afternoon breeze almost lifted a Windsurfer and its rider from the water. Its presence was unusual: few outsiders visited these days; even fewer chose to besport themselves in hazardous pastimes that might result in injury and a visit to a hospital overwhelmed by the ravages of AIDS. The board rose onto its tail, churning the stiller waters inside the reef into a slender, white wake. It was dangerous sailing. The lagoon was mined with jagged coral heads, just below the surface, and a fall could easily lead to severe laceration. Whoever was on the board seemed to possess some expertise, for, as the wind strengthened, the rider stepped back onto its very tail, pulling the sail tight onto the boom so that the whole rig seemed to be barely in contact with the water. Above her head, she heard the palms rattle as the wind gusted and the Windsurfer, now almost directly ahead of her, turned downwind. She knew the rider would be girding to take the full brunt of the onshore wind in anticipation of downwind acceleration, tipping the board to slice across the water in a fine arc of ever-gathering speed, directly towards her place on the beach.

"I'm glad it's you. I'd hate to make an entrance like that again. The coral's vicious."

"I thought you laughed . . ."

"In the face of danger?"

From a waterproof yachting bag lashed to the foot of the Windsurfer's mast, he withdrew a dewy half-bottle of Moët and Chandon, wrapped in a cooling sleeve, and a single, red rose that had become crumpled on its ride at sea.

❧

He was out of sight now, beyond the Torver woods. Six months earlier, just before his condition revealed itself, they had strolled on the Lake District's many shores: for Naivasha read Derwentwater, for Mombasa read Coniston. Looking up at the distant fells, he had recited summit names from memory—Skiddaw and Blencathra, Wetherlam and Swirl How, Great End and Scafell Pike. He had pointed at slabs of granite and labeled the routes traced by climbers' ropes with their old-fashioned grades: difficult or severe, very severe or extreme.

"One day I'll climb these hills right to the top again."

"I dare you," she said then, and wished now she had not.

DOW CRAG
from Coniston Old Man

Chapter Three

Swear to tell the truth, the whole truth, nothing but the truth. These are my notes, my observations, my record. No more than that. No less. My aide-memoire if things go well, my legacy if they don't. Perhaps I'm fooling myself. Perhaps what I should admit about these tapes is that they are my myth, my construction, my lies. But that would not tell the whole story either because I do intend them as a record, as grist to whatever mill I can make of them: my life as a gimp. After a life of turning experience into commercial portions of printed matter, how could it be otherwise? Except that this is personal. This is my testament. Meant for whose ears? Mine, of course. And if anything should happen, then for Eva's of course. And anyone else? She will hear them when all this is over, if she wishes. And what could happen? Disaster, triumph, sudden deterioration, slip, fall, summits. Whatever happens, it will be in slow motion, an underwater ballet.

It's eleven A.M. Day one. Three hours out. GPS coordinates SD 26396 98245. Weather's looking a bit dicey. Dow Crag is just one of those places. Gets

the morning sun. Chills like a freezer later on. Up at the top of the crag, from
where I'm sitting—five hundred feet, four hundred feet up, whatever—there's
cloud just sort of spilling over. Shouldn't be a problem. Famous last words. OK.
So I made one choice. Now another. I can go right, up over the shoulder and onto
the ridge. Grass most of the way. Or there's South Rake, to the left, just beyond
Great Gully. Climbers' easy way down, South Rake. Used to run down that one,
too. Now I've got to get up it. That'll bring me up onto the summit ridge. So go
for it. Prove you can do it. Next stop Dow Crag, 2,555 feet. And going with some
alacrity for the summit. Work that one out, dear listener.

The binoculars scanned the summit with cloud spilling over and
roamed down over the great, gray buttresses. She had followed his route
after he left, breaking free of the woodlands to reach the upper fells,
beyond the farm houses and narrow mine cottages, trailing him with the
thought that he might need her help to advance or retreat. Through the
powerful glasses, at the base of the crag, she picked out Joe Shelby. He
had shed his fleece and parka, tying them under the top flap of his black
and red rucksack. She knew he would be perspiring through his tee shirt
and woolen overshirt, because his illness did that—made him sweat
with all the extra effort of moving limbs that could no longer propel
themselves in the way they had been designed by the deity he had con-
veniently adopted as his own. Go right, she murmured. Take the easy
option. But, throughout this initial part of his journey, he had not taken
any of the easier choices.

She was not surprised to see him lever himself upright on his aluminum poles, swaying slightly as he sought his balance against the coun-
terweight of his pack.

She was not surprised to see him begin moving to the left, a dwarf
figure under the lowering walls and slabs and gullies of the east face.
Despite the magnification of the glasses, she saw the crag as only a
broad, incoherent mass of deep fissures and precipices, chasms and

blank faces. The summit ridge looked like the gable of a home, not really a mountain—not in the way you would look at the twin spires of Mount Kenya, or the soaring symmetry of Kilimanjaro and say: now that's what I call a mountain. But a tutored eye, a climber's eye, would have deconstructed the crag into its components—broken ground and true rock face, gullies and rakes, routes that took lines of resistance measured in varying degrees of difficulty. In miniature, perhaps, an expert would have said, but certainly, this qualified as a mountain.

When Joe Shelby first climbed here, the most tasking of climbs bore the label "hard very severe," a qualification of "very severe" that followed on from the lesser gradings—mild very severe, hard severe, severe, mild severe, very difficult, difficult, moderate—a descending scale of potential terror. Nothing was categorized as easy, although, of course, to the practiced climber, the lesser gradings were preliminaries, warm-ups, nursery slopes. Only against the climbs graded very severe and hard very severe, in Joe Shelby's day, did the climbers begin to take their true measure, weighing their worth against the technical and physical difficulties of gradient and paucity of holds, strenuousness and smoothness of rock, and, worst of all, exposure to the chasm of emptiness below, the drop that increased with every upward move, every dance across the chessboard of finger grips and cracks and protrusions that formed the inner logic of a climb. The slender holds and smooth planes of the rock, the crevices and excrescences were physical, quantifiable challenges to be countered with acquired skill and brute strength. But the exposure was a different matter, psychological warfare. No matter how artfully the climbers arranged their running belays—their protection—threading the rope that led to a second climber anchored on a tiny ledge below through carabiners and slings, the emptiness below their heels never let them forget the stakes, the finality of a slip, an error. Then, like the turning point of a great, heroic story, the moment came where the climber was "committed," making a move that could not be reversed. Beyond that single step into the unknown, there were no further options. She assumed, now, that he was committed, that he had taken a step he could not reverse, just as his condition seemed to have carried him from a world where everything was possible to one where the possibilities narrowed, progressively, implacably. If he needed a guide, it was through this new, nether world, not through the crags or the mountains, and she doubted her abilities as Beatrice to his Dante.

Joe Shelby moved in the direction she did not wish him to take, stumbling across boulders that would not have troubled a child. Damn him. Damn.

She returned to the car, lighting up a cigarette as she switched on the engine to build up warmth. He had left her with the road map and scribbled instructions of the route she was to take toward the valley where they would be reunited in three days' time: Ambleside, Grasmere, Keswick, Borrowdale. Suite booked in both our names, he had said: no subterfuges, no false names or noses. He had meant it as a joke, as if to imply their relationship still contained a seed of tremulous clandestinity when, in fact, the formula was set in habit and familiarity—he departing, she remaining. No matter how he depicted it, insisted that both had their freedom of movement, she, invariably, was the one who stayed behind. Naturally, she had her business—an electronic extension of her work in Kenya that required an investment of time and money in projecting her offerings into the unfamiliar markets of cyberspace. Since arriving in London with Joe Shelby—was it really less than a year ago?—she had learned to deal with software engineers and venture capitalists and bankers. She had learned well and successfully. Everybody said so. Her Web site was among the premier attractions in the business of buying African art and artifacts through the Internet. She had been interviewed and photographed, not just for the African editions like *Style* and

Cosmo, but also in *Forbes* and *Business Week:* "Survival on the Web: Putting Africa Online," one headline enthused. The photographs showed both aspects of her running her operation: clad in jeans and khaki in the Rift Valley, among the patients at the clinic—looking, the writer of the article said, like a redheaded Princess Diana—and in London, in business attire, posed in front of a computerized catalog of her wares. If this was success, then she had achieved it, far beyond her ambitions when she had first ventured among the Masai as a teenager, feeling that history obliged her to offer something in return for the Kimberly family's bounty—its estates and paddocks, its homestead and airstrip and the herds of long-horned cattle that were Africa's equivalent of a blue-chip portfolio. She had, one magazine writer gushed, fused technology and compassion.

Her site provided eclectic links to game-watching cameras and itemized catalogs, an archive of newspaper clippings and the chronology of primary health care projects in Kenya. You could use it to send messages or get the news headlines from Zanzibar or Zimbabwe. You could order antique masks or malachite eggs. You could even download the chants of Zulu mine workers or the thrilling rhythms of Kinshasa's virally challenged nightclubs. Its revenues, coupled with those of her boutique in Nairobi, provided a steady flow of income both to sustain her financial independence and enable her to expand the business so that her projects might prosper. But, essentially, it was an operation that did not move, conducted—to cut down on overhead—from their shared apartment, where one room, used by previous owners as a nursery, had been converted into the current headquarters of @Africa: home was where the order books were.

Eva Kimberly learned the obfuscations of business with relative ease: she would tell investors that software and ISP solutions were outsourced, rather than say she left the technical side to a bright, young Ethiopian asylum-seeker in a basement in Camden. She said her receivables were positive going forward when what she meant was: we're making more than enough to get by. From Kenya to South Africa and Zimbabwe and Mozambique she created a network of women making or buying every kind of artifact—arm bracelets and exotic kikoyis, vrai-naif paintings and wrist blades and carved masks. That was product. Her accountants told her that her net was in good shape and pre-tax looked sound, but, in the current tech climate, she shouldn't risk an IPO. That was all so much camouflage for the fact that she was making money for all of them, so why rock the boat? To her male business partners— depending on the level of privacy at which they offered their assessments—she was dynamic, smart, sexy, gorgeous, highly fuckable, pushy, arrogant. But she wondered how she ever became so entwined in matters that meant far less to her than the smell of burned goat's fat and eating from the communal pot around a fire and feeling that, for all her family's history, one small corner of the continent could make use of her talents to make things a little better.

Indeed, looking at balance sheets and business model projections, she no longer knew whether she enhanced the continent, or patronized it, exploited it as her forebears had done—only the nature of the magic had changed, from Bibles to laptops.

JADINI, KENYA. SEPTEMBER 1999

He pulled the Windsurfer into the shelter of the palm trees. From the reef, he had been looking for distinctive blue shutters and the white stucco of a gabled Cape Dutch facade—the landmarks of the Kimberly place, they had told him at his hotel. It had been farther south than he had been led to believe and the hired board was a clunky old thing with a big, flapping sail that had lost half its battens and wasn't really nimble enough to be out on the waves crashing over the coral. Scudding along the inner rim of the reef, though, locked into the waist harness and propelled by a blessedly steady, onshore wind, Joe Shelby was jubilant, as if the wind and the sun were finally chasing away the recurrent dreams and memories of burned villages, spread-eagled corpses. If that was the heaviest, least affordable price of his job, then this was the reward, the upside. "The last of the adolescent professions," an old friend still liked to call this illogical mix of elation and horror, of freedom from and enslavement to events in other people's lives. Today, his satellite phone was switched off, locked in a hotel safe, and he was free.

There are moments in everyone's life when actions become decisive, when choices are made that change the whole course of existence. Some, he had made long ago. While school friends headed for the management trainee appointments at Unilever or Shell or General Motors or IBM, he had taken his notebooks and secret writings to the newsroom of the local newspaper and followed the trail from there.

Meeting Faria Duclos in Gaza long before they ventured together into Rwanda, Joe Shelby had cast his fate in stone: he would be not just the shitholes man, but the fireman, the knight who rode into the thickest of battles and emerged with his damsel. It had been his choice, and she had reinforced it. Every single marker of their life together, every single turning point they had reached together had been set in places where most other outsiders did not go—in Kosovo, or Bosnia, Freetown or Ramallah. Now, another choice was speeding and bucking toward him as the rental board bore him along the reef on a spume of spray that caught the tropical sunlight and turned it into a thousand bright, refractive spangles. Eva Kimberly was light where Faria Duclos was dark. Eva Kimberly seemed the essence of sanity regained, her being defined in the sharpest of ways: a white in Africa, her identity thrown into relief by its chromatic environment, a woman conscious of place and time and responsibility, a reprieve from the craziness that had overtaken him and Faria Duclos on their final odyssey.

He was, he thought with some jubilation, windsurfing across the Rubicon.

TAPE ONE, SEGMENT TWO
SEPTEMBER 14, 2000, 11:45 A.M.
MONITORED SEPTEMBER 17

Fell. Just seemed to lose balance. Not far. Maybe twenty, thirty feet, slipping and sliding down the South Rake. Tore my gaiters on something or other. Sharp rock probably. One hand, left hand, useless thing, bleeding slightly. Otherwise no damage to report, Captain Norton. I just slipped because, stepping up with my right leg, my left leg couldn't take the strain. On the South Rake, for sweet Jesus' sake. So it caved in, bent, and I stuck my pole out to balance and missed what I was prodding at. Stuck the pole out into thin air, and that was it. Arse over tit. On the easy way down. Easy as gravity can make it. But no substantive harm other than to the ego and that's taken some incoming in the past six months. Like at the outdoor shop near The Strand. I went because I knew the name from way back when it was a climber's shop up north where you bought crampons and pitons, rock boots, carabiners, rope, helmets. Now it's all snowboarding and win-ter wonderland stuff. But they still had some mountain gear so I went in all the big high-roller with my corporate Amex gold card and my list after Eva threw down the gauntlet. Quite excited really, though I'm not sure what the attraction was. Making the list. Selecting the gear. Poring over the catalogs. How much does this tent weigh, or that one? Down or synthetic in the sleeping bag? Fabric or leather boots? Enough stuff on the list to take on the Mother Goddess herself. Self-inflating mattress, stove, water bottle, fleece and waterproof. And the boots of course, had to be top-of-the-range Austrian things. And what else? The GPS, with coordinates downloaded from the web. Things sure have changed since you had a little brass Boy Scout's compass and the ordnance survey one-inch-to-the-mile. Didn't tell them where I was going, of course. Didn't want to say: I'm buy-

ing all this stuff to go up the Lakes. Just kind of dropped hints about Kilimanjaro and Mount Kenya and the Mountains of the Moon. But it was the boots that got me, now I remember. I was choosing the boots. I was worried about weight and took a fabric boot in one hand and a leather boot in the other. In the left hand. Sitting down there, in the basement, surrounded by all this macho stuff—rucksacks and high mountain boots, slings, crabs. I'm weighing them like the scales of justice and I can see the shop assistant rolling his eyes: why doesn't he just buy the most expensive ones and fuck off? And there's something wrong. The leather boot in my left hand seems much too heavy. So I switch them around and now it's the lightweight fabric boot in my left hand that seems too heavy and I realize that when I hold them both out, my left arm starts to unbend and there's this weird quivering in the biceps. The big, left-handed biceps, big from rock climbing and windsurfing and working out. Under my shirtsleeve I can feel it dance and I put the boots down quick and say I'll take the leather ones and all the other stuff I've picked out, the tent and sleeping bag and rucksack and socks and gloves and walking poles. Like Boot of the Beast heading for Africa. In Scoop. Evelyn Waugh and all that. With the collapsible boat and the cleft hockey sticks. Except mine is all hi-tech fabrics and designer names. But it's my arm that's bothering me. When I come to sign the Amex bill it's there again. And it doesn't go away. Quiver quiver quiver. Like I've got little demons under my skin pulling at the muscle tissue, out of control. I remember I go to the Harley Street doctor the comic pays for and he takes one look and scratches his head but he doesn't fool me. I can see he's thinking: oh shit, I hope that's not what it looks like. But he keeps up the facade in his—what does he call them—his rooms. Not clinic, or practice, or surgery. His rooms. Having rooms puts about fifty quid onto the bill. "I'm going to call a colleague, in the London Clinic, where he has rooms." I see the cash register beginning to spin like a slot machine. "He'll take a look at you and then we'll have a chat." So it's on again to the next lot of rooms and I know it's pricy because there are no lines, no hanging about. You go up in a tiny cage of a lift and into the narrow corridors with discreet nameplates on the doors and there are none of your harridans bellowing about how you can have an appointment next year some time and who do you think you are anyhow to waste my time? And then there's the neurological routine. Spread your fingers. Make a fist. Push me away. Pull me towards you. Mmm. Straighten your leg. Don't let me straighten your leg. And the quickfire phone call Harley Street—style to the places where they have all the fancy machines to peer into the mysteries, intercept the signals along the strings of axons and sheaths of myelin that are constantly wired, constantly trilling with instructions from brain central to the outlying garrisons of the anatomical empire. Or not in some cases. Sending a patient over. EMG. MRI. Tests.

But he doesn't send me back to number one doc. No little note to say: this chap's a malingerer, this chap's making it all up, this chap needs a spoonful of medicine three times a day for ten days and he'll be right as rain. He tells me he's going to have A WORD with another colleague, Nigel Lampton, and see if Nigel can take a look at me when they've done the EMG and the MRI and God knows what else and at least Nigel will be able to rule things out because—now, don't be put off by the name—he's the top MND man in Britain and he'll at least be able to say what it isn't, exclude the worst, so to speak. So you get home and look up on the Internet what the fuck MND is and suddenly you are drowning in words like incurable, progressive, a.k.a. Lou Gehrig's and asymmetric lateral sclerosis, or ALS, which means the progressive removal of your muscular functions—arms, legs, fingers, hands, neck, tongue—until the only ones still working are the ones that move your lungs and they finally slow down so that your lungs fill up or your throat collapses and that's it. It's not clean and swift like a well-aimed bullet. It takes no prisoners. You are constantly in its sights, unable to duck and weave but it saves the coup de grace until the humiliation is unbearably driven home by platoons of Zimmer frames, divisions of complicated wheelchairs with headrests and voice boxes. It chips away, nicks you, but won't show you the exit until you are incapable of motion, your muscles withering and wasting by the second and your mind screaming: release me from this dying body, this mockery of the two-fisted, brass-balled image of myself that I never quite lived up to. I remember, once, before it all started, seeing a guy in a restaurant in Rome whose arms both hung limp at his side, totally immobile. He was beautifully dressed in one of those navy blue suits with a windsor-knotted silk tie and wide cut collar of a cotton shirt. He was groomed to kill, too. Tanned features. Black hair swept back. Like some Florentine prince. But he couldn't move his arms. Not an inch. I watched him surreptitiously and perhaps I was so fascinated because some snide little receptor already knows and is tipping me off: that's where you are going, buddy, so get used to it. And this beautiful woman is feeding him his soup, one spoonful at a time. He sits erect, and haughty, and immobile, being fed like a damaged child, or a very old person who has just forgotten all the lines. And he is peering into the candlelit middle distance of a restaurant with eyes full of a pain that only the intimates know. And, God, I don't want that. And, of course, it may not be that at all. You don't know. I still don't know. But it might be, and your arms or legs may be on the very point of packing up like the guy's in the restaurant, and you've just dropped a grand and some on designer mountain gear and your boss is indelicately suggesting a quick revisit to Grozny or Sarajevo or Gaza and you can't say no to her because you can't admit it, not even to yourself.

Chapter Four

JADINI, KENYA. SEPTEMBER 1999

She invited him to stay for a light, impromptu supper. She said a guest
room was available, unless he wished to windsurf back to his hotel by
celestial navigation. It was a rash, spur-of-the-moment offer that surprised them both. It was a tears-before-bedtime roll of the dice with
stakes she found both terrifying and exhilarating. It was something to
do with Jeremy Davenport in the Serengeti with Faria Duclos and a lot
more to do with her alone in Jadini with Joe Shelby in what military tac-
ticians called hot pursuit, meaning a chase that crosses frontiers, flaunt-
ing the laws of inviolate borders.

He could not decide whether he had inspired the invitation or simply been its recipient by default, an accidental player, collateral to her
breach with Jeremy Davenport. The distinction did not trouble him.
Since their meeting at Naivasha he had wondered how this moment of
opportunity could be brought about, how—or even if—it could be made
to proceed through the preludes and preliminaries to the acknowledgment of equal, mutual need. Now, almost casually, she had offered the

opening maneuver and she must surely have known that he would take her invitation as anything but casual. He was not at ease with the process. Past relationships had always formed magically, by osmosis, without conscious pursuit and calculation. Now he had taken a clear decision: he had placed himself in the traitor's role. He had forfeited the high ground and compromised one long-standing bond by seeking another. He had allowed his fear of Faria Duclos's craziness to lure him to the symmetry and safety he craved from Eva Kimberly.

They ate on a screened verandah where a ceiling fan turned gently over hurricane lamps on white linen. In the mornings, the light would flood in here from the east, and in the evenings, like now, the sky and the ocean blended into degrees of gold and vermilion, framed in the dark calligraphy of the palm trees, stilled with exhaustion after the ceaseless buffeting of the wind. He sensed the deeper interior of the house only from pinpricks of candlelight at strategic corners between low divans and unexplained archways where people in white tunics moved without sound. Servants. Staff. The people who brought avocado in light olive oil and smoked sailfish on bone china platters, poured cold white wine and murmured code to her in Swahili, calling her mama, the honorific that had once been her mother's. Yes, the bwana would stay for dinner, and they should prepare the guest room. Yes, they could retire now once the security team had walked the perimeter, set the alarms, just as she was doing with him.

"Have you known her long?"

"Years, I guess. Met her in Gaza. Been doing stuff together ever since." Not: met her in Gaza when the craziness first started, when she was stretched thin as the lines of cocaine that sustained her.

"Stuff?" A vague sense of amusement, expressed through an exquisitely raised, sun-bleached eyebrow.

"Well, I guess more than stuff."

"But is she all right? I mean, in herself. She seemed . . ."

"Unstable?"

"If you like."

"Crazed, maybe, I shouldn't bad-mouth her. But she's not at her best at the moment."

"And is she to be trusted?"

"With him?"

"With herself. To do herself no harm," Eva Kimberly said, trying to suppress a flush of annoyance.

"Faria has never been able to offer certainty in any regard. Her behavior is generally spontaneous. If she wants something, she usually takes it, without thinking about the consequences." He wanted to be loyal to her memory, as to a companion through dark times who has now gone a separate way. He wanted Eva Kimberly to see his loyalty, and interpret it as trustworthiness for the future, not as a commitment to what was past.

The light of the oil lamps drew out the sun-glow from her skin. She had showered and tied a kikoyi around her waist and draped a translucent, white cotton shirt over a tee-shirt top. Her hair was tied back, still slightly damp. She wore no makeup and her skin seemed the color of sand and biscuit.

"And you don't care?"

"We don't have those kind of hassles anymore."

"How so?"

"It's a long story."

"They're the best ones."

"It's not very edifying, either."

"You mean you don't come out of it very well." She smiled, another invitation to proceed.

45

So, we're in Rwanda.

He begins haltingly, over the remnants of dinner, with the barefoot servants sliding across the tile. Like her, he is wearing a kikoyi and tee shirt, borrowed gear—Jeremy's? She did not say and he did not ask—for he had not thought to pack an overnight bag when he rented the Wind-surfer from the hotel. In this part of Africa, she had told him with a laugh, the men don't wear trousers, and certainly not shorts as in South Africa or the old Rhodesia. So he is relaxed, aware of the freedom this kind of dress imparts, fearful of embarrassing himself with inappropriate shows of enthusiasm or faulty knots.

Rwanda, again. He knows the story is the price. He will pay for one intimacy with another. He will buy her trust by betraying another's secret. It is the natural progression. It is how people meet, securing one bridge ahead by burning another behind them.

But there's a preface.

So. We're in Rwanda because that's what we do. That's the life we have chosen. It is unusual. Plenty of people travel a lot—investment bankers, corporate troubleshooters, members of international agencies, diplomats. But we travel to very unpleasant places. The markers are the datelines. Every significant point in our lives is associated with one of the places where we ply our craft. You asked how we met. Well, we met in Gaza, in a sniper's nest, and we broke up in Rwanda, in a killing field. Those are our bookmarks. We have no home where events unfold in an orderly manner. We are never at home. Some of us have no home to go to. Some of us have destroyed our homes. Or we have people at home who have gotten so used to waiting for a phone call that they don't care anymore whether it will come or not. We have the road where events waylay us, ambush us. And we love it. It is a drug, a narcotic. We inhale it through every part of our being. We cannot resist the siren call of crazy airplane flights and mad cab rides and rentals and hikes and long trajectories whose sole aim is to land us at the point of intersection where history's trail crosses the highway of the present to create the future. This is where we get our fix. We want to hear the thudding rattle of heavy machine-gun fire, the howl of war planes past their target (you do not hear them before the bombs are already released and falling), the banshee wail of multiple rockets We desire collapsed buildings, broken bridges and corpses to describe. We cry out for the sheer joy of danger. We want to peer into the mirror of war and see our own reality reflected back at us, our frailty, our cowardice, the fear that tells you that—indisputably—you are living on a higher plane than all the others. We love war because in these battered, broken places we find our freedom. The only rule is survival. The only fuel is adrenaline. When we return with our notebooks and cameras we are blessed, suffused in this so special knowledge that we entered a world where the carnage and the bloodlust freed us from petty considerations. We are gods because we emerged unscathed, sated from the table of the warriors. And our addiction is a luxury. It is a fix that comes prepacked with gold credit cards and downtime in five-star hotels and seats at the front of the plane and the glory of our bylines and exclusives. We are paid to do this. Name a place we go and we will tell you about affairs that started there, close calls, loves that died, amours that blossomed. And ask what happened afterward and we will say: there is no afterward, only the next fix. The highs blur. Between them is void. As the bosses say: you are only as good as your next story; as the addicts know, you are only as good as your next fix. It is a stupid, incendiary job but we have—we want—no other. In some ways it is the ultimate soaring of the ego, but only in the sense that Icarus soared.

You follow me? I know you understand. I know this talk enthralls and captivates you. I know you are glimpsing possibilities you had not dreamed of. Or am I wrong? Please do not let me be wrong.

So. We are in Rwanda. And, yes, you know, you guessed. We are, well, what is the right word? Lovers? More than that? Less than that? Partners in lust, insanity. We are a number. We are bonded.

In the press corps they called us a number, a couple fused and soldered by serial survival. Joe Shelby and Faria Duclos.

On their odyssey to the interstices between life and death, they took no passengers, no prisoners, they traveled alone. The dynamic duo, a German reporter from *Stern* once called them, with heavy sarcasm. A Fleet Street reporter with a gift for headline phrases suggested "bonkers," because that suggested as much their mental state as their physical relationship. Their competitors feared their arrivals and disappearances because the couple seemed to have developed a knack for locating the most graphic moments of human insanity, divining horror. Had Joe Shelby traveled alone, his less kind colleagues would have accused him of fabrication—not to his face of course—because his reports, more often than not, carried a whiff of smugness, subtly hinting that they came from the places the others wouldn't go. But the Duclos pictures that accompanied his articles invariably confirmed that they had, indeed, pushed their trade to its limits.

On this last journey to Rwanda, they had gone much farther.

Imagine how it must once have been, an idyll with just a meandering footpath cutting through the bushlands, verdant, luxuriant, chattering with small unnamed animals, birds, insects. There would be springs and streams and the nomads—the Bantu moving gradually south, unconsciously toward an unbidden collision with Bibles and slavers—would settle where this greenery beckoned. Eden on earth. Paradise. Adam and Eve and the serpent freed of sin and bruises. Then the path would widen because the outsiders were coming with machines that needed broad ways scythed through the bush, and buildings built for eternity, with spires and benches and crosses. And then, more outsiders, with stores and money and taxes and jobs and strange, hot, unsuitable clothing and odd smells to skin that burned pink or was brown not black. Once, in the spoken histories, it was said the ancestors exhausted the land and moved on. Now they stayed within the cages and perimeters set down by these outsiders and there was nowhere to go as the villages burgeoned. So at every point along the path that had become a trail or road there would be settlements, places where the earth was beaten and swept to keep the serpents from huts roofed in straw, where a fire burned constantly from three logs pushed together into a hub of hot embers, where the thick tongues of foliage lapped rainwater that bred mosquitoes. There would never be silence until all slept. There would be talk, movement, fitful stirring on the hottest of days, games, intercourse.

Not today, though. Not on this trip.

The trail ran between stands of manioc and plantain, fringed by emerald grass that stood higher than a man. Ambush alley, they said simultaneously, but drove on anyhow.

At each place along the way, the village sounds—children and radios, squabbles and the thump of mortar and pestle grinding corn—were absent. The fires still smoldered but the people were gone—or newly demised. The straw roofs of the gray-mud roundhouses were burned black and stinking, the wooden uprights charred. The corpses lay spread-eagled on open ground, entry wounds in the back of the head, or huddled in ramshackle church buildings, grotesque sculptures of mother and child, pieta wrought by machete. In the overwhelming quiet, in the utter stillness of the unburied, there were only negatives—breasts that were stilled, without breath or telltale movement, or warmth. In this charnel house silence there were no smiles, no laughter, no memory, no thoughts of the future. In villages populated solely by the dead, there were no stories or myths, beyond the sagas of almost unimaginable brutality.

In life, the blood in the veins, the milk sucked from the nipple, the semen in the groin must all offer some minuscule contribution to the sounds of vitality. But here there was nothing. Whatever you touched or saw or commented upon, there would be no reaction. Even the feral dogs had fled.

"Fucking marvelous. Look at these fuckers. So dead, man." Faria leaned over bodies, stealing their images, robbing corpses of their last privacy. Joe Shelby stood back, taking notes, pleased that his hand was steady, his script likely to be legible when, later, he fired up the laptop to compose, tallying the slaughter, giving it form, context, righteous indignation. Faria and Joe. Avenging swords.

In one or two hamlets, survivors crept out of the bushlands, wild-eyed, terrorized, to have their stories, as he put it, clinically removed by his dispassionate interviewing. Bodies, mayhem, after all, were nothing new. Tradecraft dictated the harvesting of sights, smells, color, words, name, age, occupation, home address. Bring out your stories. Bring out your agony. When you visited, you were the plague harvesters passing from door to door in medieval Europe: bring out your dead.

"The soldiers came to the village . . ." How often was that the preface to the liturgy of destruction?

The day wore them down, hot and unrelenting. At each halt, they took their booty of quotations, photographs, descriptive notes, then moved on, jumping into the rental car as if propelled beyond reason. They were flying now. They were along for the ride. The story had become an irrelevance—and that, he knew, should never happen, but did.

The same lurid fascination had taken hold in both of them, as if they were pushing themselves to ascertain how deeply they could immerse themselves in horror, wallow in it, force the unseeing eyes and the spilled intestines and the grimace of dead innocents to lose all significance, inoculate them against all sense of fellow humanity. The further they progressed along the track, the fresher the bodies, the fewer the survivors. The gunshots and the screams, distant at first, grew louder, as if they were slowly overhauling the murderous caravan.

Eventually, what brought him up short was an exchange that he recalled like this:

"Can't get any quotes from this bunch of fuckers."

"Because zey are all fuckin' dead, man."

And they laughed, as if they had grown calluses on their own souls.

This was the point of divergence, the moment he awoke. What they were doing was not simply recording small, pointless massacres, but, like moths to flame, pushing themselves towards the arena of perpetration where soldiers with blood on their hands would have no compunction about adding to the day's tally.

Joe Shelby had infringed too many of his own rules.

Never go stoned or drunk. Rule one. Broken.

Always leave time to get back. The day was almost finished. Dusk would arrive with the speed that lives departed in these parts.

Never go too far. Never so far that you could not retreat. Never so far that you might be encircled. Never into whatever the clichés called it—the dead zone, the heart of darkness. In these wars, the lines were mercurial, shifting. A road was secure only as long as you could see it to be so. Turn your back and the ambush positions on the high ground changed hands. Proceed at your peril.

"That's it. We're splitting. You've got pictures. Great pictures. Better pictures than anyone else."

But she was no longer thinking in such obvious terms. The small spoon on a silver chain round her neck hung over her shallow cleavage, white and powdery from frequent use. The glint in her eyes reminded him of the sickly luminescence before a tropical storm, when light and darkness joust for dominance.

✍

So I said to her:

"Round the next corner are the people who are doing this and they won't like an audience. They'll rape you and kill you after they watch you shit yourself when they take me out. Don't be stupid, Faria."

"You are just a sheet-chicken."

"You mean chicken-shit?"

"I go without you."

"You stay with me you crazy French bitch."

"Sheet-chicken."

That was when I struck her, a hard open-handed blow across the cheek that almost floored her. I struck her. I struck her because I just couldn't do this anymore, not her way. It was too far. She was on a different plane from me. I wanted to stay alive and I realized that she didn't. I'm not proud of this. I have told no one. Until now.

From outside the netting, captured in the glow, they were the perfect couple, bronzed children of paradise. Imperceptibly, their fingers would advance across the white linen until they touched just enough for the signal to be transmitted. They would peer deeply, significantly into one another's eyes and the spark would ignite the ready tinder. Eva Kimberly knew the gift was hers, to offer or withhold. She had belonged, for many years, to one man who right now, on his admission, was beyond contact in his tented camp with a temptress of uncertain intentions. But, to her surprise, she did not really care. Aquiline, aloof Jeremy Davenport had been her consort since postgraduate times when both had returned from overseas colleges in America and Britain to restart their African lives. She had studied languages—Italian and German—though her true tongue was more likely to be Swahili—and Oxford had been impressed enough with the colonial interloper to offer her a first-class degree in those subjects. And he had returned with an economics degree of a low, third-class order that he would stuff into some drawer or attic and forget. But they had completed the tribal rite—gone overseas, sampled its narrow horizons and failing light and frigid people and found it lacking, returning to the crazy dislocated world that they knew better. Someday—always soon—they would make the commitment to another marquee on the shores of Naivasha and a wedding party and children and home.

Until now.

Was this when we met, Joe? Was it?

He was telling his stories—war stories, funny stories, indiscretions concerning big-name people she saw on the satellite television news. He was laying out his offering: look, see, I'm capable of tenderness, humor, care. I come fully equipped with a visa to the chanceries of Europe, to places where you do not fuse the claymore mines before retiring, where you do not watch every third or second acquaintance turn gray and die with AIDS or TB or malaria, where selfishness is licensed and greed is legitimate and you are not obliged to fret about your debt to an adoptive continent. Let me court you in St. Germain and the Piazza di Spagna and Unter den Linden. Let me take you to places where the dues have been paid, where you are warm and safe.

He was reciting an old-timer's story, about sending dispatches by carrier pigeon, in the era before wireless or telex or modem. He was describing how the pigeon handler holds the bird with its legs caught between index and middle finger, the thumb gently caressing the neck, holding the wings closed. How, before the bird is freed to soar and circle and find its true coordinates, the pigeon handler brushes the feathers of the bird's head with the merest peck of a kiss for good fortune and true flight. As he told the story he went through those motions, an imaginary bird calmed and cooing in a strong, manly hand, his storyteller's lips pursed in a kiss as he looked at her across the pool of light at the dining table. Then, with both hands he showed how the bird was freed and launched, the kiss of life breathing fire into its wings, free to spiral into the skies, to find its way home. And he looked straight at her, the virtual kiss lingering on real lips.

Dow Crag, England. September 2000

Beyond a certain altitude you are in the dead zone. The body does not regenerate. The climbers say this is the place where you know your death has begun to unfold. Starved of oxygen, assailed by bitter cold, the systems slow to a halt. But before succumbing, you put one foot before the other, gain one small victory at a time, then steel yourself for the next challenge, the next step to gain one more iota of height, to progress further into the zone that is killing you. There is little or no sleep. Food does not nourish. Liquid provides respite but not sustenance. At some point, entropy will erode the desire for the incremental triumphs of putting one foot before another. You lose sight of your summit goal, your aim, the passion that brought you here. You have only a limited, ever-dwindling envelope of time before desire perishes and you will, too, your eyes blinded by the glare, your fingers blackened by frostbite. You will curl up against some barren rock and let the last vestiges of energy slip away. The dead zone takes its prisoners and casualties with supreme indifference. You are in the zone where the axons wither, the signals sent so valiantly do not arrive at the muscle tissue, where unintelligible quiverings replace premeditated movement. Like a huge, tangled city whose power supply is failing, whole areas are blacked out, progressively, the light vanishing, patches of darkness encroaching on the organism until it disappears from view, its every function stilled.

Behind schedule, cursing the weight of his pack, Joe Shelby engineers one step at a time in the South Rake, alone in a world of mist and sudden chill that allows him to see only the scratch marks of previous toilers, but nothing beyond that, no sense of a point of departure or a point of arrival. At his back, he is aware of the huge, menacing buttresses, the narrow fissures, the swoop—somewhere—of scree and rock plunging down towards the still tarn. He locates a firm grounding with one of his walking poles, then swings the other with an awkward improvisation of his useless left arm. Once anchored in this manner, he raises his left leg using the thigh muscles only because the calf muscles are unresponsive. Then he orders the good right leg to follow, completing the process of making imperceptible headway. But moving nonetheless. And repeating the formula to ensure upward progression, careful since his fall, and ever more aware of the pain this adventure is causing to limbs that will not function according to their basic design. His thighs ache and his breathing is labored, heartbeat in overtime. He has not up until this point contemplated failure or lowering his sights, making do with one peak, one day, one retreat. But now he is telling himself that, in the dead zone, victory is relative. Victory is survival. There are ways down the mountain without shame. There are summits best left to others. And there is the knowledge that every upward step must be reversed. He is sweaty and breathless and cannot abide the thought that, if he fails now, the dead zone will enfold his soul.

⟋

JADINI, KENYA. SEPTEMBER 1999

He awoke confused by the absence of his usual coordinates—hotel furniture, whisky, cigarettes, bedside telephone, reading lamp. He was in a strange room, with the sound of the ocean surf pounding on a reef. The room was white with simple furnishings, blurred by mosquito netting. He had been sleeping fitfully, restless after the dinner, after sitting opposite her and trying to absorb her speech tones and laughter, the clean, perfect lines of her. He had thrown off the thin, cotton sheet and tossed and turned so that his feet protruded from the netting. His mind went back over their dinner, like after some interviews with nervous sources, when you have to exercise total recall because the source has refused a tape recorder or notebook. They had talked about being white in Africa, being an Englishman in New York, where people talked too fast and thought on their feet while he digested courses of action. He felt drowned by her voice, the unbroken lines of her body, the English accent that, in his youth, would have raised the banners of class struggle in his northern soul. He wanted to make her laugh and dusted off his best stories about pigeons and wars and adventures, censored to skirt around questions concerning his companions on those crazy drives across the desert, those wild races against rivals in the era before mobile phones, an era that almost merited its own initials: B.C., A.D., P.C.— pre-cell. Now, P.E.—pre-Eva. He wanted, somehow, to suggest to her that her life should change and he should help navigate her exodus.

"Do you ever feel you'd like to move on?"

"As in?"

"A new start. A break with the past?"

"In my own good time."

"But doesn't time march on?"

"Not as quickly for me as it seems to do for you," she said, but there was just the merest curl of a smile on her lips.

Over coffee, with the surf beating a relentless backdrop, he was the good listener. She told him, slowly at first, then in a rush of words, of the fears and exhilaration of her tribe's adoptive home, of the cruel juxtapositions of a life set half in the unquestioning luxury of Home Farm and half in the flyblown backwaters of the Rift Valley, where hope was always denied by AIDS, violence, rape. She laughed—and he laughed with her—at the old family stories, of how a great aunt had married a hunter who summoned early morning beverages from the servants by shotgun: one barrel for coffee, two for tea. She grew somber when she spoke of a particular young Masai man she had adopted only to discover that her generosity had made him a wastrel, trading pride for handouts and hand-me-downs. She grew, briefly, silent as she recited the statistics of infection that stripped the colleges of healthy students and left babies with grandparents and no generations between. In her conversations, B followed A and C followed B. Not what he had become used to from his crazy French bitch who thought in curves so that a Q might wing in after B and a Z could crop up at any time as her thoughts and responses flew like sparks from some hidden dynamo.

"I don't usually talk so much," she said.

"It's my cunning interview technique."

"Or the wine."

He sat opposite her on the divan in the main salon, where ceiling fans turned the night wind off the ocean that stalked the house through the shutters and netting. Sometimes, across the covered verandah where some invisible person had mysteriously removed the detritus of their dinner, a phantom crossed the silhouette of the palm trees with a glint of steel.

"Just the askari," she said. "He obviously feels I need protection."

"From who? Not from me."

"Of course from you. They've known me since I was a baby. They are all very protective."

"And what would he do to protect you?"

"You really wouldn't want to know, but I fear your manhood would never recover." Again the smile.

"Sounds like it's me who needs protection."

"Don't you laugh in the face of danger?"

"Of course. Always. That's why I'm here."

He focused on her hazel eyes, willing a message from them that would encourage his desire to slip her shirt from her shoulders, loose the knot of the kikoyi from her waist. He noted that her eyebrows and lashes were naturally sandy, made even paler by the sun, that her skin was very lightly freckled and that her hair glowed. As she spoke, he focused his gaze to prevent it from straying to the intimate places where he was not sure he would ever be invited. She told him about assumed privilege and late-stirring guilt, about the sunlight that soaked through her life and pain that this same life was so much the product of decades of elitism, racially based at first, then economically based. Was it the same with him? (How could she know at that early stage that it was not?) Did his family fix every moment of its own past, as if creating a pageant across the decades to justify its behavior—from the first arrival to the disastrous foray into coffee, from the horrors of the Mau Mau on a remote homestead to the triumph of survival, from the plantations to the corridors of colonial administration to the arrangements and compromises with the new order. Of course outsiders thought it all very pat: white masters, black slaves. But it was her life, she was saying, she knew nothing else and he stopped her dead in her tracks by saying: I could show you another one. If you wanted. If you thought.

In the soft focus of the mosquito netting, she was standing in the doorway, wearing some kind of robe. She seemed to be watching him, like someone trying to decide whether to join a party at which she is not sure whether she is wanted or will enjoy herself. He feigned sleep, asking himself whether she could see through the netting that he was naked. She was walking across the rush matting of the guest room, moving the mosquito netting to protect his exposed feet. Her fingers brushed over his ankle and he sat upright, swinging open the netting with a gesture he hoped was chivalrous, then kneeling to face and receive her.

And that was it, Joe. That was when we met.

Chapter Five

SERENGETI, TANZANIA. SEPTEMBER 1999

In the almost innocent, earliest years of her career as a war photographer, Faria Duclos sometimes indulged the notion that, if she survived her newly found profession, she would end her days alone with rich memories of a turbulent life, a portfolio of fine and terrible images and, possibly, a cat. She would live in a tasteful apartment in St. Germain with high ceilings and a warren of corridors leading to darkened rooms, off limits to most of her guests. She would be one of those querulous, quirky ladies in broad-brimmed hats, sought out by old flames desperate to rekindle dead embers, and by young men with existential problems. She would, by then, have detoxified and her work would be shown in well-attended retrospectives. It did not occur to her to dwell on the slow, painful messy ends associated with death in battle. Death, she believed, was an alluring mystery to unravel, not a transition to be feared. Death was a solution, not a problem, a lover to be courted, not an unwelcome suitor to be rejected. And if its visit came earlier rather than later, then so be it: it would be as welcome as any other long-awaited guest.

In those early days, a partner, a soul mate also seemed improbable. When she walked into a hotel lobby or an airport lounge, returning from assignment with the sweat and adrenaline still upon her, men looked upon her brooding black eyes and slender frame with attraction and fear. She was not the kind of girl who expected to be taken home for tea and parental introductions, not the type who would crave—or qualify for—the protection and companionship she saw other women extracting from men who seemed born to be tamed. She had learned her priorities from men whose rules were fluid and simple: whatever it was, the adventure came first. No commitment was binding. At the first hint of distant trouble, in Chechnya or Kandahar, she would simply lock her apartment, sling her camera bag over her shoulder and take a cab to the airport, calling her agent along the way to line up clients. She was free because she had never felt that anyone wanted to capture her. She was free because she never asked anyone to take her in, to set markers of safety. Joe Shelby alone had ring-fenced her demons without seeming to, spun an invisible web around her, without saying so or making a point of it. And now he had withdrawn the favor, just as she had begun to think he would not, showing himself, really, no different from other men in her life.

Her father, a Tunisian professor of archaeology, had died of a heart attack on a dig in Egypt when she was in her early teens, and she had seen little of him before that. His death merely drew a line below years of separation, de facto divorce, from her mother. At school functions, she saw other children flanked by a mother and a father. Her mother always arrived alone, if she arrived at all, and drew attention by her too-young, too-tight clothes, her racy, tarty hats and helipad-sized sun-glasses. In the empty hours, returning home to a silent apartment in Paris, she confided this to her schoolgirl diary: *I have learned that no matter how hard you love somebody, you can never love them back to you; love is never strong enough to reverse destiny.*

Her memories of her father—rarely revisited—lay in warm, rosy, special places where he still played silly games with her on a silk rug, or told her magical, made-up stories as she hovered between wakefulness and sleep. But for the rest, for the presences her school friends simply took for granted from their fathers at school fetes and prize givings, birthday parties and outings to the zoo, he was absent. She clung to his memory with a fierce loyalty and, at the same time, could not bring herself to believe that her lackadaisical mother had been in any way at fault in whatever relationship her parents had ever had. Her father's early death merely confirmed that the void and the pain would be her constant companions. And death itself became the central mystery, the single event that offered certainty. She learned its lyrics from Kurt Cobain. She laid flowers at the grave of Jim Morrison and mourned all those like her condemned to courtship with the dark angel. She thrived on the twilit, sinister poetry of Charles Baudelaire and Gerard de Nerval. Of all the music she played on headsets and hi-fis as a teenager, two songs defined her condition and she wept freely to them. They were "Knocking on Heaven's Door" by Bob Dylan and "Tears in Heaven" by Eric Clapton—a song inspired by a father's loss of a child that made her ask if her own father had ever felt that loss. Her tears were all the more bitter because heaven seemed an elusive, alien notion, not meant for her.

Her mother, a delicate Frenchwoman of independent financial means, mourned her husband only briefly before setting out to find a successor. Her choices were never good. The young Faria, packed off to a Swiss boarding school, would return home at vacations to find the apartment in St. Germain populated in succession by a rote of raddled playboys and rogues attracted by the small fortune that had accrued to her mother from her father's modest legacy and her distant ties to a prominent family of bankers. Some set out to seduce her and she allowed some to succeed. Some sought to expel her from her own home,

ALAN S. COWELL

regarding her as a willful, spoilt invader, a brat. None of them said simply that he liked her for herself, or took her to a movie without trying to
paw her. Sex, she told her intermittent diary, could not be separated
from treachery.

Even now, on this supposed photo safari with a haughty, handsome
man called Davenport, she had no illusion that she was being cultivated
as anything other than a trophy, a collectible on a par with the stuffed
antelope heads and worn lion skins that adorned his camp in the chattering bush of the Serengeti. She had known him a thousand times over,
knew his tactics and conversation down to every predictable ploy and
suggestion. But she considered the safari a peace offering to Joe
Shelby—a pause when they might both reflect on the excesses, pull back
from mutual anger, and she had no desire to break what little remained
of their faith, despite this man's assumption of triumph from the very
moment she had stepped into his four-wheel-drive Toyota in Nairobi
for the long drive south.

Boarding school led to a spell at art school, where she discovered her
limitations with oil and canvas but, citing boredom, *ennui,* made no
attempt to transcend them. One of her mother's suitors, gazing on her
near-anorexic frame and the dark, impenetrable looks she had inherited
from her father, suggested that she model for fashion magazines and she
tried that, enjoying the pouting and flouncing, the ferocious attention
and flattery, but more interested by far in the mechanical devices of the
business—the Hasselblads and motor-drives, the lenses and lights—
than in modeling itself. She achieved easy success, in demand for those
sultry, androgynous shots—usually in black and white against gothic
backdrops of turrets and towers—that depicted women as vaguely menacing, and certainly unpredictable beings in long expensive gowns cut to
the navel over a pale, shallow, vulnerable cleavage. At airport news-
stands, she saw herself peering haughtily from the covers of *Vogue* and

Marie Claire and *Elle.* She thought it amusing and scary and unlikely to last and probably ending in tears.

With her first commission check, she bought a secondhand mechanical Leica with a single lens. That, she was told, was what the masters like Cartier-Bresson used—none of these modern automatic devices with motor drives, still less digital image making. Between assignments as a model she taught herself how to process and print monochrome images, grainy representations of the Parisian demi-monde, of her mannequin colleagues in their downtime, without makeup or glamour, puffing on joints and snorting cocaine with mascara-ringed empty eyes. Alone in the ruby glow of her darkroom, her attention was devoured completely by the chemical interactions that conjured stark, grainy blocks of black and white with few interme-diate stages of gray.

The modeling business was good. It earned money and a fast life, flying in Gulfstreams to shoots from Morocco to Mongolia. She took easily to the proffered lines of narcotics the photographers produced af-ter—sometimes during—the shoots. Far more than the cloying haze of marijuana, Faria Duclos sought the bright burn of cocaine in her blood-stream, the ritual chopping of white powder, its formation into aesthet-ically pleasing lines and the sense of inordinate self-confidence it created. Even without the hunger-killing drugs, her physique was a nat-ural for the business of modeling. She seemed alight with an inner fur-nace that burned off every last calorie. Her hair became photogenically frizzy without a coiffeur's attentions, another function of her father's genes. Art school lay somewhere forgotten in a turbulent wake: with her Leica and her growing collection of other cameras and lenses she came to think that, if only she mastered the techniques of reading and manip-ulating light, she would some day produce the depths and riches of a Caravaggio canvas on film. Her upbringing had given her fluency in French, Arabic and English so that, in most places where the procession of lights, cameras, clothes, models, hairdressers and frenzy moved, she was able to win the trust of and photograph the people who had not asked to host a shoot but tolerated it, usually, in return for temporary work and outright bribes. The dogs bark, her agency boss liked to say, but the caravan moves on. And everywhere along this route the path was lined with men, of canine tenacity who would take but never love, seduce but never embrace, whose preferred terrain was the cocktail party, the moored yacht, the candlelit dinner and the boudoir. In her heart they confirmed her belief that she would never meet her protector, her shield, so she would be alone, live alone and die alone. Now Joe Shelby seemed to have joined that unsavory gallery of people who had faltered, and her sin was the worse because, foolishly, she had trusted him.

❧

Jeremy Davenport shifted beside her in the hide where he had suggested they watch and photograph a leopard circle and kill a tethered goat by a salt lick in the Serengeti. The arm placed across her shoulder was supposed to be casual but she shrugged it away. He was not too concerned, knowing that, usually, it was the sight of the attack, the blood and the bone, that coaxed forth less rejectionist emotions.

❧

She knew the precise moment that her life as a model came to an end. There had been a shoot in Jordan, where the director hired the entire ancient site of rock carvings and temples at Petra. The caravan was on its way there, overnighting in Amman, when Faria and her colleagues awoke to find the hotel ringed by protesters demonstrating against the presence in the same building of an Israeli trade delegation. Where the models, photographers, makeup teams and hairdressers had been anticipating a line of limousines awaiting them, they were greeted by a furious crowd hemmed in by riot police with shields, truncheons and rifles. From her hotel window, Faria photographed the protests and their aftermath—the police lines, the stinging tear gas and the first thrill of live gunfire. When the shooting stopped, she ventured forth, photographing the dead and the wounded with a grim fascination for the raggedness of the wounds, the sickly cocktail of blood and cordite, the fatuous abandon on the faces of corpses on the hard concrete of the hotel parking lot. She moved in close for the wide-angle images that became her hallmark. She photographed a bloodstain on an abandoned black-and-white checkered kafiyeh headdress, not realizing at the time that the blood had spilled into an approximate image of the geographic frontiers of the state of Israel. When the professionals arrived in town that night from London and Cairo and Jerusalem with their edit packs and laptops and bulging camera bags, she alone had rolls and rolls of exposed film to barter. When her photograph of the bloodstain—overlaid against a computer mock-up of a map of Israel in flames—appeared on the following week's cover of *Paris Match,* Faria Duclos was ready to leave modeling for good.

She had a healthy bank account, an apartment from her mother's dwindling fortune and an instant following among a raffish army of male photographers in headbands and flak jackets and ragged fishing vests only too keen to trade their hard-earned wisdom for a chance to court her. After the riots in Jordan, the region was aflame. The very future of the Hashemite dynasty in Amman hung in the balance. The West Bank and Gaza trembled with yet one more uprising starring suicide bombers and young, masked men wielding slingshots and rifles. Islam was poised to take over the world. She took an apartment in west Beirut near Hamra Street with her films and her cameras. She switched from her model's glittery regalia to baggy black pants and shapeless tee shirts, and tied her hair back in a rough pony tail that accentuated the gaunt, angular planes of her features. She purchased her first bulletproof vest. She had no wish to be sought out for her looks: what mattered now was the images created of others, not of herself. She made new friends among the region's traveling circus of reporters and photographers, and kept close ties to her old friends in the cocaine market. It took only a few spurned advances, and a rapidly growing portfolio of exclusive images, for her colleagues in their faded jeans and Kevlar tunics to realize that Faria Duclos was a contender.

She had no time at all for the region's convoluted sophistries—the power balances and shifting sands of Iraq and Syria, Egypt and Israel. She told no one of her own history, with an Arab father and a mother who kept hidden her remote Jewish ancestry—her own private contribution to the region's nuances. Here, there were just good guys and bad guys. The bad guys were the dictators and oppressors—whatever their faith. The good guys were the oppressed—the region's most fertile harvest: the veiled widows with their graveside ululations, the teenagers flung back crazily by a bullet in the chest. Even victimhood was ambiguous. Ultimately, virtue could be divined only in death, at that enchanted moment when the soul left the body while the spirit transposed itself into the parallel world of the afterlife. Therefore, Faria Duclos believed, she needed to be ever-present in the places where violent death was likely to occur most frequently.

Only rarely did she encounter other outsiders so close to the crossing point between this world and the next. Competitors and companions only seemed to get in the way, spoil the luxury of time that she devoted to burrowing into the situations she wished to exploit. In the Middle East, she found it just as easy to wear the chador of Islam as to pass in long tresses and modest skirts among the Jewish faithful. Where others sought a quick-fix, one-day jolt of pictures, she was happy to spend days, weeks living among her subjects until she felt she had grasped the essence of what she wished to portray. Often enough, her patience carried its own special dangers because people trusted her enough to take her into situations far more perilous than the normal clashes so typical of the region. She had accompanied Israeli special forces into Iraq and, in Africa, the Sierra Leone rebels had unusually taken her along to witness their perpetration of a mass mutilation, as if going to a soccer game. At her first encounter with Joe Shelby, she was irked to discover an intruder on her patch, because she had spent a considerable amount of time winning the confidence of a particularly brutal mercenary sniper operating from a half-built Gaza high-rise, a man who specialized in the murder of Israeli civilians, using an old and powerful Steyr-Mannlicher rifle, its long barrel wrapped in rags to break its profile and prevent glare, to spread the terror of the unpredictable through Jewish settler communities. Shin Bet, the Israeli intelligence unit, had been unable to locate him. But Faria Duclos had. And, to her chagrin, so had Joe Shelby.

From a breeze-block vantage point in the shell of the high-rise, looking through the powerful scope at dusk, the sniper had shown her an Orthodox Jewish woman with three small girls entering their home behind the barbed wire of a settlement one mile distant. The following morning, the sniper said, he would let her choose which one of the three would die.

Joe Shelby snuck into the high-rise in the early hours as Faria Duclos wrestled with the choice forced upon her by the sniper. Without really thinking through the consequences of her actions, she had sought this vantage point along the faultline between life and death, between a child's body drawing breath and a child as a lifeless object on the concrete sidewalk outside her home. But, now she had taken up this position, she realized she could not pursue her craft without bearing witness, and even becoming party, to cold-blooded murder remote from the heat of battle. She was no longer an observer, a chronicler, a dilettante among the murderers and fighters. The sniper had turned her into a participant, an extension of his own divine status as master of other people's mortality. From her studies she recalled a text she had studied for the international baccalaureate. Ahead of all her classmates, she had understood Andre Gide's notion of the *acte gratuit,* the arbitrary choice to be made without reason or reference to antecedents or morality. Now it was on offer and she wanted no part of it. The sniper—he called himself Tawfik but did so with a heavy German accent—thought otherwise.

"If you don't choose, baby, you go first, with this," he said, waving a silenced pistol towards her.

"Tawfik, we can't do this," Joe Shelby said as the deadline ticked closer.

"But you must do it, my friend."

✍

Jeremy Davenport shifted beside her. For a moment she was back in Gaza three years earlier faced with the sacrificial choice.

"What do you want to shoot? The leopard or the kill?"

"Neither," she said. "Not like this."

The leopard was hungry, sniffing at the wind, salivating at the rich odor of its prey, prowling with hackles raised. Its eyes were the most beautiful she had ever seen.

"Any minute now. Get ready," Jeremy Davenport said, easing his body alongside hers in a way that suggested his anticipation of an outcome he did not think was in doubt with his own fiancée far away on the coast and Joe Shelby on some kind of walkabout, God knew where.

"No. Not now," Faria Duclos said. She rose slowly, breaking cover from the hide, walking straight across a clearing in the savanna towards a taut, hungry leopard. She had chosen a wide angle lens, knowing that would necessitate a close-up.

In Gaza, the moment of choice would come with first light when the settlement began to stir and the children were given their breakfast and told to put on their dark, navy-blue head scarves and long skirts for the ride to school. They would follow their mother from the front door to the parked Chevy Blazer on the toy-town streets of the settlement behind its guard towers and razor wire, shy and pliant in her wake. For twenty or thirty seconds they would be exposed on the sidewalk with their bright orange school satchels on their backs. The steel-jacketed bullet would precede the muzzle crack, scything through the windless, morning air, cool enough still to prevent eddies of heat from disrupting its trajectory. The child—one, two or three depending on the number they called—would fall too fast to scream, the circuits closed down by massive trauma. A mercy killing, the sniper called it. A kosher killing for the oppressed masses of Palestine, he said with a hollow laugh.

"So. One, two or three? Who goes first?"

The sniper had spent the night with his back against the wall, carefully avoiding any movement that might draw attention to the jagged hole in the breeze-block that served as his platform. Now, with the sun easing over the horizon, preposterously big and orange, he rolled into his position, back from the hole, with the camouflaged rifle barrel resting on the lower edge of the narrow aperture. Behind him, Faria Duclos chose her biggest lens of a type that extends its focal length through the use of a bright, polished mirror as its front element.

"I will say it," she told the sniper. "One. Two. Three. Tell me when."

She wriggled back from the sniper, moving her mirror lens until its mirror caught the blaze of the morning sun.

The woman had left the front door of her home. She wore a head scarf and a long, black coat stretched tight over her pregnant belly. Perhaps he should shoot her—two Jews for the price of one bullet, Tawfik was thinking. He had her in the crosshairs and his finger rested lightly on the trigger that he would squeeze, not pull. Unconsciously, reflexively, he controlled his breathing so that the image in the telescopic sight remained steady. The woman peered anxiously left and right, scanning the streets of the settlement for any hint of abnormality, unusual silence. Then she turned and gestured to her children.

"One. Two. Or three. You have five seconds."

Tawfik the sniper was focused solely now on the image in the crosshairs. The three girls—one only slightly taller than the next, as if they had entered the world with the minimum delay between birth and conception—emerged from the house.

"Quickly. One. Two. Or three. Or I shoot you both."

Tawfik saw the children's dark, braided hair flowing from below their head scarves. He saw their shining brown eyes and white, just-cleaned teeth. He saw their bright orange satchels and worn leather sandals and dark stockings. Outside the narrow, rock-steady tunnel of the sniper-scope, he did not see the sudden flurry of movement in the settlement's guard tower, the raising of the heavy machine gun as the Israeli soldiers gestured and pointed to the flickering of bright light from a half-built high-rise across the divide in the Gaza Strip.

The noise inside the concrete shell of the sniper's eyrie was deafening as the heavy rounds clanged home and Tawfik's body exploded, captured in its disintegration by a whirring motor-drive.

She walked towards the leopard and raised her camera. The light was poor but the animal's eyes glowed a bright amber. Looking through the range finder, she saw the leopard bunched and poised as if to pounce. The light, at one-fifteenth of a second, in that moment of stasis that bound her to the animal, would douse her film in deep, natural tones, Caravaggio tones. Behind her, she heard the slide of Jeremy Davenport's hunting rifle, but knew she was blocking a clear shot unless he moved off to the side and exposed himself to the leopard. She heard the goat's hysterical cries, and smelled the stink of its urine and feces. In the perfect, frozen seconds of the leopard's indecision and her own beginnings of fear, she took four frames that would capture the animal's ferocity and wisdom. Then, quite suddenly, the leopard was gone and she turned back to Jeremy Davenport.

"You still want to fuck me?"

His hunting rifle drooped at his side and she knew his secret answer would be that he did not dare.

Returning, amused and celibate, to what had been their shared hotel room at the Norfolk Hotel, Faria Duclos found that Joe Shelby's gear—his scuffed tote bag and laptop, his whisky and cigarettes and spare notebooks—had all been cleaned out. He had left in such a hurry that he had taken both their Kevlar vests with him and she made no move to replace hers. She waited three days for a call, stretching listless by the hotel pool until the sun scorched her, nurturing some vague hope that he would call to tell her of a new assignment, a new adventure that he had embarked on in a hurry, unable to reach her, but aching nonetheless to see her, hold her, ride with her into the fray once more. Yet, when the telephone did ring and she leaped naked and panicky from the shower to grab the receiver, the voice was barely recognizable, a drunken, sneering parody of Jeremy Davenport saying: if you want to know where your boyfriend is, he's fucking my girlfriend in a little love nest in Mombasa.

Faria Duclos flew back alone to Beirut. She did not require clarification from Joe Shelby. She did not demand a face-to-face rundown on what had happened. That was obvious enough. What had happened was what always happened. Sex went hand in hand with treachery. The only constant was death. Death was the leveler, the common denominator to be explored, challenged, mined for truth. To imagine that, even as she prepared to pardon him, he was with the princess Kimberly; the sequences of treachery, the monstrousness of betrayal, were almost too much. Jealousy cast blue-movie close-ups and clinches across logical thought patterns and better judgments, offering precisely the images, the details, she did not wish to see—the intimate tenderness, the private exchanges of promises and fluids. It goaded her with an overwhelming feeling of stupidity: how could anyone be so dumb, so blind to what was happening? What had the intruder, the invader to offer that she had not? Why had she been found wanting? And, ultimately, it provided her with the obvious answer: this pain was caused only because you trusted the betrayer, and you had never trusted before, so do not trust again.

Working alone now in a man's world, she had no wish to be known as an easy lay, a castoff of the great Joe Shelby. She accepted assignments as before from the magazine that employed them both, but insisted that her instructions relating to his articles come by e-mail, through an intermediary editor, not from the writer direct. Covering the same stories as Joe Shelby, she traveled alone, trailing him like a distant phantom, revisiting the scenes he had observed only after he had left, avoiding the hotels where he stayed, aware of his every move, but making no attempt to reestablish their covenant. She heard rumors of frailty, malfunction but shied from confirming them.

Old Joe has taken his African princess to London. Shelby's hanging up his flak jacket. Joe's out on a limb, traveling alone, strung out on Scotch. Joe's sick, but he won't say what's wrong. Shelby has Parkinson's, AIDS, MS. Joe's dropping out with his bimbo in Primrose Hill. What happened to Shelby of Sarajevo? Where's Mr. Exclusive now? Whatever became of Captain Wilderness?

Trailing him, she imagined herself as a dark bird of prey on large, silent wings, circling in the thermals of his travels, the sun at her back and her quarry within sight. She had no wish to confront him, demand explanations for the finality, the brutality of his breach with her. She did not want to be told how he and his Eva were doing. Looking back to the garden party in Naivasha, she understood that Eva Kimberly was the opposite side of the Shelby equation. Studying her photograph in magazine articles about her business success, she saw what Joe Shelby must have seen in her: symmetry, order, the light side of the moon where chaos never intruded. She had the same well-formed features as the British liked to see in television announcers and the wives of royal princes, a near-irresistible pull for an Englishman of the north, a potent emblem of wholeness, arrival—the kind of woman a man would take home for tea. But Eva Kimberly would never reach out to the Joe Shelby who thrived on disorder and mayhem, who would chance his all on a turn in a remote, dirt highway, who fed on humanity's worst offerings, breathed in the smoke of the slaughterhouse as if it were incense, torn between darkness and light, purity and defilement.

She marked her progression with a trail of credit card slips, half-eaten room-service meals and forensic traces of white powder on glass-topped tables, lavatory cisterns, handout glossy magazines. She journeyed alone and fed her addiction alone. She did not replace the Kevlar vest he had taken from their shared room at the Norfolk Hotel in Nairobi. She shuddered sometimes when she thought of the particularly irresponsible risks—and then laughed, sniggered, a schoolchild caught out in a misdemeanor. There had been Kosovo and Sri Lanka and Afghanistan—any place where depravity provided the benchmark of human behavior. She had traveled by Land Rover on sandy tracks in southern Angola, and by camel across pale deserts in Chad. She ran with the Albanian rebels and huddled with Palestinians as the rocket fire of

Israeli jets made the earth tremble. In southern Sudan her airplane miraculously survived a direct hit from surface-to-air fire. She laughed as the light plane bucked and spiraled. In Sri Lanka, the shrapnel almost blinded a woman reporter walking next to her, but somehow passed her by. If she had quiet time, downtime, then Joe Shelby invaded it, corroded it, besmirched it with the memory of treachery. So she avoided quiet time. She sought out the worst and craved the one defining moment, the crystallizing image between life and death when she would absorb humanity's baseness unto her camera and unto herself. She found it, finally, in an unlikely place, in someone else's home with a corrugated green zinc roof and tobacco barns in the yard, in the high, dry brightness of southern Africa's winter, zenith and nadir at once.

Chapter Six

CHINHOYI, ZIMBABWE. MAY 2000

They had traveled together, five journalists and photographers in two cars, to investigate reports that people calling themselves veterans of some indistinct war before her time had taken over an isolated, white-owned African farmstead, threatening its owners, a couple in their early thirties with two young daughters, Emma, aged six, and Jemima, aged four. Driving quickly from the safety of the capital, they soon reached the turnoff from the main dirt track onto a narrower, unpaved lane marked by the farmer's family name—Van Deventer—painted on an old ploughshare nailed to a wooden post at the roadside. Her colleagues pulled over, eyeing a group of thirty or maybe fifty of the occupiers two hundred yards away down the farm road. The consensus was not to drive onto the farm, not to sever escape routes before the situation could be assessed. The feeling was to talk, negotiate with the occupiers, if that were possible, but only from a position that could be exited at speed. The engines of their cars turned in the stillness. The occupiers bunched as a group, shimmering in the heat-haze like some medieval band, bristling with weapons of crude and intimate destruction—knobkerries and makeshift spears, honed pangas whose blades caught the brittle light. When they moved, they moved as a single threatening group, with dust clouds rising at their feet. They marched with a synchronized high step, like a war dance, and they chanted. "Hau, hau." It was the throaty roar of southern Africa's crowded explosive townships, of massed guerrilla armies, a statement of intent. The mood among her colleagues was in favor of speedy, tactical withdrawal. Who needed photos that had been taken before? Who needed to take risks for old news?

Faria Duclos alone dissented. She recognized this moment from her own past, from Rwanda where Joe Shelby had wavered, denied her the opportunity to meet the destiny that had always awaited her. If she hesitated now, she would again be walking away. This time, she would not be diverted by his doubts and calculations.

She climbed from the car, abandoning her canvas bag full of gear, taking only two light cameras equipped with wide-angle lenses and a stock of film. Ignoring her colleagues, she climbed over the farm gate, advancing down the long empty track that led to the occupiers. She heard her colleagues call: come back. The occupiers, the so-called veterans, too young to have known real war but blooded and hardened in their own way, paused and called: be gone white trash, *hamba*. There was a voice inside her, Joe's voice, that said: turn, run, now, you can still make it; vault the fence, climb into a car, speed away and laugh and be none the worse. But that was the voice of a false prophet, a mendacious advisor. She was committed now. The options had closed and they all knew it, the occupiers and her colleagues. In the quiet, she heard a car drive away, then pause. She walked on and raised her camera, a stick figure in the heat, a woman in black advancing without hesitation, so spindly thin she seemed to slice the air without moving it, casting no shadow. On either side of her, in this fallow, dry season, the fields that would not soon be replanted with corn lay bare and stubbled, stretching to distant perimeters of bush and torn fencing. The land was silent. The track was deserted save for the occupiers. Silence and emptiness—the warning signals, Joe Shelby's alarm bells, crying danger. But she wanted danger, she wanted proof that she had not been wrong when he sought retreat. The silence had a particular quality. The stillness of the air beckoned her with knowledge of very recent, indefinable events. No birds sang. No crickets chirruped. If she failed now, then the people outside this dark circle would never know the horror of what she suspected—knew by now—must have happened. If she turned, she betrayed her own truth and the truth of her business. If she retreated, the avenging sword was forever blunted and sheathed. But that was secondary to her mission. If she turned now, they would run her down like a fox.

Through the range finder of her old Leica with its wide-angle lens, the mob still looked distant even when she was close enough to smell the sweat of rage and blood and recent sexual emission, see the dust on dull faces sculpted with runnels of perspiration. Again she heard her colleagues exhorting her to flee, return to safety while she yet might. But it was too late for that. If she turned they would be upon her. If she showed a fear she did not feel they would take it as their invitation. She would not give the mob that pleasure, that pretext to hound her. "I do not run for you bastards," she told the leader with his ganja-red eyes. And walked through them, to the farmhouse they did not wish her to see, to the incontrovertible evidence—the woman, the girl-children, defenseless in death as they had been in life, the semen still seeping from their still bodies, blood not yet coagulated on cheery print dresses, the husband shot with his khaki shorts pulled down to his ankles, over his knee-length woolen socks, with his balls in his mouth, even the dogs silenced in a pool of their own blood and feces—deep reds against pale skin, a chiaroscuro juxtaposition, the passion of Van Deventer. Hah!

She recorded the images from close range, with 19mm and 24mm lenses, so close that she smelt the co-mingling of blood and seed, sweat and evacuation. The lines of pure terror were drawn indelibly across the faces long after the departing of the last breath, a rictus that no blessing or unction would ease. To the touch, the skin of the victims was still warm. In the room around her, with its worn, comfortable sofas and old television set, its stack of folding tables for TV dinners and wall trophies of antelope heads and stuffed tiger-fish mounted on varnished timber, she felt the spirits moving around her, seeking a place in the afterworld, craving release from the manner of their bodies' destruction. The spirits sought grace, redemption. And she sought the same from them—release from the harpies and demons, entry into a world of light and calm.

With the occupiers regrouped and restive, murmuring and sullen at her back she took what she later called her family portraits—mother and daughters, man and wife, sister and sister. That was half the job done, the victim half. Now for the perpetrators. She turned and faced them, moving close to them, photographing them as a group, moving in to capture inscrutable, individual stares and slack mouths. The peril was immediate, personal. Clear and present. Between her and the men with their shark-black eyes, there was no barrier, no distance, no room for escape. They were young, frightened, angry, defiant. They carried blooded machetes and homemade clubs stained dark with coagulated plasma. They had slept and lived rough, wearing vests full of holes, and hand-me-down sneakers or no shoes at all. Some wore new headbands that resembled a farmer's Sunday-suit tie. One had placed a pair of girl's panties on his head, like a bonnet. They would move together, a shoal, inspired by one another's rage until it built to a collective frenzy, beyond individual accounting. Remotely, in the outbuildings of the farm, she heard the crackle of a fire taking hold in bone-dry thatch, heard the cries of farm workers whose turn had now come. She heard shots fired and the thud of machetes on skin. She heard screams, but kept on photographing the faces before her—the rogue's gallery, she would call it—

the bravado and fear and dullness and fury. She did not speak. She knew her spell would soon expire, but she knew she had this moment to herself as long as the magic of her audacity numbed them. Only when her entire stock of film was almost used did she walk out back of the farm, through tall, ocher grass under a blue sky marbled with white, jolly clouds, and on through the bush. She turned once, to complete the sequence, as the farmhouse itself began to burn, casting unholy flickers over the discarded bicycles around a swimming pool turning green, the strident purple hedges of bougainvillea, the rusting barbecue and the dense lawn of emerald kikuyu grass. Then, before the occupiers had chance to give chase, she ran, on across the bush, four miles to the adjacent homestead, through tawny chattering scrub and mopane trees, stopping only when she knew she had outrun them. In that moment, finally, she trembled and tears scoured hollow cheeks. She shivered with fear and wept in exultation. She felt an almost irresistible desire to urinate. She had found and crossed the threshold she had only approached with Joe Shelby in Rwanda and she was free, finally, to abandon the quest for it.

✍

PRISTINA, KOSOVO. JUNE 2000

In their world, it was almost inevitable that they would meet. Friendships formed and dissolved and re-formed easily among the close band of their peers. For all they were rivals, they congregated inevitably in the same places, in the same theaters of competition, the same bars that became known as their watering holes. So often, since the schism between them, they had been in the same towns, sometimes in the same hotels. Now, in the drear reaches of the Balkans, where the minarets and domes jostled for space in the air they breathed, what had surely been foretold came to pass. She did not know why, but he called her. She had not seen him in nine months. She had heard rumors, stories about a condition, an illness, a curse that had struck down the man he had been, and brought forth a cripple from his body. But she had not seen him. He called her to say he was in trouble, that there was no compunction but he needed help he was sorry to ask for. She was more curious about his plight than angry at his presumption, conscious more of his need for help than of his treatment of her, his hurtful rejection. She would help a colleague, of course, and he was asking for help as a colleague. But he was asking her—and no one else, least of all the thief princess bitch—and she alone was going to him and that had to have meaning. He did not say what kind of help he needed. She did not ask.

They met outside the elevator in a hotel in Pristina—a rendezvous point he requested. With a telescopic walker's pole in his right hand, he seemed curiously unbalanced, tipped over. His left arm hung from his vest, straight and motionless, and the sleeve of his shirt had unraveled, flapping weakly as if he did not have even the strength to fold it back. He leaned heavily to the right on the walking pole. His face had changed little, but the shock in her voice betrayed them both. How could this apparition be the same man at all?

"What happened, Joe?"

"I wish I could tell you."

Joe Shelby had been taught that if he studied hard, his effort would be rewarded, and, usually, it was. He had learned human destiny could be controlled by individual human will. Among his school friends, in the rough-and-tumble alleyways of his hometown, in the grimy cauldrons of habitation below the Pennine Hills, he was acknowledged as a leader. He believed that, if he conceived a plan of action, he could also carry it through. In his family, that was a luxury, a novelty. His grandmother left school at thirteen to work in a cotton mill. His father had never been able to struggle totally free from the clinging legacy of being born in a household that prized a brown wages envelope on a Friday night above college degrees. Joe Shelby's grandfather had been a shipyard overseer of working class men, but a working class man nonetheless, his cap as flat as the vowels of his northern English accent. Where Eva Kimberly traced her lineage through knighthoods and commissions, Joe Shelby's line ran through machine shops and the lower ranks, the foot soldiers, not the officers. Where her family album showed the sepia prints of gatherings on the shaded terraces of large houses with servants paraded just off-camera, his memory book traced a progression from row houses to flat, muddy beaches where three-penny donkey rides were the closest his forebears came to the sleek polo ponies and hunters of her ancestors.

Joe Shelby's father had advanced the appropriate rungs on the invisible ladder of class, from overseer to manager, but he was still a man who had grown with oil behind his fingernails and grease on his hands. On the rare occasions that Joe Shelby visited the few aging aunts and uncles, widows or widowers in their narrow terraced homes, with gas fires hissing in sitting rooms that were always tidy and lonely, he saw them not simply as old people resigned to death's approach, but as the bridge across the generations, to a time when his forebears had been as impotent and exploited as the peasants of Kosovo or Zimbabwe, their expectations truncated in time and scope by the system that made a very few rich and powerful, and a very many poor and powerless. Joe Shelby's gift from his father, really, was his freedom to choose, his freedom to leap any hurdle simply because he wished to do so, and could will himself to do so.

Now the spell had broken.

The weakness had spread from his left arm to his left leg. His foot had begun to trail. In London, he had tripped, inexplicably, on a tennis court as he tried to maneuver himself into an ungainly swing at the ball. Walking through the city, he caught sight of himself in a store window, leaning forward as if in a gale, to compensate for the awkwardness of his leg. The physicians ran tests, took measurements, required him to show his prowess at pinching and gripping. His specialists talked of second opinions, at Queen's Square in London and the Mayo Clinic in Rochester, Minnesota, in the United States of America. There was talk of putative, experimental treatments—steroids and plasma exchange, even traction or exploratory surgery between the cervical vertebra.

When the siren call summoned him back to the Balkans, he did not hesitate. Ignoring the weakness, Joe Shelby flew in, posthaste, from London, bidding Eva Kimberly farewell with a promise that the long-awaited visit that night to the opera—*Tosca* with Plácido Domingo—would definitely be postponed, not canceled. Next week. Soon. At La Scala or wherever it took. And don't worry, he told her, he would be fixed: he had an appointment, soon, at the fancy clinic in the United States, where they worked miracles. It was, he said, a last trot around the paddock before that encounter.

In Vienna he switched flights for Skopje, renting on arrival a hard-shell car with armor plating. Avoiding his colleagues, he made a swift round among the bureaucrats, handing over cash and passport photographs to update accreditations, careful to stash them in separate pockets to avoid confusion at roadblocks. Locked in the car trunk were his laptop and spare batteries, drinking water and satellite phone—a valuable cargo that could provoke envy and cause trouble. He mapped a route that would cross lines through the Balkan patchwork—a not-for-beginners trajectory that would take him from one warlord to the next, under a variety of friendly and unfriendly guns. Climbing into his hard car, he told himself that his arm was fine, that the quivering would go away, that the American physicians would fix it with some wonder drug, some slice of the scalpel just as soon as he had completed this one assignment.

He paid the mandatory calls on the United Nations career optimists in their sandbagged offices adorned with large-scale, laminated maps that reduced the fault lines of the centuries into bold strokes of red, green and black marker-pen, as if that made them more open to resolution, as if the pen strokes themselves did not define the age-old chemistry of outsiders meddling in intractable, local matters. In the four days between assignment and deadline, he maneuvered his left arm awkwardly to take notes. Crouching beside fugitives to drain the distillate of their misery, he found he did not rise as easily as he had once done when he stood up, the interview over. He assembled in thick notebooks the variants and gradations of loathing from dignitaries and peasants who drew their allegiances from some indecipherable point five hundred years earlier. With a variety of rapacious and untrustworthy guides, he secured his moment of exclusivity by locating the wooded laager where fierce, anonymous men in beards with flared eagle badges sewn on U.S. surplus tunics crouched in the forest over AK-47 rifles and swore eternal hatred of the Serbs, the Germans, the United Nations and Uncle Sam. With a shiver of sadness, he acknowledged to himself—but to himself only—that the adrenaline rush of a scoop had, over the years, become secondary to rank fear. Each war, each adventure took its tally among those who took their invulnerability a step too far. The roll call was surprisingly modest considering the Faustian pact that underlay it. But, just as Mephistopheles would surely come to claim his prize and Dr. Faustus would resist, so, too had his own bargain worn thin. How could you sup from the cocktail of adrenaline and triumph when your body betrayed you?

In a concrete hotel, in this dour provincial capital, he settled before his troika of notebook, Scotch and laptop. Somewhere, trailing him, following his story through terse exchanges of e-mail, Faria Duclos had been assigned to match his words with pictures, gliding just beyond his field of vision, just inside the stockade that Eva Kimberly had erected around his heart. She, too, would have made her arrangements, hired her hard car. She, too, would be traveling alone—all the worse for a woman, a raven-haired ravaged beauty at that—along empty roads that the world mostly ignored.

In their barracks, National Guardsmen and Royal Marines hunkered down, giving no interviews or access. After 3:00 P.M., the roads became a nightmare. Chetnik snipers, his Albanian translator, Fatima, told him, were the hazard. Muslim dogs, said Danica, a Croat stringer who also had lines into the Serbs, fertilized by common hatreds creating alliances that would, at best, be temporary.

He had been on these same roads before, on an earlier assignment, when a car in front of him took a mine, eliminating Thatcher from *Newsweek* and Slingsby from *The New York Times* in one blast of fire and metal and dismemberment that had sent him and Faria spilling into the noisome ditches as the routine, post-mine machine-gunfire hosed down the debris, an indifferent hail of .50 cal fire that kept them pinned for three hours until the gunners wearied of their sport and returned laughing to their tough-guy brandies. What had the macho-man Thatcher said, the night before, over late whiskies? "Don't think of the bang. Think of the enveloping red wetness."

He would have all eternity to mull that wisdom.

In London, Eva Kimberly drove smooth roads in black cabs with voluble drivers bearing her to the dark reaches of Primrose Hill while her heart departed on its own, Africa-bound coordinates. Most times, she answered the phone in their shared apartment when he called from his satellite equipment, and he would listen for the hint of a gin-genie in her voice then check the time difference to calculate whether she had started early or late. But she would start, sooner or later. That was never in doubt, anymore than his absences and returns. If the genie was well and truly loose, she would ask whether he had seen *her* and he would say, no, he had not seen *her* for a long time. But he did not say that *she* was never far away, physically or otherwise.

Now, sitting before his icons, he raised his hands to the keyboard of his laptop, the organist summoning the faithful to commune, to reenact the mystery of words. He closed the drapes tight against the nocturnal sniper-fire that drew tracer lines between shabby apartment houses, sending side messengers to probe any pinprick of light. Still, stray rounds nicked the concrete walls, and sometimes shattered windows criss-crossed with gray duct tape against heavier explosions. He switched on the desk light, leaving just a pool of brightness around his props—his notebook and his whisky glass, his pack of cigarettes and chipped ashtray bearing the mocking insignia of a glitzy, international hotel chain: The World's Greatest Hotels. How long ago had that been true?

The screen was bright, blank.

In his mind, he was building the anecdote that would provide the introduction to his article. Thatcher and Slingsby had been a cover: The War Junkies. An Eyewitness Account. This time, the cover would read: Mayhem in the Balkans: Should Our Troops Come Home? Even now, in New York, they would be looking at the time-zone clocks on the wall in the big, whispering edit room and they would be wondering how much longer they could wait to call Shelby to remind him that it was show time. Show-and-tell. Joe Shelby was on deadline with a fat notebook and no time in the world. All he had to do was write. That had always been the easy part.

But now he could not.

Called upon to tap at its designated keys, his left hand slid away from the keyboard. Inexplicably, his left arm swung at his side. He stared at it as if it belonged to someone else entirely. Where there had been quivering in the upper arm muscles, the biceps lay flaccid along his upper arm, useful as a beached jellyfish. He closed his eyes, as if that would focus great power and authority on his mental order to move, but the limb disobeyed. His arm died on him, betrayed him, offering no mercy, with no right of appeal before the death knell sounded. Show time, and nothing to show. His will had failed him.

He sought again to use the keyboard with both hands, canting himself over so that he could use his shoulder muscles to swing his left arm into a position remotely close to the keypad. But, seeking to move his fingers, the arm again slipped from his knee. With his right hand he took a swig of Scotch, then maneuvered a Marlboro from its pack, and lit it again with the lighter in his right hand. The blank screen mocked him. When he sought to compose with his right hand only, the words stumbled incoherently across the laptop window like one of those very old telex circuits transmitting at a quarter speed.

The guerilla commander squatted in the forest camp. Sounds like he's taking a crap.

Deep in the killing fields of the Balkans. Used that six months ago. Bad then. Worse now.

The commander tightened his grip on his worn AK-47. Fuck. Fuck. Fuck. What's wrong?

Joe Shelby knew exactly what he wanted to say: he wanted to say that this bearded man led a band of degenerates who, under the guise of nationalism, had committed an atrocity they blamed on their opponents. And the reason they had done so was to protect a prospering narcotics fiefdom. It should have been easy enough just to get that across, with an admixture of atmosphere and location and cliché to create the requisite mix of journalism lite favored by the comic. But, with his left arm refusing the simplest of orders, it was as if his ability to write had been reduced by much more than half, as if expression were a two-handed matter, requiring the full gamut of eight fingers and two thumbs to keep pace with the tumble of words and ideas generated by his memories, his notes, the very deadline urgency of what was to be written.

Remove one hand and the channel that bore the currents from brain to screen was narrowed, too constricted for the full flow of thought and language. All that emerged was a sad, halting trickle. If he spoke his ideas out loud, he had some sense of what he might achieve. But when he tried to capture those same ideas on the screen—or by taking notes with his right hand—the filter re-inserted itself. Joe Shelby was a left-hander, a southpaw, and his right hand could not write more than a scrawl, or type alone at the speed he needed to keep pace with the whirl of what he most wanted to say.

He knew from the e-mail traffic that she was in town. He knew he could ask no one else to help him without demanding a price, a counter-trade. He knew that, when he called, she would come and he would not be able to vouch for the emotions she might inspire.

"I wish I could tell you," he said.

Chapter Seven

First summit. FIRST SUMMIT. I'm here. I'M HERE. Dow Crag. 2,555 feet. Almost missed it in the fog. I've reached a summit and if the sun was shining I'd be able to see all the way over to Scafell Pike. Chomolungma. I'd be looking at Coniston Old Man across that huge hole I've just climbed up through. I'd look south way out over Morecambe Bay to Blackpool Tower—on a clear day. GPS coordinates SD 26262 97781. But I can't call anybody. No cell phone. No microwave signal. No satellite disk. Not even a carrier pigeon. Freedom. Alone, perched on the summit rocks, cold and damp and what? Triumphant. Yes, I guess triumphant. Because it was tough. And I can go down again now, can't I? Back down the easy way onto the Walna Scar Road with the compass and the map and get to a phone and call Eva and say: look, I did what I needed to do and I'm back and I've proved my point. Except I haven't. How long ago is it now since I was last here on this same old beautiful lump of rock? Fifteen, sixteen years? And in those days, in summer, when we were all hot and sweaty and thirsty, we'd hit the summit last thing after climbing all

day so that our arms felt they'd been pulled out of the sockets and we were all weighed down with ropes and crabs and nuts, and we'd tally up how many thousand feet of rock we'd done so we could measure the total to see how it tallied against the height of the North Wall of the Eiger. Then run—I mean RUN—down South Rake and the scree and all the way down to the pub in Torver. There'd sometimes be youth hostel girls hiking their way around and that would be a bonus if you got a lucky fumble and we were always lucky. And now all memory. Sometimes you have to just stop and think and say to yourself: I did the climbs, and hit the roads, and read the poems and wrote some and covered my share of boom-boom so the innings wasn't too bad. Awful. Those cricketing metaphors. Don't cross the pond, the comic reckons. But it's part of dinosaur Englishness: remember that poem? "And his captain's hand on his shoulder smote: play up and play the game." Well, I guess I played the game, but not always by the rules. I made my choice. I hit the road when some of the others were getting mortgages and houses and wives and families. And now they've got the Merc-in-the-drive pile. And I've got this pile of wet rock I'm sitting on and a quivering arm and a leg with all the power and resilience of Jell-O. The arm of flesh shall fail you, as the hymn says. But if you add it all up, would you rather have stayed and been safe or would you rather have done what you did?

The point is I got this far. Whatever happens now I got this far. The mist just cleared for a second and I saw Coniston Water and I thought of Donald Campbell in 1967 when he crashed his Bluebird trying to break his own speed record and went down to the bottom. He made it. That's what he was thinking when the boat lifted off and cartwheeled over and smashed him to bits with the impact of hitting a brick wall at 300 mph. I made it this far, he was thinking, and no one can take that away now whatever happens. But, then, look how it turned out for him.

GRASMERE, ENGLAND. SEPTEMBER 14, 2000

The mist had not lifted. The rain had not stopped. She was conscious of time moving at a submarine pace since Joe Shelby disappeared behind a veil of drizzle that explained to her why this region specialized primarily in green grass and sheep that grew so fat from eating it. The valleys were so steep that her cell phone had lost its signal. Beyond the drystone walls, uneven fields led up to a scraggly tree line that eventually petered out in rough, gray crags and seas of bracken turning from green to gold and then to a dull sepia, entwined intimately with wraiths of mist. Beyond that there would be soaring, glorious asymmetrical peaks with inscrutable names— Harrison Stickle, Pike o'Stickle, Pike o'Blisco, Bowfell, Crinkle Crags. Somewhere up there, a limping man struggled on, unable to take no for an answer, to recognize that his luck had run out, a Canute proving that the tide of mortality was invincible—so sure of himself that he'd refused to take a radio, and so deeply uncertain that he'd stopped to pray before he set off. For what? For strength and forgiveness? For three more days? For the people he always managed to leave behind as he indulged himself? Or perhaps it was worse than she thought—a moment in a cold chapel to request the extreme unction, the last rites, according to some inner voice that decreed he must perish high in the mountains, make his death as much of a drama as he had sought from his life. Was that what the Lake District's muse would require of him as the price of his self-aggrandizement?

Turn wheresoe'er I may / By night or day / The things which I have seen I now can see no more. And, again: *But yet I know, where'er I go / That there hath past away a glory from the earth.* The lines had been underlined in pencil in the pocket Wordsworth which, after some consideration of weight-versus-spiritual-uplift, he'd left behind in the glove compartment of the car. His intimations were more of mortality than immortality. But he had penciled another line with a faint exclamation mark, an ironic notation: *And I again am strong.*

She had no particular agenda. She had a day to fill before arriving in Thirlmere to the north, stopping in the slate-gray, rain-glistening town of Ambleside and turning up her collar against the wind to meander among almost-out-of-season stores that still refused to reduce their prices on boots and parkas, souvenirs and a curious confection called Kendal Mint Cake that tasted to her like pure sugar injected with some minty essence. At a liquor store, she pondered whether to buy a half or a full bottle of single malt and settled on a full bottle which she stowed in the leather grip in the trunk of the car. For their reunion, of course.

From a desolate car park in Bowness on the lake shore, where the wind flurried and raced over puddles of rainwater on the gray tarmacadam, and the rain traversed Windermere in solemn, veiled procession, she made calls on a faint wireless signal, reestablishing contact with the various strands of her business: the Web site manager and the shippers, the accountant who kept track obsessively of the cash flow and pronounced it sound. She tried to raise her store in Nairobi, but succeeded only in connecting to a recorded announcement in Swahili and English saying that all circuits were busy. She was adrift, severed from her daily business and her distant home. For her vigil she had packed a serious biography and a sheaf of paperwork, weighing down her leather grip with its cargo of practical day wear and reunion clothes with their optimistic frills and fripperies. Laying the Scotch among them, like a doll or a child, she thought: is this my baby? My muse? My sole companion? And was I like this before he initiated me into the art of solo consumption, into the slow lonely slide from sharp functionality to the blurred edges of self-pity and imprecision? Of course not. So why do I allow myself to be seduced by it now? Despairing of ever finding a familiar, friendly voice, she switched off the phone altogether and rolled slowly north on the prescribed route. By lunchtime she was hungry, as much for company as for food. She had been unable to show the same enthusiasm for breakfast as Joe Shelby had, awkwardly maneuvering his fork and knife to attack a plate of bacon, eggs, Cumberland sausage and a menacing concoction called black pudding made of blood. Instead she had nibbled at toast, toyed with muesli, and now the chill in the air gnawed at her. She had meandered to a place called Grasmere that offered white-painted hostelries with black window frames and lunch menus. The rain cascaded down from the steep fellsides, pressing her indoors to seek refuge.

Perusing a menu, she ordered a gin and tonic, then a half-bottle of red wine from some indistinct vineyard in Chile, breaking her resolution to hold off until evening almost before it was made. At the bar, an intense, dark-haired young man in his twenties who had parked his little sporty car next to hers on the gravel parking lot cast a predatory eye over her.

Freedom, she decided. This was freedom. Freedom from Joe and his brooding. Freedom from the never-spoken answer to the spectral question: what if it's incurable, like they say? Freedom to throw caution to the winds. She was, technically, free to go anywhere, do anything she wanted. Freedom from unscheduled reappearances in the boudoir. Freedom from guilt.

It was a freedom she had hardly known, still less enjoyed. Always there had been a clamor for her attention from her school friends and playmates and college associates and pupils and patients: then, after the death of her mother, the same demands were made in her long relationship with Jeremy Davenport, most of all within the network that represented the extended family—Africa's blend of support and bondage. What freedom was there in the tending of a querulous father, the peremptory demands of an arrogant lover, the calls from distant pay phones to say a clinic had been ransacked, a child had died, a girl had been raped by an uncle?

Africa did not permit freedom. Africa placed you at a fixed point within a constellation of unchosen relationships—nephews, aunts, parents—all with their demands, their needs, their assumptions of support. And she too had those same needs so that, at home, among the people she had grown up with, she understood her location perfectly, without need of his GPS devices or compasses or questions. She knew she was part of the broader landscape, while Joe Shelby knew he was alone. For him, freedom could only be exercised in solitude. But how could you be free when you hankered for a companion's voice and touch and solace, or pined for the familiar joys and irritations of friends, acquaintances, family? But, then, how could you exploit liberty to the full if those same people filtered your vision, rode shotgun on your impulses, built fire-walls around your ambitions and desires? How could you be free to exploit wealth and good fortune when the immediate assumption in your entourage was that you would share it, dilute it? That was Africa's dilemma and curse.

Before lunch, in the chilly hotel bathroom, with its little bowl of potpourri on the shelf beside a mirror framed by pink floral wallpaper, she was not displeased with what the young man saw. Save for the smudges under her eyes that, late at night, turned darker and deeper, she was still whole, still thirty-something and far from middle age. A Fer-ragamo silk scarf in rust colors offset her black polo neck and sandy golden hair, shining like polished bronze with no hint of gray. In her black, tailored slacks, her waist and thighs were snug and tight from workouts. There *was,* possibly, a certain haughtiness that people some-times mistook for arrogance, not realizing that this was the laager around her doubts. There *was,* indeed, a sharp edge to her voice when she thought people forward or insulting. But that was not what the young man had seen: single woman, of very slightly advanced years, alone and drinking. Mature. Practiced. Good tits. Great arse. Quite a looker. Obviously hot to trot. Maybe an afternoon of lubricious delight. And it would be so easy. He was not bad looking. The lunchtime beers had not yet overlaid his midriff with fat. He removed his jacket to reveal a pert enough backside. He did not limp or stumble, or maneuver with his hands to raise his beer glass. His eyes shone like a puppy's, almost disguising the lizard glint of the rutting male. He'd know some little place where a room could be had and no questions asked before they went their separate, sated ways. Who would know?

She would know. That's who. She would know she had allowed herself the thought: why does Joe not look at me like that anymore? Why has the fire that burned into the night in Jadini become such a dull ember in such a short space of time? Most of all, she would know she had allowed herself to be seen as no more than the sum of physical attributes associated with arousal.

In the dining room, she and the stranger were the only guests, their tables facing one another across an expanse of folded napkins, shining glassware, pink linen and silk posies. Polished horse brasses adorned old, low beams. Hidden speakers, turned low, broadcast generic versions of old songs: she deciphered one that began "Trains and boats and planes," but gave up trying to recall the lyrics or who first wrote or recorded it. Beyond her field of view, behind a screen, the kitchen echoed to the sound of a slammed saucepan, hissed rebukes. The manager, or owner, fussed in a desultory, vaguely offended way, as if he were seeking a scape-goat for unfulfilled expectations—a full restaurant, a Michelin star, a hint of gratitude from a life of disappointment.

The rain spattered on the narrow sash windows. She chose shrimp cocktail and venison salad. He ordered soup of the day and the roast lamb with another pint of bitter. If she looked his way, he would be looking at her, like a cheetah in the savanna, coiled and awaiting the sig-nal. Or a hyena. One smile would do it, one stretch of her shoulders to offer a glimpse of her breasts. Is this how it happened? She had never tried before, prided herself on never entertaining a one-night stand, although that had been a matter of definition in her college years. But, in fact, how did it happen? As a grown, mature woman with a career and commitments, it would be easy enough to start an affair, but how would it then end? Begin, say, with an afternoon quickie in an anonymous bed complete with worries about transmissible diseases and the availability of condoms suffusing the ineffable delight of exploring a new, naked body, an introduction to new odors, habits, requirements, dimensions. Then, wham-bam, thank you sir. On your way and me on mine, wiping away the fluids and the guilt, showering off the betrayal. Or would the phone calls start coming: I have to see you again. I've left my wife and three-month-old baby. And Joe standing with a buzzing receiver in his good, right hand saying: wonder who that was. Or, we seem to be getting a lot of wrong numbers these days.

The shrimp cocktail was all bottled mayonnaise stained with ketchup. The venison salad was stringy. The wine had brought a soothing, familiar glow that softened life's cruel edges. Then he was sitting at her table: wonder if you'd like to join me for coffee in the lounge. His accent was strong, northern, the flat vowels and muscular consonants more pronounced than Joe's. Was she to be his Lady Chatterley? Coffee? Why not? Really, Eva, where was the harm in a cup of coffee? Where was the guilt?

"Thanks, OK." She saw triumph, almost surprise, flare in his black eyes and thought: Get a grip, woman.

"But only for a second. I really have to go." Even to herself, she sounded hopelessly stuck-up. The victory kindling faltered in the younger man's eyes. His name, it turned out, was Desmond, Des to his friends. From Manchester. He wore no ring, but that meant nothing. Her name, she discovered, was Maria. From Watford. Was he heading south? Then she was heading north. Was he in business? No, just passing through, a long diversion from the M6, because he loved the Lakes, the fells, Wordsworth country. Well, then, have a good journey, Des. And thanks for the coffee.

But she had permitted herself to imagine the alternative outcome, and, as she left the hotel in the mid-afternoon rain, waving to him as he climbed into his sporty little car, she was almost overwhelmed: she had been wanted, desired, out of the blue—perhaps lusted after would be a better description; she had frittered her time on a meaningless, gratuitous flirtation that could never have come to anything. But it had satisfied a need for attention that she felt as keenly as other people did: so why did Joe fail so utterly to understand that, why did it not seem to be a factor in his calculations when he abandoned her, placing her second to the Balkans or the Gaza Strip or to the specter she feared most—the figure who haunted them, slid between them like a wraith, a genie that rose from her nocturnal whisky bottle to fill her with rage and desolation? In most recent times, of course, she had good reason to believe from his behavior that his ghosts had not been laid, as if his illness had recalled the phantoms from the past. But why could he not understand that attention, thoughtfulness, simple old-fashioned caring cost nothing but paid huge dividends? Betrayal was just as easy by default as by commission, so how often had she been betrayed, in one definition or the other? She felt a quick, violent urge to drive after the young man—like in a Bond movie—overtake him, race him so that the tires of their speeding cars almost touched on a winding, sunlit road; and finally fall into whatever bed he chose, give way to a simple, carnal urge for a new, taut, stranger's body.

Then Joe's image came to her, struggling across the high ground, limping, lost.

Well, you did well for yourself, she said out loud. Four hours of freedom and you're anybody's.

She was to stay the night—set up advanced base camp, Joe said jokingly—in a suite at a lakeside hotel still further north, over Dunmail Raise and along the somber shores of Thirlmere, an artificial lake, built from the flooding of two smaller meres to provide water for the toiling masses of Manchester ninety-six miles of gravity-fed pipeline to the south. But, in the car, with a road map unfolded over her knees and the engine turning to provide heat, she decided on a different route—freedom, indeed!—back south then, at Ambleside, taking a right turn, almost retracing her route of the morning but veering off into the Langdale Valley. The map showed a narrow track, marked with arrows apparently denoting steepness, that snaked over a place called Blea Tarn before dropping down to the Little Langdale valley and the Wrynose Pass, where he planned to make camp. She would surprise him. That suddenly seemed the most obvious plan. He had said there should be no contact until he arrived in advanced base, but she knew he would not object to seeing her, to being surprised, over-whelmed by events, as so often in the beginning, when he had parked his motorcycle suddenly at an Umbrian roadside to roll with her into a hedgerow, and the passengers crowding a small, speeding car had cheered as they passed. Or, yet earlier, when she had halted her Land Rover on a trail above the Rift Valley and straddled him in the rough grass, breasts bare to the African wind, while kites circled and a herd of Thomson's gazelles looked on with mild interest.

How could anyone be expected to stand fast against a whirlwind, a tornado like that, a typhoon that tore everything from its roots and anchors and pinnings? How could she not have fallen under Joe Shelby's spell? When she thought of the young man at lunch, Desmond or who-ever he really was, she flushed to think she already knew betrayal, not as a victim but as a perpetrator. In the warm interior of the car, her cheeks reddened.

She recalled how Jeremy Davenport had been devastated, returning from his stay in Serengeti with crazy tales to tell of a crazy woman, brimming with adventures to lay at her feet, like a gun dog with its booty, but finding her gone from Nairobi and, at Jadini, unwilling to see him except in Joe Shelby's company. Her father, too, disapproved of her new liaison—the first time he had failed to interpret her feelings, give her the benefit of the doubt. Her friends in Nairobi—the photographers and conservationists, the aid workers and society hostesses—sided with Jeremy, and had little time for Joe Shelby. At first, Jeremy Davenport had tried to brave it out, refusing to allow a trace of emotion to disfigure his tanned, aquiline features. He went about his business in his immaculate safari suits, confirming his client list, laying in stocks for his next trip to the bush with wealthy, overseas visitors—film and champagne, smoked salmon and beers, ammunition in case things went wrong. Then he launched his countercampaign, pleading, striving in vain to reestablish authority. Come with me, he said, to the new camp in the Mara, the one with the big tents with wooden floors and the crystal on the table. Just talk. Please talk. He telephoned at odd hours, waylaid her as she left her store in Nairobi, wrote letters for the first time she could remember. The dark patches under his eyes broke through his perennial tan. Surely all the years together are worth something, surely I deserve a hearing: I'm not asking for everything, just a chance to persuade you to love me again because I can't live without you; you are my life; you are everything. Just like me. Just don't turn away from me. We can go anywhere, to Paris, London, New York. We can have adventures, romance. Mauritius or the Seychelles. Please just tell me, he said, what I can offer and whatever it is I'll do it, because I can't bear this. Then there were the drunken calls, the vile insults—harlot, whore—and, a day later, the delivery of roses accompanied by craven apologies.

In divorces, they say, you either get to keep the furniture or the friends. She got neither. As if reading from a script, her friends told her Joe Shelby was a womanizer, a home wrecker, a known philanderer, too fond of the bottle and the weed, too fond of his bylines and adventures and one-night stands. He was tied to her, to the crazy one, the Frenchwoman. She was the mistress of his soul and would ever be. In his heart he would never leave her and he would always be drawn to her because they mirrored one another. But none of the cardboard cutouts matched the man she slept with, and she looked away from her friends and family, ignored them until much later when one barb from her father broke through her defenses and was never dislodged. "You know, you've broken Jeremy," he said, almost casually, as he stood and watched her pack the day before she finally departed to join Joe Shelby, first in Rome, then on to London. "He waited all his life for you. And now he's a wreck, a shadow. He will never forgive you or the shame of it. Not in his heart of hearts. You must beware of his vengeance. All your life. And you could have played it so differently."

In these short, brutish days of an English autumn, the taunt returned with greater frequency, no longer so stealthy, no longer a cloaked figure that pounced to surprise her with a whispered denunciation, but a brazen accuser: you destroyed a man who loved you, and why? Because your body ached and thrilled and your mind and soul were silenced, seduced? Because a transient weaver of dreams spun a myth for you and you clutched at it, falling from the grace that you, above all people, had been given in such generous measure?

As the Umbrian hedgerows and African savanna receded, so, too, did her inquisitor become more bold: where is your Grand Passion now? Where is the thrill of the moment that blinded you to the consequences? Remember: Romeo and Juliet died young, but you have a whole life stretching ahead of you to fill with regrets, tied to a cripple. You were Eva and Jeremy, Jeremy and Eva, a couple with a destiny of togetherness, companionship, a solid nucleus. And now you are a subdivision of Eva and Joe, a particle freed of gravity and weight.

CRINKLE CRAGS

Chapter Eight

She turned the car south, winding past Rydal Water, where the poet had lived and written of his daffodils and the bliss of solitude. She did not want the bliss of solitude. Solitude merely encouraged her accuser. She wanted a passion that could transcend a wet tent and a crippled man. But the only passion she could muster was anger at the rapaciousness of these people, these Lake District merchants with their milking of other people's achievements—the Wordsworth Hotel, the Beatrix Potter gift-shop, Dove Cottage, Lakeland fudge. Joe Shelby told her that, years back, in the winter, the Lake District closed to all but the truly commit-ted—the climbers, the walkers, the hill farmers in their mud-spattered Land Rovers carrying hay bales and snake-bellied sheepdogs. In those times, he said, in winter, the pubs were cold and unwelcoming and the fells were lonely, empty places where the streams cascaded and the path-ways turned to rivulets and the peat moss lay in swampy ambush for the careless walker. Now it was year-round cash register. Every cotton baron's mansion and oversized Victorian vicarage had been turned into a "country house hotel" with five-course dinner menus and a full English breakfast. Prosperity brought people here all year round on "weekend breaks." Every walker had a full outfit of expensive gear, stowed in shiny cars parked outside hotels that had no closed season. It was the new, market-driven England, the one he didn't recognize but still found tugging at his soul. Up there, he was looking for the old one to see if that had been packaged, too, as an exemplar of the market's power. If he got to the top, he'd probably find someone selling Kendal Mint Cake or Peter Rabbit figurines.

The road was infuriating. Even if she had wanted to pursue Des in his sports model, the way ahead was blocked by small cars each containing a matched set of pensioners, dawdling, tootling, maintaining a steadfast twenty miles per hour along a twisting blacktop that did not permit overtaking, even in a powerful car like hers. She imagined each vehicle loaded with the day's newspaper and homemade sandwiches and a thermos flask of sweet, milky tea to accompany bland conversations that followed routes devised over decades to skirt around touchy subjects or painful issues, borne on the familiar sights that the road revealed: isn't that where we picnicked, before the kids left home? Isn't that where X caught a fish and Y fell into the lake?

But was that so unfamiliar? Back home, in Africa, you would drive past a tree or a rock and realize that, unconsciously, you had been seeing that same object for so long that it had become part of you, part of the frame into which you dovetailed your existence. That was where she would have finished up with Jeremy, bumping along a sandy track, past the same broad acacia tree in the same sunstruck Rift Valley, watching a herd of nibbling giraffes that had been there—one generation or another—forever. Joe Shelby made no room for such certainties. He led a double life. She sensed it, knew it now. They—the old team that preceded her—were too often in the same places; their bylines gave them away. And there had been far more damning evidence that she did not

wish to dwell on now lest she cease to believe his protestations of innocence and be made a fool.

After the dawdlers in the cars came the cyclists, in bright yellow
slickers and crash helmets, pedaling all over the narrow road, waving at
her with righteous anger when she blasted the car horn to pull by.

At Ambleside she followed the road signs for Great Langdale, past a
spectral rugby pitch in the mist, through a place called Clappersgate,
adjusting the heater controls of the car to de-mist the windscreen as the
rain sluiced across it with ever greater vehemence, as if it was all personal, not just weather. The hills above her might not even have existed
and her vision extended only to the narrow stone walls and the wooden
gates leading into fields where the shrouds of mist turned the sheep into
ghosts. She glimpsed a road sign telling her she was passing through
Elterwater—"Please drive carefully through our village"—but it might
just as well have said Ouagadougou or Mogadishu, places that seemed
more familiar because of the rambling, doomed continent that
embraced them. Alone in the car, her memories strayed not quite randomly, searching out the milestones, the turning points, the intersec-
tions of circumstances that propelled a decision she would not have
been called upon to make if he and his Frenchwoman had not arrived at
Naivasha. The classic scenario—the intruder, the rogue molecule, crashing and banging to produce fission. But if there had been meltdown—
and, of course, there had—why had she not seen from the very start that
she would never be alone with the man who carried her away from her
beloved Africa? Why had she trusted him to bury his dead the way she
had consigned Jeremy Davenport to the netherworld of new history?
Why had she ignored the jealous tracker's signs—the distant, wistful
looks, the lacunae in the narrative? Months earlier, when he returned
from the Balkans, something had changed and she had chosen to ignore
it, attributing the silences to his preoccupation with illness and decline.
Considering what came later, that, surely, was the moment for the

inquisitor's icy gaze and stiletto questions. For there had been a new element after his Balkan visit, an unspoken rebuke, as if she had been secretly compared and found wanting. But she had done nothing. From the very beginning she had looked only in the direction she wished to, averting her gaze from the snares, the tripwires he declined to remove from their common path.

CAPE TOWN, SOUTH AFRICA. OCTOBER 1999

In the first weeks, right after Jadini, he insisted she accompany him on his travels, take time out from her business. First it had been Rome, then a mysterious excursion to Jerusalem—her first taste of the hobo life in which he invested so much passion, took so seriously. "And to think they pay us good money to do this," a colleague of his, a Canadian reporter from a big-time American television network, told her over drinks at a subterranean bar in Jerusalem, at the hotel where the journalists, the shitholes men and women, stayed to await the latest outrage. Once, she thought she caught a glimpse of her—the Frenchwoman—in a rental car parked outside the hotel in the pale, limestone backstreets of east Jerusalem. But, before she could make inquiries and for no discernible reason, the orders changed. Tel Aviv–Johannesburg–Cape Town. Jadini was her turf, her arena, where she set the rules, and he was the novice seeking initiation. Cape Town switched the markers.

Comic likes boom-boom. So boom-boom's good for Joe. But we'll be OK in the Nellie. So much gobbledygook, so much energy diverted into high-octane travel and adrenaline for the purposes of what? Ink on a printed page with colored photographs that became the detritus of long, tedious airline flights, to be tossed aside, gathered by the cleaners, pulped.

The Nellie, she knew, meant the Mount Nelson Hotel, under the great wall of Table Mountain, Africa's grandest hotel where the staff at reception greeted him with a discreet, knowing welcome, casting a speculative eye over her as if she were only the latest trophy brought in from the hunt. The other guests observed a basic dress code but Joe Shelby stuck to his jeans and vest, believing devoutly that a Platinum Card overcame all etiquette. Main suite, he insisted—comic's paying, for Chrissakes—on the garden side, if you please. And, from the bar at the sound of his voice, a matching apparition made an entrance in faded jeans and olive tee shirt and scuffed Texan boots, cropped black hair and a deep tan from too much time in the bush: meet Du Plessis, soldier and photographer, tracker and adventurer and never trust yourself alone with him. The southern Africa guy—sixteen wars and still snapping. One of *his* people. One of his collection of spirits who seemed to glide past humdrum obligations, believing themselves called to the higher vocation of observing and recording, using other people's catastrophes to vindicate their rejection of the common laws and duties governing the lives of lesser beings. They floated, his people, from hotel to hotel, never owning anything or paying the bill or accepting responsibility for anything beyond the indulgence of their own foibles: they lived in a world of rental cars and hired rooms, expense accounts and adrenaline that demanded an ever greater fix of catastrophe from those they fed on. It was not her way, and it grated with her: she had been raised to discretion, to quiet solid wealth fixed in place by property and land and the sense that it was poor taste indeed to flaunt riches among people sliding ever further into poverty.

"How's it, Joe? Hey, Eva. Welcome to the deep south. Big boom-boom. Let's hit it." Du Plessis spoke in the clipped, hybrid tones of southern Africa. In the social order of the continent's white minorities, that denoted a lower class than the officers and gentry who had colonized further north, in Kenya in particular. She held his taunting gaze that fell on her as if to say: don't think I haven't seen you before. She looked back scornfully into mocking eyes that said: don't imagine that you are the first bimbo Joe Shelby has brought here. And don't think that you belong in the places we go.

Eva Kimberly was well-traveled: her father had seen to that. They had taken rooms at the Oriental in Bangkok and the Savoy in London, the Plaza in New York, the Crillon in Paris. Even Jeremy had sometimes shown a lover's extravagance, putting them up once at Brown's in Dover Street rather than his usual cramped club quarters that came cheap as part of the reciprocal arrangement with Nairobi's Muthaiga Club. But she had never been in a hotel suite quite like this before—the brocade and antiques and high ceilings and the sheer size of the place, big as a squash court. Two bathrooms, of course. And a sitting room with a well-stocked bar and deep sofas and flower arrangements at every turn, a writing desk in the bay window, looking out over the palms and roses and bougainvillea of the gardens and the swimming pool.

As he unpacked his tote bag, Joe Shelby suggested that she might want to make business contacts in the city while he and Du Plessis went to work in the townships. Look, he said, there are people here who are really into all the same stuff as you are. Web cams. E-commerce. Synergies. Talk to them while I'm out in the townships. But she wouldn't have that, not after the way Du Plessis had looked at her.

I'm not some popsy, some bimbo, some Jeffrey Archer floozy, Joe Shelby, she said firmly. I'll talk to them when I feel like it, but as for the townships, you forget that I grew up in Africa, and I'm not afraid of Africans.

So wait 'til you meet these Africans, he said. Generation X. No bwanas and memsahibs here. Still, it's your choice. But you'd better wear this, he said: from his bag he pulled a Kevlar bulletproof vest. It was not new and it was not her size. She could guess whose sweat and smell had stained its collar, but said nothing, pulling it across her chest as if it were her totem of victory.

From Crossroads, they traveled to Guguletu—Gugs, Du Plessis

called it—and on to Khayelitsha and the Cape Flats, piloting the rental car around smouldering barricades, navigating by the columns of oily smoke rising from burning tires, some of them—horribly—fast around the necks of randomly incinerated victims. The photographer had gone on ahead in a separate rental car, calling in by cell phone like a tracker on safari, directing them from this kill to that, from one barricade to another, from township to squatter camp.

And these were not her Africans. They were young men wild with inchoate rage at someone's failure to deliver on the promises made by someone equally indistinct. They were saying: where are the jobs, the money, the BMWs, the life we fought for? Where is the land for us when the whites sit fat and pretty behind their high walls and security fences, around their pools and tennis courts and barbecues, while we scavenge and steal? They were not her Masai, her warrior sons and sisters, her meandering Kikuyu, her wily Kalinjin. They were not her people of the limitless savannas, the sweeping Rift Valley and the big skies, but the product of loose associations in mean shacks, half of them HIV-positive and spoiling for a fight with the next Big Lie to come their way: freedom and prosperity, health and jobs, justice and peace, security and longevity—lies, all of them. They wore torn trousers and ragged vests and cracked hand-me-down shoes without laces. Their eyes shone with rage. She cowered from them when they approached the car, grasping knobkerries driven through with six-inch nails.

Joe Shelby was not especially impressed. No scoops here, no big exclusive, too many hacks, he said, watching with amused indifference as a car full of his colleagues came under a barrage of rocks and gasoline-bombs ahead of them on a broad railroad bridge in Mitchell's Plain, where people of mixed race had been dumped by apartheid and never left when the race barriers came down again.

But what about the ordinary people, Joe, aren't they always the ones that suffer?

Good point, very good point, he said, backtracking from the front lines of conflict between an angry, flowing, unpredictable mass and a police force that used pretty much the same tactics as it always had, pulling back from the stray rounds and crackle of gunfire and the appalling, itching, scratching stench of CS gas.

Cowering behind lace curtains in a neat house with a yard and gate that mimicked the far grander estates of Cape Town's whites was a middle-class, mixed-race couple, he a teacher, she a sales clerk. Eva talked them in, sliding past their fear, their objections. She softened them for his gentle, prodding, never-intrusive questioning that did not seem to be all cynical manipulation. They told him how they shuttered their homes and lived in darkness for fear of marauding gangs, out on the Cape Flats where the currency was crack cocaine and the anger never eased. They told him how they struggled to keep a few rands back from the protection money they paid to the minibus drivers who carried them to and from work, avoiding the gangs and the gunmen and the shakedowns. They admitted, finally, that their own children—their hope, their pride—were out there, somewhere, now, with the mob, running wild, never going to school, and they did not know where they were and would not be surprised if they came back in a coffin and might even be glad that the struggle was over. But where could they go? Where was safe? This was their home and it was a home from hell with even their own children turned into unrecognizable monsters. They sang their song for him and he called on his cell phone for Du Plessis to make his way to their coordinates. To her surprise, Du Plessis showed tenderness, empathy, and she took that to mean he had some inner understanding of what it was to grow up on the wrong side of the tracks, to be excluded. He spoke to the couple in their native Afrikaans, the language bequeathed by the first Dutch settlers. As if this were a wedding or a baptism, he sat them for a stylized family portrait, in front of their glass-fronted display case with its framed photographs of their lost children, and large television and overstuffed brown sofa with its antimacassars and fringed velour cushions—a vertical shot that would make the cover story: "The Innocents—the scramble to get by in a blighted nation."

Bingo, Joe said, as they left. You're a star.

But not a photographer, she murmured and, for a moment, he looked inexplicably hurt.

Back at the hotel, she bathed for a long time, listening to a classical radio program that played Vivaldi and Mozart to accompany Joe's tip-tip-tapping on the laptop and enthusiastic vending of his story to an editor in New York. The Innocents—caught between the lines of Africa's newest conflict.

Their room-service dinner arrived with great fanfare on a trolley attended by four separate retainers to spread the white linen tablecloth, pour the Cape Sauvignon from its ice bucket, retrieve the crayfish from its warming trays and spoon vinaigrette over the salad.

"Where you guys from?" Joe inquired as he riffled through his wallet for an unnecessarily generous tip—guilt money, she surmised.

"Guguletu, sir," the lead waiter said.

"We were there today, weren't we Joe?"

"We are there every day, madam."

That night they made love in a wide bed with a passion that was not the spontaneous coupling of the Italian hedgerows or the Kenyan savanna, but a darker, anguished lovemaking of the kind only survivors understand, more familiar to him than to her.

"What would she have done? It was her flak jacket wasn't it?" Over breakfast, delivered by the same fugitives from the front lines, she tried to keep her voice light, as if she'd inquired about the weather forecast.

"Faria? She'd have said: let's go for the boom-boom."

"So I failed boom-boom 101?"

"No way," he said with a big grin. "You got me a cover. You took me out of the darkness and showed me light."

"Bullshit, Joe Shelby."

"No bullshit. It's true. I'd have gone for more boom-boom, the defining moment, the blood. You saw Du Plessis. Where do you think he'd have dragged me? Right into the middle of it. You showed me the real people."

"Then I feel sorry for the others."

He shaved, showered, dressed and lifted both Kevlar vests from the floor.

"Coming?"

"Where?"

"Du Plessis says there's more boom-boom."

"But you've got your story."

"No, you've got to be there. You've got to be up at the sharp end because that's where people show themselves. That's where you find out. And anyhow, it ain't over 'til the fat lady sings."

"And when might that be?"

"When the final deadline tolls the knell on Friday night."

"Then give me the numbers of the business people. I've had enough boom-boom for one week, thank you very much. You don't mind?"

"Mind? I love you, Eva. I love you for whatever you are and whatever you want to be. And I love you for giving me the idea yesterday."

"And you don't think I'll be letting you down?"

"One idiot is enough."

"Two with Du Plessis."

"He's two all by himself. That's why we go in separate cars."

"You know, I may not be too good on boom-boom 101 but I think I've figured Joe Shelby 101."

"Meaning?"

"In my part of Africa there's a saying: the wife who stands between a warrior and a lion is a foolish wife."

"Really?"

"Not really. But work it out."

LANGDALE, ENGLAND. SEPTEMBER 2000

Langdale, it transpired, had a New Dungeon Ghyll Hotel and an Old Dungeon Ghyll Hotel, and a place called Wall End. There was Great Langdale and Little Langdale and the Langdale Pikes, though they were covered in mist. A sign at a campsite ordered: "No noise after 11 P.M." Another, near a cattle grid across the narrowing road, told her: "Road unsuitable in winter conditions." Unsuitable for what? Driving? Skiing?

In a gap between squalls of horizontal rain, she pulled over to consult the map and grab a fresh pack of cigarettes from her overnight bag, along with the bottle of single malt for their reunion. She wedged it between the front seats of the car and lit a cigarette, opening the window to blow out the smoke on draughts of cold, damp air. He was out there, somewhere, in this awful weather. When the cloud cracked open for a moment, the valley unfolded as a deep U, its floor an uninviting bed of boulders, glacial moraine. Leading off it, trails led to the high ground like pale surgeon's scars drawn across flanks of coarse grass and the ubiquitous rocky outcroppings that left no ridge or hillside unbroken, as if the weathered granite refused to be hidden. Then the cloud closed again. She switched on the engine and the headlights, nudging the car forward onto a narrow track that seemed to head in the roughly southerly direction she needed to cross over the shoulder of land between hills that would bring her to the junction with the Wrynose Pass road. She thought of denying herself a bracing nip from the whisky bottle, but succumbed.

Smoke break. Not easy. The wind's dropped a bit but the rain's settled into a drizzle. Soaks the Rizlas. And with this arm refusing to cooperate, it's a bit tricky. The cigarette looked like a cross between a beginner's spliff and a piece of toilet paper. Tasted about the same. Water's low, but this is the final stage for today. I think. GPS coordinates 27053 00961. That should put me on top of Great Carrs. There's supposed to be the wreck of an airplane up here somewhere. So that makes two wrecks. The GPS is fine but it can only point you between A and B: it doesn't tell you what's actually between A and B. Like the crags that the map shows on both sides of the path. I've worked out a bearing on the old compass, though, north for four hundred yards, then veering north-northwest ten degrees to get onto Wet Side Edge and allegedly a path zigzagging down to Wrynose. Camp One on the icefall. Tempting to think of hitching a ride to a B&B and a hot bath and a couple of pints of bitter. Call Eva. Call somebody. Because one thing I hadn't quite reckoned with: there's no one to talk to up here. Come to think of it, there's no one at all.

WRYNOSE, ENGLAND. SEPTEMBER 2000

Right from the beginning, he had denied it, refused it. When his arm weakened, he merely readjusted his body into a deformed crouch to be able to get both hands to the keyboard. When his leg weakened, he told people it was a war wound and left it at that. When his bosses called to send him to his usual shitholes, he said: fine, great, on my way. His tote bag was never really unpacked. The Kevlar vest was his second skin. But she knew he was scared, running from reality, accepting his assignments, telling no one at head office that he should not really be doing this. He'd seen the doctors in London and the United States. They had offered him a choice between utterly grim and just plain average grim and he pretended nothing was happening. Like this silly expedition. If he was proving something to himself, so be it. But all he was proving to her was how pathetic the male ego really was. Where did he think he was? The north wall of the Eiger? Everest? Quite probably. He had a professional gift for embellishment and, in his own mind, he would doubtless enhance this experience, if he survived it. But why did he seem to assume that she would simply be there, a disconnected spectator, somewhere on the sidelines? She had not been raised as a carer. She could extend her heart to those in need, in the Rift Valley, among the Masai and the Samburu, but that did not make her some kind of Nurse Eva. Why did they shy from the strongest possibility, the nearest they had to a diagnosis: that this was incurable, that his mobility would be ever further reduced until—and this was part of the nightmare—he would require someone to dress him and tend him, feed him and wipe him, push his wheelchair, manhandle him into a passionless bed, wait with him until the final set of muscles around his lungs expired and he died an invalid's death, without a warrior's glory, a slow progression not a simple, clean cutoff of the kind he had so often chronicled in his reports. He would not wish to wait that long, but maybe they would not oblige him. Maybe the doctors and nurses and administrators and lawyers would deny him the morphine pump or whatever they used to camouflage euthanasia. She did not believe that she could bear that—the watching and the decline, the withering away of everything he had ever been. She was no Florence Nightingale. Nor was meant to be. The courage and stoicism were just not there. Perhaps even love did not stretch that far, if people were honest with themselves: for love intervened at a specific moment, a specific coincidence of needs. It did not necessarily contain the seeds of transformation to cope with a completely different set of circumstances. If he had been ailing when they met, would she have abandoned her life with its known rhythms and expectations for him, for—say the word, woman—a cripple? Of course not. But this was Judas talk, whisky talk. Pray it was no more than that.

At the junction with the Wrynose Pass road, she halted, the right-hand indicator light blinking in the mist, and took a quick, furtive nip from the whisky bottle, observed only by a lone, lost sheep. The roads were so narrow she needed a three-point turn to swing right. If she could intercept him, she would say: stop this nonsense now. Right now. We are going to a hotel. You are going to get warm and we'll discuss where to go from here. She turned. The road she had just traveled had been extremely narrow and this one was only a fraction wider. But it led upwards in what she thought to be the right direction. The radio reception faded in and out. Just before it subsided altogether into a hissing silence, she caught a crackly weather forecast: something about storm fronts and the Irish Sea and warnings of something too indistinct to decipher. Her cell phone in its cradle had not picked up a signal for hours. She almost began to miss the Honda Civics and Ford Fiestas with their aging cargoes of pensioners in putty-colored parkas and tweed hats. The mist wrapped itself around the car with feline stealth. She had an eerie sense of weightlessness, as if she could not quite tell whether the car was going uphill or downhill. One moment there would be a clear, steep upward gradient, then the road would even out or descend. Eva Kimberly switched on the fog lamps but they seemed to make no difference. The more she progressed, the more impenetrable the grubby wall of cotton wool ahead of her seemed to become, and there were no landmarks. The paved road simply gave way to ragged green grass and gray shapes that might have been boulders or sheep. She sensed rather than saw a steep drop-off to her left, where the mist seemed to swirl as in a cauldron. The windshield wiper slid back and forth but it was not clear whether it was up against rain or simply the mist condensing onto the car. At one point, to the right, she thought she saw a small obelisk, a sculpted geometric intrusion into this hig-gledy-piggledy, barely seen jumble of rock and grass and patches of bracken as dull as old, dry tea leaves. But if it had been there, it was soon gone. Was she climbing or descending? Did the pass attack its summit in one solid, uphill grind or meander, choosing between ups and downs? Now she seemed to be descending, sharply, the big car running away from her so that she scuffed the tires on roadside rocks as she struggled to find a lower gear. She stamped so hard on the brakes that the ABS system kicked in, too late to prevent the rear of the car from swinging wide, crashing into a rock on the roadside with a brief howl of metal and a tinkling of glass from the brake and indicator lights. She thought of halting to inspect the damage, but the car still seemed to be running smoothly. There was no ominous grating of steel on rubber. The road ran quickly, clearly downhill now. She peered through the windscreen. Had there been a signpost, off to the left? There was not supposed to be a signpost, but her road map was small-scale and did not show every road beyond the highways. She swerved to cross a bridge. Was there supposed to be a bridge? But the narrow lane ahead of her was climbing again, so perhaps she was still on track in this strange, alien land. In Africa, the mists burned off, the rains were ferocious but soon vented their rage. They did not cling like this. They did not settle in for the duration so that you could never imagine sunlight or warmth again. The storms announced themselves with great thunderheads building white and gray into a blue sky. Sometimes, in the cloying heat before the rains, the very earth would part to release a subterranean army of flying ants that broke to the surface and knew instantly to fly on gossamer wings, whole squadrons and legions of them that people leapt at to catch and fry. But not here. Here the earth was dead, denying all bounty.

The road leveled and she pulled over onto the squelchy grass, careful to leave two wheels safely on the tarred road. She stepped forth into the mist, lighting yet another cigarette, pulling the thick sheepskin coat around her. She glanced at her watch—a gift from him in gold and steel. The rear of the car, just on the passenger side corner, was a mess: dented, scraped metal and fragments of orange and red plastic, all that was left of the brake and indicator lights. A bare bulb in a shiny, silver surround blinked on and off where she had signaled her intention to pull over, a lonesome beacon summoning no one. The hours had run away since lunchtime and finally she admitted she was lost, not simply geographically, but as if the land that had nurtured him denied her, mocked her with its contempt for the outsider, the alien. The air was liquid, seeping into her hair, her eyebrows, lacquering her coat with a silver veneer of droplets. If she waited long enough, surely the clouds would part, lift. She scanned the map. Clearly enough she could see now that there were two passes, not one. The one called Wrynose—where he would camp—was the first. Another—called Hardknott—was the second. She would bet good money she stood now on the second. What point was there now in the grand romantic gesture? What point had there been in the first place? How could anyone expect to revive a passion born in sunlight on the soaked fells? In a bivouac tent, for God's sake. Why had she wasted her time?

She charted a long, onward route that would end in a civilized hotel suite, a deep bath and room service dinner. Without Joe Shelby, who had brought her here. From the map, she could see she would be late arriving but that did not matter: he had booked the suite with a credit card reinforced with a faxed confirmation. She would call ahead once the mountains released her into cell-phone-signal country. There was no doubting now where she was. The road ran on ahead through places with typically impenetrable names—Boot and Eskdale Green, Gosforth and Egremont, Cleator Moor and Cockermouth—fat chance of that, Joe Shelby, she thought, and sniggered—Braithwaite and Keswick. Once resolved, she restarted the car, spinning the wheels in the grass as she pulled back onto the narrow paved road, nudging down below the cloud line and, after some confusion and false starts in an area of small lanes around Santon Bridge and Plumgarth, she hit the A595 highway, heading up north. Somewhere around the notorious Sellafield nuclear power station—which looked about as appropriate in these wild parts as an elephant in a flower bed, a turd in a punchbowl, a bull in a china shop—her cell phone sprang back into life, startling her with its ring-tone.

"You have a message," a synthetic voice informed her. "To hear your message, press one." Driving with one hand, she did as bidden, wedging the phone between jaw and shoulder to get her second hand back on the wheel before the car veered over the white centerline. When the message began, her hands tightened on the leather steering wheel and she pulled over to hear it again, to be sure her senses were not deceiving her.

"Hi. It's me. Jeremy. Just in London for a few days, squaring the punters, meeting the agents. You know. And. Well. Maybe this is the wrong thing. Time. You know, to be calling. You tell me, Evie. But I just wondered if you'd like lunch. Or a cup of coffee. Walk in the park. Anything, really. Best behavior, of course. No tears. If I could just see you. Just for a moment. I'm at Brown's. Remember? You see—"

The message died after its allocated moment in wireless ether.

Jeremy. Dear Jeremy. Timing never was your strong suit. But you have learned something about it now.

Chapter Nine

Rochester, Minnesota, is a town that lives on undiagnosed and frequently terminal illness. In winter the snowdrifts scud across the highway and the all-year residents stay indoors or huddle over shot glasses in half-lit bars showing football games on television sets mounted high in the corners. In summer, only the sport changes. More than just about any place on earth, its population is heavily weighted towards the medical profession because this is the home of the Mayo Clinic. Even the hotels in Rochester, Minnesota, are linked to this great institution by covered walkways that run above the streets, as if the sick are already at one remove from terrestrial life—not exactly knocking on heaven's door, but not too far from it either. At most times of the day, you will find the cavernous central hall buzzing with patients on their way from one appointment to the next, some clutching urine samples hidden in paper bags like a drunk's liquor bottle, hurrying with the same dedication as children who just won the goldfish at the fun fair and are taking it home in its plastic globe. Most people of a certain means who have been seriously sick know of the Mayo Clinic. Along with the laboratories and consulting rooms associated with London's Harley Street, it is held to be the world's preeminent diagnostic center, where maladies that have baffled the rest of the medical profession may ultimately be resolved. Look around, as you walk through the halls and corridors and consulting rooms, and you will not see anyone who is not gravely, bafflingly ill—except of course the nurses and physicians. And even medical doctors who have been unable to cure themselves gravitate here to seek the truth from more specialized colleagues. Within the medical profession it is held to resemble a conveyor belt along which its paying clients are subjected to all the necessary tests and examinations. At the end of the conveyor belt is a desk where you pay your bill and receive a diagnosis offering hope or despair. The complex has ministered to kings and presidents, and there are share-dealing companies where you can sell your stock to pay your bill or, as appropriate to the diagnosis, realign your portfolio for the purposes of avoiding estate duties. Looked at from a cynical viewpoint, you could say that its clanking magnetic resonance imagers, its humming laboratories are simply a vast cash register, an alchemy that turns sickness into wealth and sometimes health. But, from a benign perspective, this place is the final salvation, the last hope for a miracle cure. If the experts here can't cure you, then you may as well start to think seriously about your relationship with—or acknowledgment of—a Divine Being, and your attitude to the mortality you never quite believed you shared with the rest of the human race.

Joe Shelby flew in via Kennedy and O'Hare, lugging a tote bag filled with books he had never had time to catch up on: Baudelaire and Wordsworth, Dylan Thomas and Eliot. The cabdriver from the Rochester airport, he noticed, did not inquire as to his business: maybe the limp told the story: another invalid, another inscrutable case that, hopefully, was not contagious. Joe Shelby checked in at an anonymous, restful hotel and braced himself for his first appointment by seeking out normal people—people, that is to say, normal enough to belly up to steel-topped bars behind a crumpled pile of dollar bills to be bartered for booze and baseball games on the TV.

The normal people, of course, realized that he was not normal: he did not wear normal tartan shirts and took his wallet from a bush jacket whose cartridge pockets contained expensive German pens topped with distinctive white stars. He spoke in a strange, limey accent and he walked kind of weird. When he paid for his drinks, or drank his drinks, or just toyed with the glass as he stared at a point a thousand miles beyond the bartender's mirrored display of half-empty bottles, gazing past his own reflection, he did so with his right hand. His left arm hung vertically and if he wanted to move it, he would swing his shoulder to induce movement into the motionless limb. Obviously a patient, a transient, not worth a nodding acquaintance in response to his murmured greetings. After two or three whiskies, Joe Shelby began to acknowledge that, somewhere along the line, he had crossed an invisible frontier whose visa requirement was physical disability; he had become one of the outcasts that people stare at surreptitiously on the sidewalk to see if they have a clubfoot or some metal apparatus from infant poliomyelitis. He knew, of course, that his heart beat true with two-fisted testosterone, just as most men in their late thirties know they are seventeen years old and always will be. But to others he already belonged to that different land of Zimmer frames and wheelchairs, whose denizens are obliged to confront the angry, impotent codes of their condition—the immobility of multiple sclerosis or the shakes of Parkinson's disease, the wasted muscles and clawed hands of any number of neuropathies. It was a world that, in their heart of hearts, most whole people wished not to see, turned away from, or, in some historical eras such as Nazi Germany, sought outright to banish, exterminate. Unwittingly, without seeking membership, he had joined a club whose codes and premises lay in hospices and medical waiting rooms, MRI tunnels and physicians' illegible notes, hospital wards and undertakers' offices. His selection of poetry books revealed new meanings. His fellow citizens were not the drinkers at the bar. They were the patients at the clinic—*mon semblable, mon frere:* Baudelaire, he recalled, had written those words in the introductory poem of *Les Fleurs du Mal,* the flowers of evil, but he had been describing the brotherhood of *ennui.* T. S. Eliot had borrowed the same lines in "The Waste Land" to evoke the fraternity of those whom death had undone: "A crowd flowed over London Bridge, so many, I had not thought death had undone so many . . . to where St. Mary Woolnoth kept the hours/With a dead sound on the final stroke of nine." Here, in Rochester, Joe Shelby was invited to join the brotherhood of those whose bodies had undone them, who awaited death to undo everything they had ever prayed for. It was an invitation, he was discovering, that came without an RSVP—the rest of the world, the healthy people, replied on your behalf.

"And, when we breathe, death descends into our lungs, an invisible river, with mute cries."—Charles Baudelaire.

For a little over four days, Joe Shelby underwent his initiation. He gave of his blood, drawn deep red like a dark Pinot Noir from the crook of his arm, he provided urine samples after fasting with various stipulations about whether the liquid should be from midflow or some other stage of expulsion. He became expert at pissing, fasting. He hated his fellow patients because they mirrored the reality he did not wish to see in himself. He contrived, in one examination room, to secure an advance peek of the seven-inch needle that was inserted into his spine to draw fluid to establish protein levels, seek out evidence of cranial malfunction. And wished he hadn't. The clanging, thumping tunnel of the MRI scan was old hat to him now; as an invalid, he was a pro. He knew well enough where the electromyographic experts would place their needles in the reduced flesh of his left biceps, in the triceps and the brachial plexus. He understood the way they measured the impulses from the central nervous system of the brain and spine and out to the peripheries, running like messengers to distant outposts along pathways of neurons and axons, sparking synapses as they hurtled briskly and purposefully at 250 mph. He knew the questions the machines were asking. How quickly did the couriers run? Did they encounter obstacles on the way, conduction blocks that showed the system to be disrupted by rotten cells, torn myelin, neurotransmitters that failed to make the leap between neurons and axons? On small green, glowing screens, his nervous system was translated into jagged peaks and deep troughs, lines to be printed out on long screeds of paper, as at the supermarket checkout after a particularly expensive shop. When the needles were inserted into his biceps, his forearms, his shoulders and hands, he could see them leap and twitch with involuntary movements that had never been there. Watching the men and women in white watching him, he realized that what they saw was a web of billions of nerves of different kinds that ran systems and reactions, a spider's gossamer of strands branching out from the anterior horn cells of his spine, relaying impulses to far-flung toes and fingers. When they examined him, he knew they would follow the prescribed rituals of their profession, checking for muscle tone and weakness, reflexes and spasms. Just as in his profession there was always a basic set of questions to be answered in even the briefest of articles— who, why, how, when, where and often how much?—so, too, the neurologists followed their set route of inquiry: the questions, first, about the onset of the disease and the symptoms, the extent to which he smoked cigarettes and drank alcohol (raised eyebrows, usually, at this stage: that much? Really?). Were his parents alive? No. What had they died of? Cancer. Had he been sick before? Not really, unless you count odd encounters with malaria, bilharzia. Bilharzia? Mmm. Had he been sick as a child? No. Did he have allergies? Only to doctors' bills—just joking. No. Had he ever had syphilis, poliomyelitis, been exposed to AIDS? No, no and maybe—these days, who could tell? In Africa, who could cast the first stone?

And only after this interrogation did they request that he strip to his boxers. Then they would require him to perch on an examination table and just look at him with the vaguely disconnected air of someone who has come into a gallery to escape a wet afternoon, taking only a passing interest in the sculptures. He knew they were looking for the telltale signs of wasting in the muscle, quivers which they called fasciculation. They would ask him to relax his arm and leg and then jiggle or turn them to discover whether the muscle tone had turned spastic or flaccid. They would test his strength, in his fingers and wrists, at the biceps and triceps, the shoulders, legs, ankles, toes, making him pull or push against their counterpressure. His left arm, predictably, scored worst: he could not even lift it into position to pull against them, and they logged a zero or a one on a scale of five for those whose limbs could not even overcome gravity. They spread his fingers and closed them with their own. Cock your wrist and don't let me move it down. He had been here before, in Harley Street and regarded himself as a quick study: now they would run a sharp object along the soles of his feet: and they obliged, interrogating his body, requiring it to provide answers to two lines of questioning: anatomical and pathological. By combining their simple tests in certain sequences, they could establish first of all the location of the disruption to his nervous system, then its nature. That, at least, was the theory. It was true, Joe Shelby figured, that for all the expensive scans, analyses, electrical testing, their art came down to the traditional magic of observation and the exclusion of options, the narrowing of choices. They worked with a feather and a pin, medieval totems. They peered from the outer skein of his being into the unseeable nexus within. Ultimately, they made their guesses on the basis of irreducible assumptions and that was the route to diagnosis. It may have been science, but a good part of it was intuition, experience, the institutional buildup of wisdom from observing thousands of people whose systems had crumbled.

They made him close his eyes and screw them up to see if they could force them open. They made him clench his teeth while they used their little hammers in a vain quest for reflexes. Close your eyes and tell me which way I'm moving your toes. Up. Up. Down. Up. Does this pinprick feel the same here as here? And here? Follow my finger with your eyes. Touch your nose then touch my fingertip. Any problems sleeping, eating, shitting, fucking? (His words, not theirs.) No, no, no and no. They sent him along to a department where physiotherapists dispensed the accoutrements of cripplehood, the badges of the unsavory order into which he had been inducted—plastic supports for enfeebled ankles, small foam collars to enable palsied hands to grip spoons or pens or toothbrushes, splints for wilting wrists unable to defy gravity.

Among themselves, they used juju words—the membership codes of their own club—such as pronate and wrist extension and anterior horn cell; antiganglioside antibodies and conduction block and radiculopathy; innervation and distal latency; then looked at him as if to say: don't you bother your little head with these things; leave it to the grown-ups. He came to recognize the quick, sidelong, heavily significant looks that passed between senior and junior doctor at some point of particular illumination, the glance that said: this one's a hopeless case and, for future reference, here is the sign of his hopelessness.

As a practiced patient, he could see the basic line of inquiry. From the outward, physical appearances of his body and his recounting of symptoms, they could begin to trace the malady back along the invisible pathways of his nervous system, using each set of physical examinations to conclude or exclude, tracking the illness back from the fingertips along the strands of myelin-sheathed nerve cells, back ever further through the cervical spine into the cerebral cortex.

And somewhere along these mysterious pathways they would find what was wrong, surely, for this was the greatest clinic on earth and no one knew better.

In the evenings, between test and result, debate and conclusion, Joe Shelby made his phone calls back home to Eva across the time zones and, closer, to his editors to make sure they did not take him off the shitholes list simply because he could no longer run or raise both arms to surrender. He lied to all of them. He told Eva he was feeling fine, while with every day, he sensed the feared specter closing on him. He told his editors the Mayo looked like figuring it out and he'd be cured. They were pleased. He read poems and his previous medical notes or flicked through endlessly tedious TV channels, or drank himself to sleep while news programs murmured the siren calls of his profession: wars and earthquakes, pestilence, flood, the curses that framed the human condition. Once, very late, with raw whisky souring his breath, he made a call to Faria Duclos and could not recall whether he told her either his truth or his travel plans, but sensed she understood, even cared, despite the monstrous way he had treated her. She had a right to know his news, he figured, because she had seen him in the Balkans, and helped him. She had taken his dictation and together they had transmitted it to New York and she had, therefore, saved him before they both moved on, barely shaking hands, not quite sure where to pigeonhole this encounter. She understood him because she had known him better and longer. And—only the whisky drunk would admit it—he turned to her because, of all those things, she would not take his burden as an insupportable yoke of her own.

He pored over his last report from Nigel Lampton, the tall, scholarly British neurologist who had taken over his case in London from the guru of Harley Street because he was *the* man on motor neuron disease back in Britain and he did not think Joe Shelby, whatever else, had been afflicted with it. But Joe Shelby sensed from the whispered conversations in Rochester, Minnesota, just where the American specialists were leading their inquiries—not into the weakened muscles and fingers and ankles, but back from there, into the very core of his nervous system where the cells at the fulcrum of all voluntary and involuntary movement interact with the conductive axons, passing along the signals from the brain that issued the commands: move this, move that, walk, lift, talk, breathe. It was in those minute cells in the central nervous system that the nightmare resided.

Motor neuron disease is defined as a progressive, incurable, degenerative disease of those cells. No one knows what causes it. There are theories, but no proofs, camouflaged in words like electrotoxicity and free radicals, meaning simply that at some stage, something like a virus invades the system, attaching itself to these critical cells without which the two subdivisions of the nervous system—automatic functions such as breathing, active decisions like walking or masturbation—do not work. People these days are used to the notion that all illness may be cured: AZT will arrest AIDS, chemotherapy will batter cancer into submission, a pill or infusion of steroids will hold back the malign course of rheumatoid arthritis, stem cell research will grant eternal life if only the crazy Christian right will permit it. But no one knows how to stop motor neuron disease, or cure it, or treat it. There are medications that are supposed to slow it, but physicians dispute their value. It has different names, such as amyotrophic lateral sclerosis, ALS, or Lou Gehrig's, progressive muscular atrophy and progressive bulbar palsy. It gets you like this: progressively, as the cells in the upper and lower central nervous system decay and cease to perform their function, the muscle groups they command weaken until the very acts of breathing or swallowing are affected. At first it may be simply a weakness in the arms or legs that does not respond to treatment. Then the weakness is transformed into a kind of paralysis: the muscle groups under the command of the motor neuron cells stop responding at all. The localized problem in a wrist or ankle spreads to an entire limb. The fingers droop like willow fronds, then curl like claws. Falling into total disuse, with no signals reaching them, the muscle groups atrophy, waste away. In the final stages, you cannot speak, swallow or move. But you know exactly what is happening. Your brain functions, your eyes see, your ears hear. You know you are dying and will die when your lungs clog or you choke, or you contract pneumonia. But there is no reduction of consciousness. Your mind lives in a mummified cocoon. Your brain allows you to perceive the stages of your vegetation. A monster has insinuated itself into your body, spreading its tentacles from the rotten cells of the central system to the peripheries that depend on them. Everything you ever were has gone, except your ability to perceive your degradation, your pitiful failure to be a normal person. Your final days will be spent in a wheelchair with perhaps some form of computer screen you can use to communicate by tapping out messages with a pointer held between your teeth. Your head will loll and be held in place with a brace. You will look at your fingers and toes and arms and legs and realize they may just as well belong to a stranger for all you can move them.

Before the onset of his weakness, Joe Shelby had never even heard of the disease. It's not a big killer like AIDS or cancer or heart attacks or road travel. It affects maybe one or two people out of every 100,000 each year, usually—but not exclusively—people older than Joe Shelby. But, almost as soon as he heard of it, he heard, too, of the debate that bound its sufferers to the euthanasia business: why continue, like this, without hope or dignity, when the outcome was foretold? Why not take a cocktail, an injection, and be done? There were some mysterious survivors—Stephen Hawking, the British physics professor, bent and twisted in his wheelchair, communicating without speech but thinking like a dynamo, was probably the most notable. But imagine the others, the terminal, hospice patients in their still twilight, calling to be heard where no sound came—Baudelaire's mute cries again—crying silently for release. The disease defied everything Joe Shelby had been brought up to believe: I will, therefore I can. This disease said: you are powerless against the destiny I, in all my blossoming evil, have conceived for you. The disease sets its own pace but, usually, is inexorable. In its quickest form it will pass along the limbs with the speed and destructiveness of brushfire, giving no chance for flight or rescue. Its only certainty is that it will claim its victim and offer no mercy. In his hotel room, one drunken night, the TV showed a replay of a movie called *A River Runs Through It*. Its final scene shows an old man who has raised and buried his family and fulfilled life's missions. Now he awaits his own demise, at peace with his river, tying his fishing fly to his line with thick, fumbly fingers, his torments behind him. Joe Shelby sobbed in great heaves, confronted with this vision of what he had always imagined he would become, now slipped from his failing grasp.

On the fifth day at the Mayo Clinic, he was given his final appointment with two neurologists. Later, his recall of the conversations was dominated by the way the encounter ended when the more senior of the two physicians looked at his watch and said: "That the time? I'm out of here." Perhaps that was just a way of saying: look, buddy, we hand down these sentences all the time.

Joe Shelby had braced himself to be tough. His tote bag was already packed. Whatever the verdict, he had booked himself a late flight out of Rochester, Minnesota, through Chicago, on to New York and a connection via Frankfurt to Tel Aviv. Lufthansa. Business class. Already he was wearing his jeans and bush jacket and high-sided suede boots that provided some support to his ankles. No way he would be put out to pasture, he told Eva over the phone when she protested that he should come back to London first. I need to show them I can hack it, he said. Show them, or fool yourself, she said. But there was no way he would go home to mope or rejoice, whatever the outcome. He had to send a different signal to his bosses. He had a job to do. Medical stuff was an irksome interruption, but no cause to abandon his commitment to covering the world's nastier events. All week the TV chronicled the latest worsening in the Middle East, the new *intifadeh,* as they called it, the newest uprising of so many no one could count anymore. Watching it, he craved the ring of gunfire and the dying cries of "Allah-uh akhbar" as if they might offer an antidote to the nightmare. You are a fool, Joe Shelby, if you think your bosses want this, Eva said. You are a fool if you think war will heal you. But he quoted back to her: the wife who stands between a warrior and a lion is a foolish wife. Then we are both fools, she said.

"Please sit down, Mr. Shelby."

"Joe."

They had, he guessed, developed a routine, a patter. Good cop, bad cop, doling out vestiges of hope and despair, putting the message across in a way that said: look, it happens, OK? We see it all the time. You're not the worst. But no one will cure you through their own tears. It doesn't work like that. No one can cure you at all.

"OK, Joe. Like your articles by the way. Great stuff from the Balkans. Just tell me if you want me to cut to the chase, as it were."

"Go for it."

"OK, Joe. We've taken a good, hard look at you, and, frankly, we're still not sure."

"But?"

"But we are leaning towards a motor neuron problem."

"Meaning?"

"Well. Motor neuron disease can be pretty obvious. What we call barn door MND, meaning you can't miss something as obvious as a barn door. You don't present like that. But there are signs, first of all that you don't have the symptoms for more benevolent neuropathies related to the autoimmune system. I'm not saying it's impossible, but the usual signs—certain electrical responses and antibodies—aren't there. I know Professor Lampton doesn't sign on to this altogether, but that's our thinking. OK so far?"

Joe nodded. His mouth had gone dry. He wanted them to say, as his father had done in boyhood games, that he would be given another innings, that he was not yet out, eliminated. But they were not heading that way.

"So that leaves the other possibility of an indolent form of motor neuron disease whose prognosis is not very clear. And again I think we'd all like to see you again in six months, or whenever Professor Lampton wants to send you over, to take another look. Maybe we're wrong, but the symptoms do suggest some kind of ALS."

"So you are saying I have motor neuron disease?" So why not put on the black cap to tell me?

"It looks that way."

Joe Shelby gulped and felt a prickle of tears behind his eyes. He felt the skin on his face go cold then break out in a patina of sweat. Motor neuron disease was the death sentence, the final indignity. You could laugh all you liked in the face of this danger and it would not go away: it would laugh straight back until it devoured you and sent you to the grave with soundless cries and soiled pajamas. And he was damned if he would allow these white-coated physicians to see the fear their sentence had produced.

"So. Like they say. How long have I got, doc?"

"Hard to say."

"But if you *had* to say."

"If I had to say, and it could be quicker or slower, one year, three years tops."

"And in that time?"

"In that time, you'd see a progressive continuation of the kind of weakness you have now spreading to other muscle groups."

"So I'd be in a wheelchair?"

"At some stage."

"And then?"

"There are support groups, Joe."

"Do I look like someone who wants a support group?"

"I'm sorry, Joe."

"That the time? I'm out of here."

Joe Shelby looked back on the journey away from the Mayo as if it had been a black hole, a period of time that had simply disappeared. He recalled sending a faxed copy of the diagnosis to Nigel Lampton, his neurologist in London. He had vague memories of writing a check to the clinic and booking a cab, transiting airports and showing his passport and boarding pass, drinking and, at one stage somewhere over the Atlantic, weeping into the mirror in the cramped toilet of a creaking old 747. He traveled on reflexes bred of long practice: check in, board plane, fasten seat belt. His mind could do no more than rearrange jumbled words—three years tops, wheelchair, support groups, one year, out of here. Out of everything worth defining as a life. They were saying: we believe you have an incurable condition called motor neuron disease that will kill you at its leisure; there is no cure, no treatment, nothing we can do save cash our checks and move on. The manner of his death would be ugly, heralded by disability, deformity and—most terrifying—dependence on others to assist with nutrition, excretion, hygiene, mobility, communication, expiry. He would be a vegetating shell, a living corpse draped around a brain screaming for release. Like some counterenergy, he would be the antithesis of his true self and he had not the courage to confront that prospect the way he had once surveyed the battlefronts. He could barely breathe or mumble the words, but forced himself to whisper them for his own inner ear only: motor neuron disease, judge and jury; motor neuron disease, the final executioner.

Three years tops. I'm out of here. Three years tops and I am truly out of here.

Then he was in the maelstrom of Ben Gurion's arrivals area scanning the crowd below the palms, in the cloying heat, for the one, single face he most wanted to see there among the tumult of soldiers in ill-fitting olive uniforms and Orthodox in their ringlets and agents in dark shades whose only prayer was to intercept the suicide bombers before it was too late.

TEL AVIV. AUGUST 2000

She saw him, but waited for him to notice her, to establish that he was traveling alone. She could not guess what this sudden attention meant: he had sought her out in the Balkans so that she could type for him, hold him in some seedy hotel with cigarette burns and less easily identified stains on the carpet. He had called from some place in Middle America, giving his flight plans down to the arrival time. It made no sense—not after nine months of silence in which she had tired of the bullring, tired of the endless, searing highs of her coke habit and the brittle, snappy dawns when the chemicals released her, dropped her back, cruel and abrupt, down to the hard, cold earth.

He glanced around to see if he was being observed before crabbing towards her through the crowd at Ben Gurion, leaning heavily on his telescopic walking pole that had become the unwanted badge of his condition. No one made way, of course. This was the Middle East where everyone labored under the burden of their original innocence, too busy tending their own pain to see beyond it to a world that really did not need this unending blight. She moved toward him, different than when they had first met in these parts, of course—older, slightly haggard as if the years had sculpted her, pared her flesh down to an irreducible core of fierce angles and big, vulnerable eyes that had seen more than they should have. The pit of his stomach churned. He recognized the quality of passion that had bound them. There is a difference between calculable love and the fire of destiny, between affection that can be explained and the inexplicable magnetism of like souls. A sudden fear seized him: would she acknowledge him again as she had in the Balkans, or had that been a one-off, a curiosity: come see the geek, the gimp? Would she see the past beneath the skein of damaged nerves and muscles? Was there such a thing as an essence of him that transcended his physical state, his condition? Another inner voice said: they should not be meeting. They should not permit the illusion of being together. There was peril where their fates crossed, a hazard like the striking of flint on stone that produced fire, indifferent to what it consumed. His breath caught, not just from the conscious effort of movement or of carrying his Kevlar vest and laptop, his supplies of Scotch and cigarettes, notebooks and expensive pens. She had come to meet him. She had responded where he had no rights of expectation, no rights of anything at all.

He had worsened. Sweat ran across his face. His body seemed hinged at the waist, the legs stiff, uncooperative and the trunk canted forward, the bad arm hanging as he wrestled to keep his tote bag over his right shoulder while he manipulated his walking pole with his right arm. Once she had called him a coward to his face, on the day he had struck her and broken her faith in him, but she saw no cowardice in the lurching figure before her, still obstinately clad in his faded jeans and vest as the crowd closed and opened and eddied around him, pushing, shoving, forcing him to grapple for balance against an invisible force field of negative energy that had filled the vacuum left by his departed strength.

🖋

Camp One. Wrestled with this crazy tent. Like trying to throw a wet bedsheet over crossed fishing poles. One-person bivouac tent, they told me in the store. More like an MRI scan tunnel in nylon, or an oversized condom. Still, you get in, lie flat. Self-inflating mattress self-inflates, sort of, and you are comfortable, sort of. But out of the wind and the rain, thank God. Headlamp on to see what you're doing. Clothes damp but warming within the sleeping bag. Managed to brew tea, cook one of these dehydrated meals that tastes like cardboard. Have a smoke, jolt of Scotch from the aluminum water bottle. Luxury.

I came down to the pass quite well, considering. I'd forgotten just how painful the downhill is, how much your knees take a pounding and my thighs are really aching, compensating for the lack of strength in the calves and ankles, I guess. But it was quite welcoming, really, to see that little carved three-shire stone, they call it, like a small obelisk, presumably from the days when Lancashire, Cumberland and Westmoreland met up on the top of the pass. Three counties, now one. Cumbria. But the stone's still there, like a little beacon, welcoming the traveler. I'd half thought that Eva might have broken the rule and met up with me because this is after all the last place where the road crosses the route and with the weather like it is, I'll be up in the thick of it tomorrow night at Esk Hause, twice the altitude of here and a lot more exposed. Managed to pitch the tent between two hillocks so it's quite sheltered. In the bosom, so to speak. Almost room for two in the one-person bivouac condom, if you get cozy. But I made the rule, I suppose: no contact until advanced base. And this is my last chance, my last hurrah. My Everest. And Eva has reason enough to steer clear.

More Scotch for the confessional. Holy water. Forgive me father. For I have. Because, of course, everybody knew we met up in Gaza that last time, after the Mayo. Not exactly Plan A, though. Supposed to be a secret tryst after that fucking doctor—I'm outta here, baby. Didn't stay secret for long.

The day after I flew in and she was waiting for me at the airport we talked our way past the Erez checkpoint and trundled on down in a hard car to Khan Younis, or what's left of it. Really old by local standards. Refugees. Flotsam and jetsam. The dispossessed of the earth. Wasn't really our number. Too many other hacks around. TV crews with those new mini-dishes that let them go live from the summit of Everest or wherever. Technology. Certainly they were going live at Khan Younis, and so were the Israelis and the Pals—live ammunition, fire at will. Big boom-boom. Couple of tanks pounding the wreckage of an apartment house. Spirited answering fire from off-target RPGs and at least one .50 cal machine gun. Old thing. Degtyarev Shpagin like they used to have on the duschkas in Beirut, in fact named them after the Degtyarevs, long before the Somalis thought of technicals. Only a matter of time before the Israelis called in airstrikes or gunships so it wasn't the best of places to hang around.

She—F, I'll call her—F was pretty well up on it, no loss of tradecraft, even if she isn't as stricken by her death wish as she once was. Nimble. Quick. Spotting the shifts in the lines before the combatants. A real pro. And still operating with those short focal length lenses that get her up real close, real in-your-face stuff: Palestinians with rocket launchers, kids with slingshots, one preteen spun around by a bullet in the arm, pirouetting with ineffable, balletic grace until he went down badly. Somehow or other we lost contact. I guess I'd moved on, anticipating which way she'd go and figuring that with the limp and the stick I looked a bit too much like a very large, slow-moving target. So I took cover behind the remains of a wall, and maybe I'd been away too long, but they came around on the flank, the Israelis and started firing past me because I'd got myself caught slap bang between the lines with the Pals letting rip one way and the Israelis the other. Rogue impacts kicking up little fountains of dirt right at my feet. I mean close. Too close. There was only one way out, and F was yelling at me to take it. Take the gap. Because the probabilities were that I'd take some serious incoming if I didn't move, which would make all the Harley Street and Mayo Clinic mumbo-jumbo somewhat academic. So I had to break cover. Not far. Twenty, thirty yards, maybe—length of a cricket pitch—and not really in the direct cross fire, but exposed. Like on a climb. That moment when you have to move your feet and hands up higher, knowing that from then on you are committed, you can't reverse the move because it's physically, technically irreversible, that whatever the rock throws at you from then on, you have to take it, cope with it. But you can't go back. So that's what it was, and in the old days it wouldn't have bothered me, the old doubled-up sprint across the open ground, fast as you can go and glad to be the first one out because no one has time to range in on you. But this was different. I shouldn't have been there. And I had to be there to accept it. I should not have been in a position where my condition made me a liability to myself, most of all to others, to her. But without going there, I would never have come to terms with the limits. So I cranked myself up and I guess I was vaguely aware that one of the TV crews had drawn a bead on me from some place back from the lines. I saw the correspondent order the camerawoman to home in on me. And I tried to run and I kept thinking of those zinging little signals from the brain, moving into overdrive because of the adrenaline that tries to pump extra blood into your muscles and fill you with oxygen to feed them and get you the hell out of danger. Except that my signals didn't arrive. Nothing got through. Like someone had cut the telephone wires so no one knew to call the cavalry. And I could not run. I limped. I crabbed. I shuffled. My bad arm swung like an ape's. I think there were some stray rounds. I heard something crack into a wall: zap zap zap. I remember thinking I had to try harder, but just as I tried, my left foot didn't pick up properly when I moved my leg so it was kind of dangling loose and hit some rubble and I tripped and I was down in the open which is not where you want to be. I don't think anyone would've deliberately shot me, but you never know and there was a lot of loose shit flying and the next thing I knew while I was trying to get up was F dropping her gear and running out from cover and not even wearing Kevlar and she's got an arm under my shoulder and hefting me up with a lot of power for someone as skinny as she is, and together we're limping and stumbling for cover and I'd forgotten about the TV camera filming all this because there was some serious fire going down and when we finally got to cover we both hit the deck and I threw my good arm around her and said: you crazy French bitch and she just let out a big whoop and a laugh and planted a smacker on me, right on the lip. Right on live television around the world on CNN, dear Jesus.

LONDON. AUGUST 2000

It is one of those balmy days that reminds her of home and makes her think that, perhaps, this new world is not all so bad. It is the kind of weather that makes a city swelter and makes its dwellers beg for escape to the sea or the countryside where insects hover over mirror-smooth chalk streams and trout rise with languor, dimpling the water as it flows. If she adds the pluses she can make something of them: he has, finally, begun to take his illness seriously and will visit his British neurologist for more tests; despite the poor business climate, she has survived well enough to hire a third full-time teacher for her school in the Rift Valley; on days like this with not too much summer traffic and birdsong through open windows from their roof garden, she can imagine worse destinies by far. The doubts linger, though. He has not given a full accounting of his stay at the Mayo Clinic, and insists there is no definitive diagnosis; he has not said convincingly why it is so important to be in the Middle East. She is ignoring the gaps in his stories from the Balkans, from Rochester, Minnesota. For no evident reason, she feels she must strive for contentment, even if that is built on an enforced ignorance. Today she has pottered. A girlfriend from Nairobi, in town, insisted on lunch somewhere expensive and exclusive enough to sound good to her friends back home. Jeremy Davenport, she learns over the rughetta and balsamic vinegar, has cleaned up his act, finally. He is busy with clients and his tours have been well received in the trade press and one or two other publications. Coyly, she extracts the information that he has no new romantic interest. Nairobi is little changed—crime, scandal, luxury, threat, all in equal doses. Her father is progressing with plans for Naivasha on the assumption that she will attend, perhaps alone, as hostess. Everyone misses her *dreadfully*. Over the seared tuna with a fresh Sancerre, she is brought up to date on liaisons and murky business behind the guarded perimeter fences of Karen and Ngong. When she returns home, she discovers that the wine at lunch— a breach of her own rules—has conjured a taste for afternoon liquor. She resists but knows it is futile. There is no one here to police her, to frown disapprovingly or offer an alternative. Given the heat, she chooses gin from the cabinet and pours too much for safety over the ice cubes, barely leaving room for the tonic and the Angostura bitters. Their apartment is big and roomy, befitting a well-placed youngish couple. A large curved window looks out directly over the fields of Primrose Hill and, leading back from it, a polished parquet floor runs the length of the building, back toward French windows open to an artfully arranged roof terrace where there is an oiled wooden table under a square white Italian umbrella and a small, pleasant garden in full bloom. Opening off this one long room, opposite the glassed entrance foyer, and alongside the newly designed kitchen-cum-dining area with its own access to the terrace, there are less public quarters— a main bedroom suite with dressing and bath rooms, a second bedroom with its own shower and other facilities. A large, rear-facing third bedroom has become the corporate headquarters of @Africa. A smaller box room has become Joe Shelby's study-cum-TV room where he has shoehorned a rolltop desk and a sofa in dark green leather and a television set that she flicks on now, the remote control in one hand, her glass in the other. She settles back in the luxuriant sofa, kicking off tan loafers that she wore over bare feet with her summery linen trousers and sleeveless white blouse. Most men she meets, seeing her so precise and elegant and in her prime, think Joe Shelby the biggest fool for putting wars before her. They do not figure her for a lush, a secret boozer.

Indeed, these are not terms she would use herself. But she is not surprised at the hunger with which she consumes her drink, only too eager to obey the inner voice that promises transportation to wonderland: drink me, drink me. The news announcer is mouthing platitudes when a sudden, explosive red banner at the base of the TV screen announces live coverage from Gaza where Joe Shelby has promised he will not get into trouble but has got into trouble right in front of the camera that is focused shakily on him, pinned down in debris and rubble with billows of chalky smoke rising from rocket strikes and the insistent clatter of live automatic gunfire that reminds her of their one day in the battlefields of Cape Town. The ice in her glass rattles in harmony. The drink sloshes onto her blouse and chills her breast. The announcer is saying: we bring you live coverage of a gun battle in Khan Younis in the Gaza Strip where it looks as if a noncombatant, a reporter, we believe, is pinned down under fire. Before he fell he seemed to be limping badly but it's not clear if that is from a bullet. And, oh my word, it seems as if a colleague is attempting a rescue.

Eva Kimberly is transfixed. Yes, it is her Joe Shelby, pinned down. And yes, a colleague is attempting a rescue. A female colleague, all in black. A woman with familiar wild looks and skinny legs and crazy eyes. She is running to Joe and Eva is watching, a voyeur. The Frenchwoman is forcing him to stand as the bullets ricochet and ping around them and kick up small tornadoes of dust at their feet. In London, sitting bolt upright now on his green leather sofa, Eva Kimberly is the spy, the outsider. She cannot grasp the obscenity of this technology that transports her thousands of miles, across Europe and the Mediterranean, to share their porno-camera intimacy. She cannot accept the wizardry that has catapulted their togetherness into her home, willy-nilly, unrequested, unwanted, denying the Big Lie he constructed over the telephone from Rochester, Minnesota.

No, he had not gone there to send a message to his editors, or respond to the urge he felt to restate his own credentials to himself. It was her, the Frenchwoman, after all this time, after all the betrayal and the progression of his illness. When it came down to basics, he had chosen *her* without even hinting that a choice was being mulled, that a competition had been held in secret conclave to select a winner and a loser. Now, on the television screen, she has levered him upright. The camera shakes. Her earth moves under her feet. Her *House & Garden* apartment in Primrose Hill is carried into the killing fields. Every bullet and rocket chips away the myths of togetherness embodied in the yellow-wood furniture from the Cape and the intricate silk rugs from Damascus and Diyarbakir. She hears the furious rounds whining from *their* roof terrace to the percale cotton of *their* bedsheets, spreading defilement at the altar of their union. She hurls her glass of gin and ice cubes at the television set but her aim is bad and it ricochets, striking the shelf where he keeps his framed happy snaps of himself and his (exclusively male) colleagues in N'djamena and Juba, Grozny and Baghdad. The flying tumbler smashes into the photographs, shattering into shards that mingle with the broken glass of the picture frames.

They played the clip over and over again, picking at her scar. Mesmerized, she became familiar with every detail of the clanging gunfire and the pockmarked battlefield, the sight of him running in that awful, ungainly, ugly way and then falling, right out in the open in a broad gap between two breeze-block buildings whose symmetry had been destroyed by insistent waves of gunfire and fighting. Then, the woman darted out, time and again, from her hiding place, like some evil insect, wild-eyed and running at a crouch until she was beside him—beside *her* man—and lifting him to his feet, and then limping and shuffling back to cover with the TV camera zooming in close to catch the total concentration both of them devoted to the business of escaping the open ground for cover. And, worst of all, when they played and replayed the clip, that moment, that awful moment, when they fell together behind

the shelter of a battered stone wall that had once been part of somebody's home. You could still see the debris of the furniture, the broken
sticks of chairs, a sofa that had been pummeled with gunfire so that the
stuffing poked out from blue-striped ticking, the twisted frame of a
large photograph of the Al Aqsa mosque with its golden dome. He said
something to her and she laughed and then—and then kissed him, full
on the mouth. You could see it. On the television in front of the entire
world. He kissed her and she kissed him back and they hugged like babes
in the wood, cocooned so closely, so privately that no one would ever
intrude between them.

Throughout that evening, under the high ceilings of the apartment
in London, Eva Kimberly paced back and forth, across the polished
wood floors with their Bokharas and kilims. All this—their Roman
prints and tasteful oil paintings on their walls in the soft beige they had
chosen, their hi-fi with its powerful speakers, their ficus trees and book-
cases with Africana originals of Stanley and Livingstone bound in
maroon leather—all this he had forfeited for a broken sofa in the rubble
of someone else's life. When she called him, her voice unsteady, slurred
and raging from too many gins and too much hurt, he had lied—lied
outrageously and insistently. And you could always tell, whatever people
said, when people who said they were alone were not alone. The echoes
were never quite right. There was always the surreptitious click of a
bathroom door being closed, the rustle of a chair or bed being vacated,
the catch in the voice of someone who was lying to an audience of two—
the deceiver and the deceived. She made him say the Judas words. Are
you alone? Yes, I'm alone. Do you love me? Yes, I love you. Is it finished
between you and her? Say it. Say her name. Say you feel nothing. Yes, it
is finished between me and Faria Duclos. And you feel nothing? How
can I say that—she saved my life.

Through the high windows, she watched as the night darkened and
the streetlights came on, marking the footpaths on the gentle green

flanks of Primrose Hill, casting pools of light over strolling lovers. Why had that woman been there to save him? Why not leave him, with his folly, to die the coward's death his betrayal deserved? And, worst of all, why had it not been her, fleet-footed in the rubble, rescuing her crippled hero, her fallen giant?

TAPE TWO, SEGMENT TWO
SEPTEMBER 14, 2000, 5:00 P.M.
MONITORED SEPTEMBER 17

. . . needed another belt to go on with this. Because I guess I lied that night when Eva called to say she'd seen the footage and was I OK but what the hell was I doing with that woman and I said it was just a coincidence and she had been reaching for her cameras not embracing me and there had been no kiss—in a war zone for Chrissakes?—and she saved my life after all and maybe I should wipe these tapes when I get down. If I get down. If I go on. But it wasn't. It was not a coincidence because, right then, when I needed her she was there. And there was a kiss and it was magnificent and a restatement of being alive after all the crap they'd given me in Rochester. I don't think Eva believed the official version but at least it was something, a fiction, a fig leaf or whatever. When you come up with a lie on that scale, as every adulterer knows, then your only subsequent course of action is to stick with it, defend it, robustly, admitting no doubt or hesitation. She was just there, I said, she's a war photographer and there was a war on. It was stupid of me to be in the same place, I said, but I didn't ask her to be there. And, of course, I had done just that, which was about the biggest betrayal you could ask for. The biggest since I'd betrayed F in Kenya on the coast, at least, so there was some kind of symmetry, payback. But it was betrayal, it was and I admit it and plead guilty, and for whatever happened after that I take the fifth. And a last hit of old Johnnie before lights out.

JERUSALEM. AUGUST 2000

After the Gaza incident the talk was that they were a number again. Sightings were logged. Gossip built, swirled. The two were seen together exiting the grand Room 5 at the American Colony Hotel, once their known habitat, tryst and bolt-hole. Fact. They were laughing. Fact. Joe Shelby's eyes were pinholes and the coke lines were thick as puff adders. Fact. He limped. He stumbled. He didn't care. He laughed and, in the bar, Ibrahim poured him scotch while she burned like a light on the next barstool, his Florence Nightingale with a lamp bright in her bloodstream. Fact. If people asked who she thought she was to be running around with another woman's husband, she replied: Nurse Diesel, and thought that hilarious. Du Plessis was on hand, too, his consigliere, always a sign of trouble, trawling for bloodshed among the faiths. Joe Shelby filed a dispatch and his byline appeared alongside one of her images showing him crouching and running under fire, an Editor's Note to say: our guy was there. Fact.

Only after he returned to London did Faria Duclos pause to ask the question: what did he really want? Only she could have told the secrets of Room 5 and she did not choose to do so. The secrets were hers, perhaps all that would remain now. Chancing upon Du Plessis over a late breakfast, she said: what do you think Joe wanted here? You've known him longer than any of us. And Du Plessis said: he wanted you to answer the question he doesn't dare ask himself.

NAIROBI. AUGUST 2000

In Africa there were many who knew her and him and who saw the live television footage from Gaza. One of them was Eva Kimberly's father, Neville Kimberly, who raged at the barefaced betrayal of his cherished daughter by his putative son-in-law and felt a sharp constriction of his chest that he preferred to ignore. Another was Jeremy Davenport who watched the footage on a portable satellite receiver at his bush camp in the Serengeti. He followed the drama in Gaza with cold and calculating eyes, then his mouth curled into a lopsided grimace that suggested he recognized this precise moment as one he had been awaiting, much as a tracker awaits the moment when the prey lowers its guard.

BOWFELL
from Lingmoor Fell

Chapter Ten

"Jeremy? It's me. Eva."

"I didn't think you'd call back. Thank you so much. Where are you?" His voice was almost contrite, as if he were the offender.

"In the Lake District somewhere. And you?"

"London. Sorry. I had to call. I hope you don't mind." He was hurrying, as if he feared she might ring off and had rehearsed his words. "It was just . . . after I saw that footage on CNN, I thought, well, my heart went out and I thought you didn't deserve a spectacle like that and I just wanted you to know that, I suppose. That—"

She broke in to say that, no, she did not mind, it was sweet of him to still think of her. But she did not really, right at this moment, want to revisit either the moment she had discovered Joe Shelby's Big Lie or the moments when his illness had persuaded her to offer a second chance. Hearing Jeremy Davenport, after her tormented, wrong-footed day in the hills, she felt something like relief, or even joy, that someone preferred the sound of her voice to the bleat of a Lakeland sheep or the lash

146

of English rain. And there could be no harm in a telephone call, not compared to the mysteries Joe Shelby had declined to explain in his accounts of his journeys to the Middle East and the Balkans. Morality was relative: physical presence ranked higher in the league of venality than phone chat, virtual romance.

True, she and Joe Shelby had promised one another that they would try to come to grips with the curveballs, the pitfalls. True, she could accept that so much of what had happened—in Gaza in particular—resulted from his affliction. And, if she stretched gullibility to the breaking point, she could believe his protestations that, in Kosovo and Israel, he had kept the ultimate commandment sacred. Both of them knew that whatever it was that survived between them, whatever they might hope to rebuild, it would not withstand the buffeting of a third-party liaison. And anyway, there was something faintly pathetic about her agonizing over these men—one miles away on a mountain and the other hundreds of miles away at the end of a telephone line. That, surely, fell within the rubric of permissible misbehavior.

"How's Kenya?" She was reaching for a bright, conversational tone. She had checked into the hotel at the end of a long, somber driveway arched by dark firs, fringed with rhododendron. She had bathed and ordered a sandwich for delivery on room service, but had not felt hungry when it arrived on an oval steel platter, overwhelmed by a mountain of fries and a forest of salad. She had thought she would not call, then checked her cell phone message again and heard a voice so full of memories that she thought: what the hell? First a stranger at lunchtime, now an ex with supper. She was becoming quite promiscuous and toasted the idea in single malt from a bottle that must have sprung a leak.

"Good. Good. Lots of high-end types, despite all the publicity in the press about corruption and crime and so forth. Need to scare them up a bit. That's why I'm over here, then going on to New York to talk to the A&C people. Eva, can I see you?"

"Perhaps that wouldn't be such a good idea, Jeremy."

"But where are you?"

"That's for me to know."

"And me to find out." They laughed and then there was silence.

"But you are alone."

"How did you know that?" she said. The admission slipped out before she realized that he did not know, was merely sounding, scouting. He was thinking: yes! He was thinking the prey was exposed.

"You rat," she said, but there was no real malice. "How's Pop and the farm and everybody?"

"All missing you. Enormously. Me especially. Now the short rains are over and the bush is sparkling and full of exotic creatures. But none, of course, as beautiful as you."

"Jeremy . . ."

"But I have to tell you, Evie. I'm sorry. I know it's pathetic."

"It's not pathetic." The whisky had molded her voice to a soft burr that she tried to clear away with a cough in case he mistook it for the kind of intimacy that people sometimes develop during phone calls that stray into forbidden territory.

"Eva, you know I'll find you."

"Jeremy, you mustn't. Really. I'm fine. OK, the TV thing was a bit of a shock, but there was an explanation for it. Really. It was just a coincidence. And it did save his life." Even as she spoke, she wondered why she was shying from calling Joe Shelby by his name. Or referring to *her* as anything other than *it*. As if schoolgirl tantrums could make a difference.

"Is he with you?"

"No, Jeremy. He's . . . You shouldn't ask. Really. It was nice of you to call but everything's fine. Honestly."

"I just don't want you to be alone. Please let me see you, Evie."

"Not just yet, Jeremy. It wouldn't be right. You know that."

"No, I don't know that."

After the phone call, she felt suddenly hungry and found a cold steak sandwich surprisingly tasty. Far to the south, in London, Jeremy Davenport called the dialer trace number that allows British telephone subscribers to ascertain the number of the last person to call them. A metallic voice provided the information he needed. After a few seconds' hesitation, he called it, hanging up after a receptionist answered with the name of a hotel and its location. Then he was calling reception at his own hotel to ask if someone could please provide him with a road atlas, specifically one covering the Lake District. The clerk was more than happy to oblige. And would the concierge help arrange a rental car, a fast reliable model with good legs? Of course, Sir.

In her voice he sensed what he had most hoped to hear after the television broadcast from Gaza: the self-confidence had been breached. Like a wounded animal she left a blood spoor of vulnerability and hurt. He knew those feelings from her abandonment of him. He knew the pain of slinking away, licking a wound until it callused into the rude scar tissue of survival. And, of course, he was intimately attuned to the hunter's code of cunning and dissimulation that led to the coup de grace. Ever since the day, one year earlier, that Jeremy Davenport had discovered Eva Kimberly's betrayal, he had been sidling towards this moment, wearing the cuckold's mask of resignation to hide a stalker's resolve.

Chapter Eleven

Day two. Dawn, pre-dawn. Great time for a hangover. Condensation lines the condom and my breath is like ectoplasm. Almost set fire to the whole damn thing starting up the Gaz stove. But Earl Grey redeems all. That and rehydrated breakfast mulch. And a somewhat complicated roll of paper and tobacco. Legs felt like stilts when I got up for the morning call, stumbling in the rain and a punishing wind. And I'd forgotten the indignity of the morning constitutional, crouching behind a boulder with the wind whistling around the zone of paramount privacy. How the hell did they cope with that on Everest without total refrigeration? The novelty now is the difficulty of rising again, squatting there paralyzed, legs too feeble to push me upright. So you lean forward, tilt 'til your good arm can provide assistance. The Wrynose moon.

Sometimes you wake up and say, or pray: today it will be better; today the evil will have departed as mysteriously as it arrived. You awake with the fantasy of recovery: it has all been a dream; you are in a hotel room somewhere, panicky and sweaty but whole. My God, it was so realistic—I actually dreamed I was disabled. You imagine that some shaman, some nganga, far away, has withdrawn the pins from a crude clay doll, thrown bones, lifted spells, muttered magic, chanted charms. You will feel the weakness drain away like pus from a lanced boil. And then—as at this very moment—it is not like that at all and you maneuver to get out of bed, prop yourself up to clean your teeth, hold the toothbrush with two hands. Your leg feels that little bit weaker so you are unsteady like a drunk and there's one more thing you can't do—change a lightbulb, climb a stepladder, wipe your arse, hold a tennis racket, climb onto a motorcycle. You pray.

I pray.

I pray most of all that I'm heard. And I know now that if I do not ask now I will not be answered.

I know there's a God and I know God is telling me something, and I'm working on the code to understand the message. I know that some day in some form these prayers will be answered, maybe not in the way I'd anticipate or prefer, but in some way. Or not. Because there's the other voice, the one that says: who do you think you are fooling?

They say you go home to die, so maybe I'm propelled to some point that is a spiritual home, like an elephant's graveyard, and I'll just sit down there and say: OK, take me, Lord, and thanks for the ride. These days, I imagine life as a spring in a green, grassy mountainside, gushing, bright, sparkly, pure. And every day you can drink of it, even as the power of its issuing is diminished, even as the flow weakens, falters and in the end it's just a trickle. But it's a trickle of life, the essence, the great gift, and you'd be a fucking idiot not to try and drink to the last drop, the lees. The point, I think, is that you are tempted to say: oh, I'll wait for X to be right before I do Y. But what this illness teaches you is that X will never, ever be right again, so you'd better get on with Y while you still can. It's the lesson of old age, foreshortened. If you don't do it now you may never do it, whatever it is—a project, a mission, a vocation. And the word "never" has a kind of finality that you never—there we go—understood before. Never means what it says: not ever again in the whole span of the universe—time or space. So if I don't get up the mountain this time, I never will.

WRYNOSE PASS, ENGLAND. SEPTEMBER 2000

What she had taken for a symmetrical boulder was in reality a small, carved obelisk marking the confluence of three old counties at the summit of Wrynose Pass. The day before it had seemed like one gray rock among others. With the improved visibility of the morning, Eva Kimberly recognized her mistake—surely a forgivable error for an outsider, an offcomer used to rather more dramatic landmarks: the cone of Kilimanjaro, say, or the Serengeti migration. If she had known what to look for just a few hours earlier, her life might have taken a different turn. She would have persuaded him to call off his folly and she would not have encouraged Jeremy Davenport by responding to his message. So blame the fog, blame the mist and the rain. Or blame Joe Shelby for being who he was and what he had become. Blame Joe Shelby for mesmerizing her, then forgetting the spell.

She parked the car and pulled her coat closer. Her hair whipped in the wind. Her skin felt faintly prickly and the roof of her mouth was furred. She had left the hotel in haste, without showering, without coffee, pulling on yesterday's clothes, raking a brush through her hair. In the rearview mirror, when she adjusted it, she looked a wreck: eyes tinged with red, the dark stains spreading below them. Who'd want her like this? Not Joe. Not Jeremy. And what a relief that would be for all of them.

The cloud seemed to have regrouped rather than dispersed, taking up position high on the flank of the hills above her—an army in ambush position, poised to rush down on its prey. On the ground, just above the marshy patch at the summit of the pass she began to discern the telltale signs of careless residence: an unsightly tuft of tissue not quite buried, a flattening of the wet grass, the discarded butt of a handrolled cigarette. In the bush, he would not have lasted five seconds without detection. But this, of course, was not the bush and Joe Shelby was not trying to disguise his progress: he was saying I was here and you were not. You drove by and left me on this damp patch of land.

From the top of the pass, a rough narrow trail curled and zigzagged steeply to the north—back in the same direction as the hotel she had fled, seized by a pressing wish to see him, to hold him as a talisman against the other man who had spoken from London the evening before with a siren-call across time. Jeremy Davenport was a hunter and must have sensed her weakness. And she was seeking cover with Joe Shelby, who had departed and left her with none, even as she offered salvation.

Underneath the door of her hotel room, an early morning fax message had arrived while she slept a fitful sleep interspersed with moments of semi-wakefulness when she could not gauge where dreams ended and realities began. She cast about on her pillow to reassure herself that she was alone, then tried to recall who, in her dream, had been at her side. She did not hear or see the fax arrive. She knew only, as she read it, her nightgown crumpled and her hair awry, that it was far too important to be left until Joe Shelby's scheduled arrival one long day later. The message arrived on the letterhead of Nigel Lampton in London. It was addressed to both of them. It said, in doctor's scrawl: "Hold the Mayo! I may have good news. Call when you can—Nigel." Immediately, she called the neurologist in London despite the early hour, hearing the practiced modulation of his reassurance, rehearsed through many discussions of terrible news. She scrawled what he said on a notepad but a lot of the technical jargon was jumbled, incoherent. When she read back his message, the words that leaped from the page were "probably not MND" and "treatable, if not at present curable." At another point in her jangled script she had written "little known condition" and "full three score and ten." She did not need to make a note when he said, sternly: he should not delay the attempted treatment. There could still be unpredictable deterioration, from one moment to the next.

In the hotel room, she thrilled and hurried. She must tell Joe Shelby before he sought his Valhalla on the hostile uplands. She must tell him there was some hope—a commodity he had thought to have exhausted. She must tell him that the progression of his illness might accelerate without warning.

Now, at the summit of the pass, she called out, praying that Joe Shelby would not be too far away, would be playing games, anticipating her remorse, her panic to reappear somehow from a wraith of mist or a cluster of rock. Higher up the fellside, the cloud opened and closed, tantalizingly, like a veil drawn back then abruptly shut. Eva Kimberly thought she saw him, moving slowly in the cleavage of a valley between two rounded expanses of mountainside. She called again and ran forward, the sodden earth sucking at her suede loafers—what a stupid choice, but she had been rushing, not thinking or planning when she left the hotel—spattering mud on her tailored trousers. The water from the ground spilled over and froze her feet, and she tried to ignore it. If only she could see him—one positive, definite sighting—she would ignore the cold, the wet, and follow. The track was rough, treacherous, and her feet gained little purchase. Her shoes were designed for the topsides of sleek yachts or the cobbles of Rome, not for the worn trails of these lands. Again the mist parted and she saw slight movement, a dark shadow against a hillside stained in flat, neutral tones of olive and gray where all brightness had been leached by the clouds. She thought she recognized his backpack, his parka, his awkward, ungainly gait, his twin poles seeking anchorage on the untrusted ground below him. She thought it might be him but could not be sure. She thought it could be any lunatic out in atrocious weather, pursuing some inscrutable agenda. She shouted his name at the top of her lungs, but the damp air seemed to swallow her words, robbing them even of an echo. She thought that anyone who knew them both would think her a fool—a fool to have believed his explanation of the ridiculous television spectacle from Gaza that she and all her friends had seen, a fool to have believed the way he insisted that his life had been saved by a coincidence, no more than that: there was no debt of gratitude to the Frenchwoman, no requirement to undo his betrayal of her at Jadini and Cape Town and many other places; there was no hangover of passion, no hankering for their hotel-room life. She believed and did not believe, believed because she wanted to, because the alternative was uncharted, frightening territory.

She believed because, when she dreamed of him, she dreamed of him whole and caring. She dreamed of his body coiled and lithe as it had been when he had surfed into view in Jadini. She dreamed of his confident, easy smile, his assumption of control over events, his unassailable self-confidence as they drove together to Guguletu or performed feats of endurance and creativity in the big bed of the Mount Nelson Hotel. She knew he dreamed of it, too. Inside, he was still that same man, and that was why the sight of his reflection pained him by confronting him with the new Joe Shelby, who stumbled and limped and could not run and whose self-confidence had transmuted into rage. She did not need anyone to tell her she was a fool to be standing here, calling to a man beyond reach. But if she was a fool, then he was doubly so, firstly to have embarked on this voyage of self-justification and now to pursue it without knowing that his heroic precept—a gauntlet thrown down to God and mortality—was false after all. "Treatable, if not at present curable"—hardly the stuff of the life-and-death epic he had wished to be his memorial.

She returned to the car and lit a cigarette. She brushed her hair and began to repair the damaged landscape beneath her eyes, then dribbled eyedrops to remove the redness. On the passenger seat, the overnight fax mocked all her efforts to deliver it to Joe Shelby, to pass on its message from the physician they were counting on to undo Rochester's malignant spell.

Chapter Twelve

JERUSALEM. SEPTEMBER 2000

It is a day of accidental truce. The momentum has faltered. The commanders in their breeze-block, sandbagged bunkers cannot muster energy for the initiation of hostilities. The foot soldiers rest over rifles and machine guns and rocket launchers, watchful but inactive. They smoke, drink tea, play backgammon, attend the obligations of their mutually exclusive faiths as they await the clarion call to battle but do nothing to hasten its sounding. It is a coincidence, a mutual, fleeting exhaustion, an undeclared, incomplete cease-fire that will not endure. Perhaps it is no more than a chance overlap of hostile intents that has produced quiet while further carnage is plotted. The politicians, who turn the gauges of conflict with a crafted phrase, a deniable provocation, find themselves baffled: they have called for peace in their public speeches without really meaning it, and yet, for a day, miraculously, it is here.

Those who chronicle the war's progress chafe at inactivity but relish calm. In this downtime, their antennae need not be attuned to the crackle and zing of incoming fire, they do not have to worry that every breath will be their last, or flinch from the hostile gaze of every high building that might be a sniper's eyrie, or ponder whether every empty, rubbled street might be the highway to premature reunification with their Maker. Yet, they pine for the joy of peril. They know that war is the only real yardstick: on the battlefronts, the fat of pretense and dissimulation is cut away; all that counts is the imperative of survival. It is a world they never want to leave because in this world, set apart from all others, they are permitted to live by their own codes, not those imposed by the societies that produced them. And outside of this world, they are nonentities, faces glimpsed and passed by without recognition on Fifth Avenue, ciphers among the crowd flowing over London Bridge to where the bells of St. Mary Woolnoth kept the hours.

In Jerusalem, the official versions, purveyed by radio stations and anonymous officials, offered up "relative calm," meaning the fatality count had notched up in low single figures and there had been no particular escalation to ignite the interest of a jaded world—no nightclub bombing of teenage girls in miniskirts, no napalm, no especially young babies with neat bullet holes through their smooth unknowing skulls. There would be anguish somewhere out there, in the refugee camps of Gaza and the West Bank and in the apartment houses of Tel Aviv, but there would be no great hunger to share it in the newsrooms and edit suites, in worlds where people had their own priorities. In the earliest days of this newest conflict, the tally might have excited some interest. But horror's threshold is never lowered: the benchmark is always the next atrocity. Without incremental expansion of the carnage, the adrenaline of the outsiders does not run, so meaning is restricted to the insiders.

On this quiet day, when there was no pressing need to go looking for trouble, Faria Duclos sought out Du Plessis in the familiar garden of the hotel courtyard. Since Joe Shelby's departure, after Gaza, she was restless, groping toward a decision. Du Plessis was no father confessor but he was the only one who knew Joe Shelby as he had been. The hexagonal stone fountain sparkled in the late summer sunlight and the geraniums drew vermilion patterns onto bright old limestone walls and arched doorways. He had found a shaded corner table to nurse a beer, take respite from the heat and the sporadic gunfire that had become uninteresting, rehearsed. His flak jacket, stained with sweat, rested against the leg of a white, wrought iron table. His cameras hung from his chair. He was using long-focus lenses, the kind that do not require the photographer to move in too close. He had covered sixteen wars. Each new conflict made him more irritable with the combatants, and exposed signs of carelessness and unnecessary risk taking on his own part—the danger signals. This war annoyed him in particular because both sides seemed so patently incapable of finishing the job. Wars needed a beginning, a middle and an end. The Middle East was lodged permanently in the middle. In his own part of the world, the end had not been to his liking, but it had drawn a line: white rule finished, black rule began. Life went on. His past lay buried somewhere in the bush of Zimbabwe and Angola and the Congo, along with his combat fatigues and rifle. His future lay in his cameras. He used long lenses because he wanted the income from the seventeenth and eighteenth wars before he retired to a wine farm in the Cape. With his hair cropped short, he was looking more and more like a retired mercenary, a legionnaire past his prime. The gilt of youth was off him and there was a malice to his thoughts about his younger, more enthusiastic competitors. It rankled with him still that Faria Duclos had performed heroics he would gladly have undertaken himself to save Joe Shelby's life. But she had moved first, and he accepted that both of them had a special bond that went beyond shared space for words and images.

"Thinking of writing a novel," he said with heavy sarcasm as she sat down opposite him. "The secrets of Room 5."

"There are no secrets."

"Tell that to the marines."

Since Joe Shelby's brief sojourn, since what Du Plessis called the Gaza kiss-and-tell, since the desperate attempts at the old craziness, Faria Duclos seemed to Du Plessis to have mellowed. In the days Joe Shelby had spent holed up in Room 5 at the American Colony, Du Plessis had watched him try and fail to reconstruct his old persona. It had been a sad chastening experience: how could you play the two-fisted, devil-may-care war junkie when you could not even prop up the bar without a leg buckling, an arm hanging useless, incapable of raising even a shot glass? And since he had left, Faria Duclos had changed too. She had taken to tanning and swimming on the quiet days. She seemed, in turn, cool, distant, excited, like someone preparing with trepidation for the journey of a lifetime, or for a decision she knew she should have made long ago. Whatever else had happened in Room 5, Du Plessis thought, Faria Duclos was no longer indifferent to her own health and safety. He had observed her eating more than salad. She had been seen to toy with grilled steak, poached fish, an order of fries. The flesh was returning to her gaunt cheekbones. When she swam in a bikini—in private times at the hotel pool when she thought herself unobserved—there was perhaps just a modicum of flesh building on her xylophonic rib-cage. Du Plessis had even caught her in the hotel gym, asking a personal trainer for tips on exercise. Exercise! In this job, you got exercise enough just staying one step ahead of the unfriendlies—and Jerusalem had more than its share of those, whichever way you looked. Most of all, the way Du Plessis saw it, Faria Duclos wanted a blessing, a sign that the direction she had chosen was the right one. Maybe he was wrong, but he believed—as much as he believed anything—that she and Joe were a unit, a number, that neither would ultimately allow to be sundered.

Now, with her black hair drawn back tight and glistening, her dark eyes clear and sparkling, it was barely surprising that she had figured on fashion magazine covers: her features, olive and faintly oriental in the uplift at the corner of the eyes, were haunting and vulnerable, imperious and aloof, hinting at unknowable secrets that could only be unlocked in the perilous zone beyond her full lips, her tight, slender body—almost boyish with small breasts and a backside that would not take two full man's hands to grasp. If she had not been Joe Shelby's girl, Du Plessis would have made his play long ago, but she was Joe Shelby's girl and that was that. The thought brought him a measure of relief: she was Joe Shelby's girl and so he had an excuse for avoiding the certain rejection that greeted everyone else. She was Shelby's babe, and so he had no need to compete with him for her. In Du Plessis's book, she was the kind of woman, the kind of photographer, who should be labeled a health hazard: accompanying this person in the vicinity of combat can kill. But, for all he was viewed outside his circle as a loose cannon, a crazed roustabout, Du Plessis had powerful loyalties. The fact that she was Joe Shelby's girl meant not just that she was off limits, but that he had a responsibility to see them whole, for Joe had erred and required help in rediscovering his true path. There were some who thought Du Plessis cunning, devious, untrustworthy, loud-mouthed, prone to gratuitous violence and devoted to drink and misbehavior. But he would not see harm or misguided circumstances come to Joe Shelby. Or Faria Duclos. And now she was asking his advice: should she follow Joe Shelby, as if he were a phantom beckoning from the cusp of another world?

"Joe is having a tough time."

"Joe's a cripple. But he's still Joe. And you're still the babe. She's the princess. You're the babe."

"Not like that. We changed. We all changed. You changed, Du Plessis. Don't tell me different. We do our wars, we get our scoops. But in the end it becomes a routine. It's what we do. Like Joe says, we go to shitholes because that's the only place we're at home, where we can escape all the usual rules, the regulations and the regimentation. What did he say once: you go to war to get some peace. War's simple. Live, die. Good, bad.

No one out there will tell you to pay your taxes or drive on the right side of the road, or change your knickers or clean your teeth or give up smoking. They'll tell you not to endanger them, not to draw fire, but that's all. Everything else is irrelevant. All these petty laws that get you parking tickets and interest payments. Out there is cloud cuckoo land."

"And the entry visa's getting more expensive."

"See? It's getting to you, too. You know you'll get it one day. You know that you can't just go on forever sticking your neck out. Look at Joe in Gaza. OK, he fell. But it could have been anybody. There was no second guessing. There was fire coming from at least seven points. No one knew what was friendly and what wasn't."

"So that would have made us collateral damage?"

"Exactly. We are collateral. That's all. But collateral like in a mortgage or an assurance. We are what the comics put up against the risk of someone else having a better picture. Just collateral, hedging. That's all. And we've done it."

"Been there. Got the fucking tee shirt. Sixteen times over."

"After that thing in Zim. On that farm? I was scared. Like I've never been. Jesus. Before, I thought there was something wrong with me, thought I hadn't been given the fear gene. But I was frightened that day, because it was the first time the images really came alive for me—jumped through the range finder and under my skin and I was thinking: Jesus, these stiffs are still warm and the killers are standing right behind me, looking at my ass and tits and it'll take just one little push to shove them over the top again. That's when I realized that fear is projection, imagination. You know? You know. Don't try that dumb look with me, Du Plessis. You know what fear is when you imagine yourself in someone else's position, when you imagine the next moment when the bullet smashes into your skull. Fear is your imagination. And the other side is this: fear builds up, like a bank account, with compound interest. Every little incident is a deposit, and then you get the interest so your fear account is a bit fatter and you go on to the next shithole and make another deposit, and in the end you think: I've got a lot of fear, enough fear. Fear is debit. Fear is in the red. Fear has to be repaid. And that's when you start to think: how long can I go on making my own luck? How long will it be 'til it's my turn, 'til someone calls in the markers? Just look back over the past few years. Where do we meet up? Where do people like us hang out? Everything important that ever happens to any one of us happens in some place that no one in their right mind would go to. Where did I meet Joe? Gaza. Where did we break up? Rwanda. Where did we meet up again? Kosovo. Where do I see him after that? Khan Younis. We spend all our time in places where kids carry rifles, talking our way past roadblocks, watching people kill people. We think we're smart to get ourselves to places where no one else wants to go, except the crazies who live there. That's no life."

"Oh, sure. I can see you doing calendars and Bar Mitzvahs and weddings and baby's first portrait. Goo-goo-ka-chook. And let's have the bridesmaids in this one."

"You are a philistine, Du Plessis."

"A realist you mean. I've seen fear, real fear, not through a camera lens. Through a fucking sniper scope, through the sights, when you're shitting yourself in the bush and you're scanning the tree line and you suddenly realize there's some gook there with his AK pointing right at you and you see his eyes and he's scared like what you are, but you pull the trigger first and—bingo—those eyes go out like a candle, man. That's fear, man. When you're in it, part of it, on the line. Not some fucking observer tripping in and out with your cameras."

"Sometimes I think you are full of shit, Du Plessis."

"But I know."

"Know what?"

"The secrets of Room 5."

She blushed and he caught it. He laughed, uproariously, and spilt beer on his olive tee shirt. It mingled with a line of sweat. He knew by now what she wanted him to say.

"I know you, Duclos. Everyone thinks you're the big tough chick who's hacked it in every war that's ever been invented. I've seen guys run a mile rather than get in a car with you in case you take them on one of your hell runs. But inside you're just a babe. Inside you're looking for Prince Charming and you don't mind if he's a cripple or a gimp, just so long as he's the one for you. And if he can't walk properly, then he can't run away from you anymore. Right? Look, he came here. He looked for you. You found each other again. Like two little lovebirds."

"So what do you suggest?"

"Go see him, man. Block him straight. Ask him to choose. Shit or get off the pot. You know what I'm saying. You say you know what fear is, but you're crapping yourself in case he turns round and says he'll stick with his princess. But how long has he got, for fuck's sake? How many months are there before he tops himself because they want to put him in a wheelchair? Take what there is while it's still there, man. Do you think the princess can hack it with him? Do you think she can bring him back to life for whatever life he's got left? Show him a good time. You're the babe, the real one. You know where he is. There are five hundred flights a day out of this dump. If you want a break, take a real break. Take the gap. Hire a car and find him. Otherwise I'll put the secrets of Room 5 on the Internet. And remember what Dylan said: when you've got nothing you've got nothing to lose."

Mock-crooning, he finished the verse that they both knew well: go to him now, he calls you, you can't refuse. And then the chorus, familiar from late nights over whisky bottles, the lament of the lost and the self-pitying: You're invisible now, got no secrets to conceal. How does it feel? To be on your own. Like a rolling stone.

"You never liked her, did you? You never thought she was Joe's type."

"That's not the point. I know you. And I know Joe. And that's all I'm saying. You'll never rest until you know why he came here. Why he came for you. You know he needs you. But you don't know whether you need him."

"Shall I tell you the real secret of Room 5, Du Plessis?"

"Like I don't already know?"

"No, you don't. The real secret is that it's no one else's secret. Not yours. Not hers. So work that one out. And, yes, I want him again—but he has to give a sign."

"Listen. The only secret you have to work out is whether to get on BA straight to London or transit Paris to pick up a frilly dress on the way." Du Plessis thought that was very funny indeed and ordered another beer.

THIRLMERE. SEPTEMBER 2000

She realized now what must have happened and rebuked herself, half in self-reproach, half in relief. He had made camp and struck camp, then caught a lift into the valley with a car or a sheep truck or a tractor or whatever. The person she had seen high on the fells—or thought she had seen—was a chimera, a specter conjured by the mist and rain. A shepherd, or figment—the abominable rainman, a phantom.

She was becoming familiar with the route, back over Blea Tarn and through Great Langdale, then turning left onto the A591 at Ambleside for the narrow, winding road past Rydal Water and Grasmere, soaring over Dunmail Raise below the slopes of Helvellyn to the east, alongside the forbidding waters of Thirlmere in the pine forests to the west. Since he had not taken his mobile phone, he would have no means of contacting her, so he would make for their rendezvous, advanced base, traveling by hook or by crook as he did in his former life as a correspondent, talking his way past the visa officers, bribing, cajoling, blustering to sidestep passport or accreditation rules. He would know what had to be done. He called it his tradecraft. If he could make it from Ouagadougou to Tashkent without a stop or a visa or a hiccup on the way, he could certainly make it from Wrynose Pass to Thirlmere, although why he had insisted in choosing one hotel for the eve of his expedition and another for its conclusion remained a mystery. Perhaps he wanted bookends, beginnings, endings, lines drawn in the sand, or at least the mud.

The weather forecast was uniformly grim, without promise of bright periods later. At the summit of the pass, the temperature had fallen. Even in her jaundiced view of British meteorology, the clouds had taken on a heavy, menacing look and the sheep in the enclosed fields huddled for warmth.

Eva Kimberly turned into the narrow lane that led to advanced base. The tones were somber: dark rhododendrons dripping fresh rain and a breath of mist on the air, leached from an unbearably oppressive sky, so distant from Africa's great openness and light and high clouds that formed and reformed in fantastic sequence. The gravel crunched beneath the tires. As she parked and clambered from the car, the branch of a pine tree chose that precise moment to disburden itself of accumulated raindrops, spilling gouts of cold water onto her. She did not mind. Her head had cleared and she had a purpose: Joe Shelby had proved his point, now she would prove hers. She would oblige him to respond A.S.A.P. to Nigel Lampton's missive. She would oblige him to soak in a deep bath and recognize that, in one day, he had achieved as much as he would in three. He had scaled a summit, an important summit. He had achieved his benchmark. He had survived and delivered his own redemption. He had made camp in his beloved mountains, communed with them, lain with them in exclusive tryst, embracing the earth, the rock. Now he would embrace her and the physician would restore hope.

She gathered up the fax message and made for the hotel entrance. She would locate him, bearing good tidings: enter breathless messenger, stage left.

The place he had chosen as advanced base was a comfortable country auberge, a converted mansion, not a glittery five-star establishment. Painted white with black window frames, it stood out sharply from the green and dark olive and gray of the lake and mountains. There was no formal reception, simply a small, antique desk in a hallway where the owner or one of his staff might be summoned by a tingling handbell. The two big lounges led right and left off the hall, comfortable spaces with deep armchairs and long sofas arranged around oak coffee tables where the hotelier served morning coffee and afternoon teas made up of scones and butter and jam and cream. Both rooms commanded views out over the lake, through pines that had been planted to frame a jagged ridgeline on the opposite shore. Just inside the hotel's front door, a wall mirror reflected her disarray. The makeup applied at Wrynose Pass had run disastrously. Her hair was plastered to her head. The dark stains had reemerged beneath her eyes. She smelt coffee and cigarette smoke on the air, from the lounge on the right. She contemplated fleeing to their sanctum to spruce and rebuild, but there was no way of passing the entrance to the lounge without being seen. She ran a hand through her hair, grabbed a tissue from her bag to wipe away the most obvious damage. In any event, he had seen her worse than this. He had seen her hair wet from the oceans, from hotel shower rooms. He had seen her face naked of all embellishment on many mornings when he brought her coffee and reveled in her warm disarray in the secret world beneath the down comforter where waking dreams and real touching mingled juicily. It did not matter today—at this moment—that Eva Kimberly was not gilt-edged, manicured, polished, shiny for Joe Shelby. It mattered only that she should see him, hold him, anchor herself again after the unraveling that twenty-four hours could bring—from her flirtation to her straying on the pass to her conversation with a man she had no right or qualification to talk to. And, anyhow, after a night in a tent and a day in the rain, Joe Shelby himself would hardly look his best.

Words would not be necessary. A big smile, a congratulatory smile, a big you're-my-hero-hug; then the production of the message—hey presto! A miracle, rise up and walk. The clouds have lifted. The end is not nigh. We can start again, and you can gather your strength to return to these mountains, not in the fall, but in spring, in the time of buds and lambs and blossoms. We will not live under this sentence. As in her dreams, he would be whole. He would not limp or stumble or be awkward and hopeless. Let's bathe together, wash away the despair, snuggle and cuddle and giggle in a big bed, with the curtains closed on those dark hostile mountains and chill lake, and the gas fire hissing in the rose-glow.

The fax message was the governor's reprieve, the release from Death Row. Eva Kimberly threw her shoulders back and arranged her face into the best smile she could muster.

"Hello, Evie. I hope you don't mind."

"Oh my God!"

Chapter Thirteen

RED TARN, ENGLAND. SEPTEMBER 2000

He was above them all now. Offering a cue or an omen, the clouds parted briefly to expose the broad, broken flanks of Crinkle Crags leading across to Bowfell. The small, blustery patch of water was named for the rust-colored, rough grass fringing its modest shores, bent to the prevailing wind. Even here, the gusts were strong enough to sculpt the wavelets into infant whitecaps. The ground around—black with peat—had become marshy, the trail rocky and perilous for him to negotiate. Without his walking poles, the balancing from one uneven stone to another would have been harder to accomplish—and this so early in the expedition, so far from the real challenge of Scafell Pike's summit ridge where the boulders were notorious for their awkwardness. In the cleavage of mountain between Crinkle Crags and Pike o'Blisco—a name that always seemed alluring and mysterious—he paused, pulling thermal clothing tighter around him.

From this high ground—suddenly, tantalizingly—he could see the path that led down to Langdale, to tarred roads and telephones, meals on plates of bone china that arrived from hot, busy kitchens, newspapers, normalcy, ordered fields and toy figures moving about in farmyards. Here, again, was the option—to abandon the project or stay with it, a decision to be taken alone because the fells were deserted, quite unlike the mountains of his memories where there was always someone to hail and greet, close by or in the distance or across a valley. On the climb up from Wrynose Pass he had encountered no one to wish him good day or inquire about his route and objective that day. The day before, too, the mountains had been curiously quiet. And perhaps the emptiness was its own message to him: why venture here where no others venture? What did they know that he did not?

But there was no real choice. In reality, there had never been a choice. The illness did not permit alternatives.

From the Mayo Clinic onward, he had been told he could only weaken. The dream of recovery or even treatment could only recede. The path back to his youth could only become narrower, less distinct until the sickly, diseased underbrush and cloying blind mists swallowed it for eternity. If he did not make the summit of the highest mountain now, he never would because he would never be cured. With every day he would weaken and, no matter how strong his will, his body would simply refuse to obey the order to place one foot in front of the other on the treacherous trails.

They had told him as much at the Mayo, and when you got that kind of news you did not ignore it: you made your dispositions, like a doomed general setting the field for the final defeat, standing firm with the banner that you would defend until the necessarily bloody end. You made your arrangements. You prepared for the heroic ignominy of the last stand. You told yourself to display neither fear nor self-pity. You sold your stock, rearranged your portfolio, transferred assets, made provision for the partition of the estate. You shortened your schedule, paring away the irrelevant, the unnecessary so that only the most pressing priorities remained to be achieved in an ever-shortening time span. You took your cue from the very old who saw the end approaching with ever greater acuity. You threw away your long-term planner because the long term was no longer a concept: long-term was a mockery, a luxury reserved for people who did not even realize it was a luxury. And if you had set yourself the target of climbing England's highest mountain while you still could, then you did not shirk from the squalls, the gusts, the sudden, unforecast snow flurries that would persuade a walker at any other time to seek the refuge of the valleys. You took imprudent decisions because the essential element of time had played tricks on you so you did not have all the usual considerations to take into account. And, in Joe Shelby's mind, there was another thought he tried to ignore because it would not help him get where he wanted to go: if they were right, at the Mayo Clinic, if there was no appeal against their sentence, if it was all simply a matter of procedures to be gone through, stations of degeneration and immobility to observe—from cane to frame to wheelchair to the final gurney into the mortuary—then it did not really make any difference whether the inevitable happened in some sanitized, whispering hospice with a blessing of morphine in the still last moments, or up here in a roaring icy blizzard where, at least, he was still under his own power to set the altar and sing the final requiem into his tape recorder: if nothing else—his legend would survive where he had not. And, when they found him, they would know that he had departed for the parallel world with his preposterous comparisons to Mallory and Irvine intact, vainglorious to the end, never submitting to the netherworld of shadows and sickliness, but striding towards his destiny in the company of his true heroes, laughing in the face of danger.

Joe Shelby turned northwest towards Crinkle Crags and the weather laughed back in his face. A sharp blast of cold, horizontal rain stung his cheeks and he fumbled to draw on waterproof gloves and an alpinist's fleece balaclava, gaiters to keep the rain and mud from spilling into his boots. The process took forever, constantly thwarted by the difficulties of maneuvering his disobedient fingers. Pulling a glove onto his left hand, his fingers buckled under the strain, refusing to separate so that two of them lodged in the space designed for one. He took the glove for his right hand and clamped it between his jaws because his left hand had no power to pull it over his outstretched hand. The velcro and straps and zips of the gaiters almost defeated him and he cursed into the wind, on the verge of his tears because the decision to go on had been challenged so soon and by such trivia. With his good hand he checked his GPS location and heading. After the moment of visibility, the clouds had closed, but the track was well marked and the ghosts of climbers past accompanied him, guiding his steps. He walked bowed and tilted. The muscles in his thighs, so far unaffected by the illness, performed the functions abandoned by his debilitated calf and ankle muscles, but they ached as they bore the unaccustomed strain.

The disease lurked on the peripheries, then moved in closer as the cells in the central nervous system decayed, behaving like drunken signalers, refusing to accept messages, refusing to open up the cable lines, the circuits. The muscles in his upper left arm, his lower legs, his wrist and fingers were all there still, sleeping, flaccid, because the signals did not come through to summon them to activity. Each step was a campaign, a conscious computation of deliberate acts, devoid of the automatic, unconscious spring of his youth. Where the track had eroded into slabs of smooth, worn granite, he placed his feet as ponderously as a climber on the highest Himalayan slope, manipulating his walking poles as if they were ice axes on a perilous traverse in the dead zone where the body entropies. His progress was painstaking. He had resolved to rest for fifteen minutes every forty-five minutes, but, in truth, the pauses between each step were their own miniature rest periods. Still, it was progress. That was what he told himself. It was progress because every step, however slow and however clumsy, took him a fraction closer to his goal and after he attained that goal, he did not care to think what would happen. The systems were closing down, like a very sick child in fitful slumber, shutting out extraneous stimuli to focus on the single, overriding goal of survival.

THIRLMERE. SEPTEMBER 2000

"Jeremy?"

He had changed in obvious ways but not so much as to be unrecognizable. Short hair made him seem more boyish, less haughty than the loose, flowing mane he had cultivated in the past. But the same old deep tan contrasted sharply with the pale Britons flitting through her life, evoking memories of bush and woodsmoke. Something about the diamond clarity of his eyes said he had cleaned up after the drunken bawlings of their severance. Something about the hardness in those eyes said he still bore scars and uncertainties. He sprang to his feet from a deep sofa in a single flowing movement, lithe and expectant. There was no limp, no hanging arm, no awkward struggle for balance. In slender blue jeans and a down vest he looked slightly out of place in this stuffy, old-fashioned hotel, like a caged animal brought in from the wild, wary and constantly poised for flight. And, my God, he was good-looking. She had somehow forgotten that part when her thoughts strayed back through the veils of guilt to their time together.

"Can I bring you coffee, madam?"

The maid broke the spell. Mercifully.

"Yes. Please. Jeremy?"

"Yes. Another pot, please."

Smoke curled from a cigarette half-smoked in an ash-tray on the coffee table where he had been sitting when she entered the lounge. An early edition of *The Financial Times* lay half-read on a sofa, next to a set of car keys bearing the tag of a rental company. She remembered his worn leather briefcase from many journeys, stuffed with client lists and supply inventories and, sometimes, with gifts for her from remote places— Parisian perfume or Italian silk, silver from Zanzibar, and, once, a diamond from South Africa, destined for a ring that was never made. There was no suitcase, no overnight bag at his feet. Next to the car keys, though, was a room key from here, from this hotel, from advanced base, from Joe Shelby's chosen refuge.

"How did you—"

"Jungle cunning. Juju. Bush rules. I shouldn't have. I know."

Leaving London before first light, nudging the powerful Mercedes saloon through the grim, grimy reaches of Camden, losing his way briefly at Kentish Town, he had told himself not to dissect his motives or allow any vestigial chivalry to corrupt his mission. Concentrate, he told himself. Concentrate on avoiding the billows of spray from the roaring trucks on the highway. Concentrate on the spoor, not like in Africa where a broken blade of grass, a smear of blood or a mound of warm droppings provided clues, but here in this alien world of artificial signs: M1, M6; so different from the open, dirt roads, the bouncing, half-seen trails through the high grass of the savanna. Concentrate on keeping speed down within the limits proscribed by this nation of fatuous, restrictive rules: do not drive too fast, do not live too fast; drink when they tell you, do not eat using your fingers, do not shit in the bushes or shoot the fauna. Above all, do not be distracted by memories of the fireside at Main Camp, with the soft light flickering across her sunburned face, or of riding together across the broad plains above the Rift Valley where the Thomson's gazelles scattered before the thundering hooves and she rode effortless and straight-backed as if part of her bay stallion. Do not allow these memories to divert you from the mission. Do not forget the simple overriding fact that you deserved far better from her and were wronged. Focus on the trail, the route map, the unfamiliar names at the roadside, joke names from the slapstick of a forgotten mother nation. Wigan and Manchester, Liverpool—The Beatles!—Preston and Kendal and Shap and finally Penrith and the turn to Keswick on a narrow, twistier Judas-road that would betray you with a hidden curve, the unsuspected appearance of a blind farm tractor. Concentrate, now, on miming delight as she walks into the room. Ignore the disarray and note her face scrubbed clean and bright by wind and rain and her eyes glistening with shock and—yes—happiness to see him.

He reached for her hands and took both of them in his large, tanned paws, scanning surreptitiously to ensure no ring on her left hand blocked off the pathways of his planning.

"I had to come."

"But you shouldn't have," Eva Kimberly said without seeming to him to mean it.

She showered quickly and changed into light-colored slacks and a very pale brown silk blouse that brought out the glow in her russet hair and hinted at but did not overstate the voluptuousness of her contours. She reconstructed her face with only the lightest touch of makeup. She regarded these preparations as her Kevlar, her defense against the waves of guilt, confusion and half-forgotten excitement that welled in successive formations, as relentless as the ocean itself. Of course she should have told Jeremy to leave. But she had not. She had agreed to have lunch with him, and would break the news then. Of course she had not planned this encounter and so did not bear responsibility for its happening. Except that she had returned his call only hours earlier, lighting a beacon, sending a rescue flare that he had seen and responded to. Of course it was disgraceful that she should be primping and priming herself when her disadvantaged lover was lost and alone on the high mountains. But there would be no harm because this dalliance would go no further than a light lunch and a coffee and, simply, a little boost to her self-esteem. When you had loved someone as she had once loved Jeremy Davenport—a first love, an innocent love that built without threat toward unskilled consummation—then of course you could not simply erase that section of your life. It was part of you. The past had meaning, but did not imply resurrection. If the new arrival in the lounge had been an old girlfriend from the tennis courts and cocktail receptions of the Muthaiga Club, she would simply have rejoiced in this renewal of intimacy. Why, then, feel guilty simply because the old friend was male—a male predator whose diamond eyes offered, with one bold, hunter's sally, to wipe out the sadnesses that had befallen her, to take her back where she did not expect to be taken?

✍

Multiply by ten and you are at 28,000 feet. Call it First Step, Second Step instead of Bad Step and you are on that other, higher ridge. Offset the weak limbs against the effects of altitude and you have a comparable climb rate. He set his poles awkwardly because the left arm was too weak to function perfectly. The rucksack weighed him down like old oxygen cylinders. Mallory and Irvine, in one way or another, created their own end, took the decisions that would lead to it whether they wanted it that way or not. But he wanted it his way. He wanted their single-mindedness and their drive and their focus on the overriding goal. He wanted their purity, their nobility. He wanted it to deny death, not hasten it. Joe Shelby was thirsty and his lips were dry. He was surprised to feel snow melting on them. Looking up from the worn path ahead of him that wound over the rocky knuckles of Crinkle Crags, he saw that the weather had closed further on him, isolating him in a world of his own strained breathing and thumping heartbeat, wrapping him in a cold, gray cocoon of cloud and ice. He had no photograph in his pocket, no bundle of letters or pack of Swan Vesta matches as George Mallory had done. And if he had been carrying a photograph, whose visage would it show: Eva, faithful Eva, or another more splintered image?

⮎

"You've changed somehow. Not in a bad way."

"Maybe. I don't take things for granted anymore."

"Things?" She had not lost that ironic twist of an eyebrow.

"People. You."

Lunch was salads, mineral water, best behavior, taken in an almost empty dining room with only a solitary male traveler reading a book over a plate of trout and almonds, pausing occasionally mid-page to eavesdrop while pretending to be engrossed.

"Maybe he's a secret agent," she whispered.

"Or a lawyer."

"Yours or mine?"

The same maid who had brought coffee now served at their table, a moonfaced girl from the hill country who blushed slightly when Jeremy Davenport smiled acknowledgment of her work before she returned to the kitchen, bearing soiled dishes and smutty news. It's not her husband, said the cook—an interloper with a southern accent and no way with the girls. And it's not her big brother, said the maid, not unless he's a very naughty brother, the way he looks at her. The way he looks at her, the cook said, would burn your knickers off. The maid blushed deeper, scarlet, thinking it would take more than a look to burn off the school-issue doubloons that her mother made her wear for work. Not like the lady's. Turning back the bed in Eva Kimberly's suite, the maid had seen all kinds of finery spilling from her leather grip—flimsy stuff with little frills, tiny straps, translucent fabrics and silky delicacies. And the perfumes in the bathroom—fancy, French stuff that you only saw in the glossy magazines. And the whisky bottle, empty, discarded in the waste bin—casual debris, as if she did not care who knew of her weaknesses among the lower orders fated to attend her, wipe clean the slate of her excesses. A fast lady indeed, for all her London looks and smart clothes and posh tones. For all she pretended she was better than the rest of them. No way. She was no better than the local girls at the dance hall, out for a fumble with the farmhands and tour guides in the out-of-season chill. Her husband booked the room, the cook said. The governor told me. Said he'd be arriving in a day or two from the fells. So she's just filling in time. Filling in something, said the maid, reddening again at her own vulgarity. Can't blame her, though. He's a fit enough bloke. And she's not so bad herself, said the cook. Though he's more my type.

"Wonder what they're laughing at," Jeremy Davenport said as the sound of half-suppressed giggling wafted through the door that led behind a silk screen into the sanctum of the kitchen.

"Us, probably."

"Us?"

"You and me. Two people having lunch. They probably think we're having an affair."

"Well . . ." Jeremy Davenport did not finish what he had been going to say. What he had been going to say belonged to the past, the old devil-may-care Jeremy who thought through his gonads and harvested life's opportunities with very little thought for their consequences. Once, he would have said: Well, let's really give them something to talk about. But now he sensed he was on tracker's ground, needing the wind to shift before moving in. Trackers were smart. Trackers concealed themselves. Trackers were patient if they wanted to achieve what they desired. In the old days in Africa, he had heard of military scouts who held station immobile for hours and days at observation points in tree branches or on rocky knolls, spying out their enemy's ground in silence and stillness before calling in the cavalry, the air strikes for the kill.

"How's Joe? I heard he wasn't well." He had not used the name before, and it sounded strange and false on his lips, but he told himself this was part of the new tradecraft, the scouting, the feigned sympathy, the quest for the point of least defense.

In the nasty weeks and months after the betrayal, Jeremy Davenport had refused to use Joe Shelby's name, calling him that hack or Captain so-called Wilderness or the northern loverboy. But, months later, when the gossip mill in Kenya began to turn with word of an ailment, a malady, possibly terminal, it had been Eva Kimberly's father who called him to suggest that, perhaps, his daughter might need some support, a shoulder to cry on, because her partner might, well, not be long for this world if the quacks had got it right. And, at that point, Jeremy Davenport remembered the virtues of patience and stealth in the stalking of the most skittish and precious of prey.

"No. He's not well." She was surprised he asked and surprised even more that he waited to listen. "He's had a bit of a shock. A diagnosis. He's not the kind of person who's used to losing or being told he can't have what he wants or do what he wants. I'm sorry. I shouldn't have put it that way. But you do know what I mean, don't you."

"It's OK. I know what kind of guy he is. I've met him. I know the story. It's not as if I'm an outsider. I introduced you, and how much of a cliché is that? But I'm here for you if you want to talk about it. It doesn't hurt the same way anymore. More of a permanent dull ache, really. You always were a pain. Sometimes."

He smiled to say he bore no malice, that his words were brave camouflage on a broken heart. In the past betrayal had been a simple matter of physical deceit. Now it was much more thrilling—an entire game of charades, of playacting, made all that much simpler by her assumption that he was a person from her own tribe, someone with the familiarity

of small intimacies that have accumulated over the years: the first successful jump at the gymkhana, the first preteen dance and the countless
unscheduled encounters at parental lunches and beach vacations; the
first sense of moving in the same circles, on the same trajectory; the
long, hot afternoons on the verandah, sipping lemonade and murmuring secrets; the first, fevered touchings that led to the first true sexual
experience. Joe Shelby was a great, broad splash of bold, violent color
that had swamped her life. Jeremy Davenport was a pointillist creation
of a thousand small brush strokes. The welling in her eyes came easily.
The lonely reader two tables away lowered his book and stared at his
water carafe to listen the more closely. Jeremy Davenport took her hand
across the table and behind the silk screen the maid said: he's home and
dry. Anything but dry, said the cook.

"He's so angry, Jeremy. So different. He's furious with the illness and
that makes him furious with everything else. With me. It's as if it's not
just his body that's crippled, it's his soul. He doesn't realize it but he's let
the illness take over his whole being, our whole relationship so that
there's no room for me anymore. It's his obsession. He's always been
able to make things work for him. He's always been a winner. People
have always looked up to him. He was always a leader. In charge. You
could see that when you went anywhere with him: where do we go
today? What's the story? Everyone asked him. He knew. And if things
didn't work out his way, he'd just move on. But this is something that he
can't escape by waving a credit card or jumping on an airplane or writing
for his beloved comic. Jeremy, it's so difficult. He can't understand why
it's him. He can't work out why somebody like him—a doer, an
achiever—suddenly gets relegated to the also-rans. That's not really
funny. It's not the also-rans, it's the never-runs. He can't run. He can
barely walk. He can't understand why he's been rewarded like this for
everything he has tried to do: tell the truth about places, make the world
notice. And it's his ego. Captain Wilderness. Laugh in the face of dan-

ger. It's all been made a nonsense. And I don't know what to do, Jeremy.

"I can handle sick Masai kids and AIDS in Muthare Valley and gangsters raiding my clinics. But I can't handle this. It's not what I signed up for—don't be hurt. Please, just listen. I can tell you the truth. I know. You of all people. You know I've always coped pretty well, ran my business, ran the charities, looked after Pop and the farm. But I don't know what to do now. He won't let me in and he won't send me away. I'm in limbo. Of course, I ran off with him. It wasn't nice. It wasn't done in a way I'm proud of. But he's not the person I ran off with and I can't just pretend he is. I think at the back of his mind he thinks that if he just fights it like he's always fought to be first, to be on top, to be so bloody clever and different that he'll beat it. You saw the TV, Jeremy. You saw that woman. It was the last bloody straw because he's locking me out and inviting her in. And now there's this stupid message from London that might change things and I can't tell him."

She took the overnight fax from a pocket and showed it to Jeremy Davenport. It was crumpled now and had been written in a physician's scrawl. Tears fell on it, making it all the less legible.

He deciphered: "Hold the Mayo. Call me, Nigel."

"What does it mean?"

"It means that he might be treatable. But I can't get up there to tell him and he's in such a stupid frame of mind that God knows what he'll try."

"But at least it means you are off the hook."

Jeremy Davenport squeezed her hand and offered a napkin for her to wipe away the smudges under her eyes. He had not imagined she would be so trusting of him, so free in her assumption that the secrets could be shared with him. As she described the man who had ruined his life, he found he was thinking of one of his best-subscribed walking safaris among the mountain gorillas. High in the Virunga mountains, there was one beast—a great, 350 pound silverback the guides called

Ndume—who had lost one of his mighty paws in a poacher's snare. And as soon as other patriarchs became aware of his disability, they had no qualms at all in taking away the females who had once been his wives.

In the kitchen, cook was offering four-to-five on sin before supper but the rest of the staff thought the odds too much in his favor.

GREAT END
from Allen Crags

Chapter Fourteen

Lunch had been too intense by far. Eva Kimberly wanted a break from it, a lightening of the mood. She suggested they drive into the town of Keswick below Skiddaw mountain to get her car fixed, if a mechanic was to be found with the spare parts for the job. He concurred, sensing the wind shifting, moving slyly to keep the whiff of his true motives from her. She drove. He commented on her skills on this wet, rainswept road compared to the open bushlands where she had learned to wrestle an old Land Cruiser through ruts and drifts and mopane scrub, where the wait-a-bit thorn lay in permanent ambush. She smiled, recalling those days, restraining herself from falling into his poacher's trap: do you remember when? Do you remember that day, when the Land Cruiser stalled and you came by on your big, red motorcycle to fix the winch cable to an acacia tree and pull the truck out and put your arms around me while the giraffe looked on? No, she resolved. No memory lane leading into a booby-trapped time warp.

The mechanic thought he could bodge it in a couple of hours, at least good enough for the indicator light to flash orange and the brake light to flash red. They meandered and dawdled. They looked at storefronts full of boots and fleeces rather than look one another in the eye. Along the damp streets, the local mountain rescue team was out on a fund-raiser, men and women clad in hooded, red parkas, boots and gaiters, moving in pairs, rattling collection boxes. To show they were no ordinary walkers, they carried rucksacks festooned with climbing rope, crampons, ice axes. A flier across the main street proclaimed: Keswick Mountain Rescue.

Eva took a twenty-pound note from her wallet and folded it into the lid of one of the boxes.

"Very generous, madam. Thank you."

"Superstition, actually." She smiled at the man in his red parka, a wiry rescuer who walked with the easy confidence of long days on the crags and mountains, and spoke with the authority of a leader used to calling the decisions.

"How does it work?" Jeremy Davenport wanted to know. "I mean how do you know when someone needs your help?"

"Funny, really. But a lot of it these days is with cell phones, specially in places like Skiddaw where you've still got a signal from the valley."

"And on Scafell Pike?" Eva Kimberly registered the rescuer's surprise at her unlikely knowledge.

"Not too worried about that today."

"How come?"

"Because no one in their right mind would be up there for us to rescue. Most of the walkers took one look at the weather this morning and headed for the pub. Especially after the gale warning."

"Gale?"

"Out in the Irish Sea. Gale warning. With the possibility of blizzards inland." The rescuer caught her alarm. "Do you know someone up there?"

Eva Kimberly glanced only briefly at Jeremy Davenport.

"Yes."

"Do you know the route?"

"He's supposed to camp at Esk something tonight and Scafell Pike tomorrow."

"Jesus. Does he know what he's doing?"

"He knows. It's more a question of actually doing it."

Jeremy Davenport broke in. "What are the rescue arrangements, the actual rescue, normally? Not in this case. Just generally."

"Well, normally we'd use the chopper. And we've got prepositioned stretchers. One at Styhead, just down from Esk Hause. But obviously in this weather the chopper's out. No visibility for it to maneuver, and those valley walls are pretty steep. So we'd go out by foot in a fairly large group to quarter the area we've been sent to. How's his equipment?"

"Good, I suppose. State of the art. Tent. Sleeping bag. Food. Stove. All that sort of thing."

"That's one consolation. I'm wondering if we shouldn't scramble now. Meet him at Esk Hause before he tries for Scafell Pike. Has he got ice gear? Crampons? Ice ax?"

"No. Just walking sticks. Why?"

"Just that this weather is a freak. The barometer's gone barmy. And the thermometer. We wouldn't normally see this weather until December, January. If the weather forecast is right, those lovely autumn mountains will change into mini-Alps overnight. It'll be bitterly cold and very treacherous. Ice on all the rocks. Snow drifts. Cornices on the ridges so you'll have to be careful not to get too close to the edge. And on Scafell there's a lot of smooth boulders underfoot that'll be very easy to slip on. I don't mean to alarm you. I'm sure he'll take the right decision. Even for us, it'd be dangerous and we'd think twice about mounting a search unless you absolutely insisted. At this hour. By the time we rounded everyone up and got going it'd be getting dark and we'd have to reckon with a bivvie somewhere. Has he got a whistle?"

"Whistle?"

"Handiest thing there is if you want to signal for help in bad weather."

"No. No whistle. I don't think."

"Torch?"

"Yes. A flashlight. On a headband."

"Can I just say something?" Jeremy Davenport looked at both of them. "If you ask for a search and they find him tonight and he's fine and tucked up in his sleeping bag, waiting it out, he'll never forgive you for doubting him, Evie. And if the weather hasn't let up by tomorrow, then perhaps we could call the mountain rescue team then, if that's all right with you, of course."

"That's fine with us," said the rescuer. He handed them a slip of paper with the contact numbers. "It's your choice. You know him best. But it's his life. Don't forget that. These mountains may be small but they're serious mountains. Call us. Anytime. Ask for me. You might need us. And thanks for the donation."

"It's beginning to look more like an investment." Eva Kimberly smiled and the rescuer seemed to take in her message. His eyes said: I don't understand everything that's going on, but count on us anyhow.

Jeremy Davenport put his arm around her shoulders and they walked on. She shivered.

"We never told him about Joe's illness," she said.

"No. We never did. And we didn't ask for a search, either. Look. I don't know him that well, Evie, and, God knows, I have no reason at all to look out for his interests. But I know something about the male of the species. The male needs dignity. If you pulled him off his beloved mountain, he'd have his illness to cope with without dignity and that would be unbearable."

"I suppose you're right."

So it's best to leave him up there, beyond help, with the weather worsening.

Esk Pike. Just below it, rather. Tea. Sugar. Tobacco. Matches. Solid fuel. Water from the last spring back above Red Tarn. Not easy one-handed. Not easy, period. Because dealing with this is Jekyll and Hyde. You pretend you're hacking it: look, I brew tea: see Joe brew tea. You want people to think of you as courageous in adversity, the plucky soldier, putting on a brave face, laughing in the face of despair. Nobility on a Zimmer frame. Guts and grit with a limp and a laugh. Like a comedian on a seaside pier. Show must go on. You project this image. You lie. You say you're OK. You even convince yourself sometimes. But, inside, when you're alone with it, you know you are not OK. You get angry. You hate joggers and athletes and personal trainers and deadbeats who wreck their own lives but still command their own limbs. You hate the way they take their strength, their coordination for granted. You hate the symmetry of their walk. Left right left right. So easy until it's taken away from you, bent and warped like Quasimodo. I did that, you think. It was me. Me out there jogging along, daring anyone to disrupt the perfect pace you've set for yourself, covering the ground as if you were a human metronome. Left right left right, lungs in tune, breathing steady, ground cushioned by the latest in fancy running shoes, the sunlight tanning your legs and a good sweat pushing out all the toxins. That was me and now this is me: foot dragging, lungs screaming, the sweat stinking of rage and fear. In the airport, they push you aside as they stride on with their little wheeled suitcases and their cell phones: yes, I'm at Heathrow and tell so-and-so I'll make the 10:30. Once you rose above it. You were perfect. No one overtook you. At work or play. You sniffed at hospitals, you scorned medical care, you floated, cocooned in your self-confidence, tolerant, amused by the rest of them, vaguely sympathetic to the unfortunates who did not share your immunity to terminal threat. But now you hate. You hate the ones who can explain their illness, who've been given a cause, who can categorize their downfall by reference to a logical sequence of events.

You rage at those bastards who go around infecting each other at their sero-positive parties: you want to say—how dare you make your self-pitying demands for cocktails of drugs and treatments and AZT when you've made yourself sick, for God's sake, when you know precisely down to the last lesion and drop of rotten semen how you infected yourself. And all the while the rest of us with MND and MS and all the rest of the mysteries are crying out in the darkness and saying: why? Why did this happen? Explain it, doctor, please. And you know all about self-pity. You don't just say why, you say: why me? Why not that prick in his gelled hair and punk clothes who has never striven for excellence, never fought for the summit, cruised through life thinking the world owes him a living? Strike him down, Lord, not me. Oh, yes. You have your dark nights of the soul, your inconsolable reach for despair and you remember that even He said: Lord, why hast thou forsaken me?

Joe Shelby switched off the tape recorder and eased it carefully into a pocket of his rucksack from which he withdrew his GPS navigation device only to find the screen blank and refusing to register the coordinates of his position. He rose awkwardly, knocking his lightweight stove into a deep cleft between the rocks from which there was no retrieval.

Chapter Fifteen

THIRLMERE, ENGLAND. SEPTEMBER 2000

Eva Kimberly told herself that teetering on a brink did not imply tum-
bling over it. She scolded herself for successive days of mild dalliance,
then reminded herself sharply that there had been no physical betrayal
of any kind and that she had instigated none of these episodes. And
even if she had, would that have been so unusual for a woman of sufficient years to know her mind, and of sufficient youth to do as she
wished? Bathing and dressing in clothes she had planned to wear for
another reunion, she told herself she was nervous not simply because
she had crossed into unfamiliar terrain by entertaining a jilted lover, but
because the tryst was set in a hotel booked by another man, where all the
waiters and maids seemed to know she was receiving a stranger and disapproved mightily. But what harm really was there in all that? Dinner
was not infidelity. The eyes of the kitchen staff did not constitute a
global television audience on CNN. People should not throw first
stones, leap to conclusions. The wind and the snow flurries at her window reminded her of the other man wherever he was now, who might

for all she knew stumble across the stormy threshold, midway through dinner, encrusted with ice—or be marooned somewhere, doomed by her decision to leave the Mountain Rescue call for another day. She reminded herself of the preparations he had undertaken—the no-expense-spared quest for the most perfect sleeping bag, the lightest, most impermeable tent, the stove and the supplies of high-protein diet. Assuming only that he still had the physical power to use his equipment, there was no reason to suppose that gear designed for the Himalayas should not perform its function on these modest hills, whatever the weather. But the presumption of bodily strength nagged at her: even if Nigel Lampton was offering a different diagnosis, he was not guaranteeing different symptoms without some kind of treatment. The progression of the disease had gathered pace. Every worsening had been detected after rigorous physical exercise, and the project he had embarked upon was by far the most strenuous he had attempted since the onset of his condition. The assumption, therefore, had to be that he might not have the physical power, that he might not be ensconced in his Everest-grade sleeping bag and expedition tent. And what presumption followed from that? That he might perish, immobilized by hypothermia as the storm gathered while she cavorted at his advanced base with another man intent on a different project altogether.

She closed the heavy drapes, denying the dark, contorted pines where she would have preferred to see still palms above a white coral beach. She imagined the lake beyond her vision whipped into angry, churning whitecaps where there should have been the evening swell of turquoise water caressing pale sand. She poured a very small bracer from a half-bottle of vodka—purchased after telling Jeremy Davenport she needed to refresh her supply of cigarettes—to blank out the thoughts of the weather worsening with every foot of altitude until, up there, it must surely be a maelstrom. But how could she be made guilty by the weather? How could sleet and gales be her accusers? Of course guilt does not need a physical act in order to make its introductions. The mere fact that she had allowed herself to think of tonight's dinner as a prelude was already a kind of betrayal. And treachery took many different guises. She recalled an older friend, a settler's wife, who discovered that for fifteen years her husband had entertained a clandestine relationship with an old college flame, seeking her out for intellectual companionship and mental stimulation, companionship but never sex. "I'd rather he had just screwed her and be done with it. I could have at least understood that," her friend said. What hurt was not just that the relationship had been deliberately hidden from her, making her into a dupe—that much was true of all adultery. Far more, the woman said, it was that despite their shared, well-tended home, their tanned and boisterous children, their vacations in Mauritius, their dogs and cats and choices of wallpaper, their intimate, bedtime togetherness, she had been found wanting in the most fundamental way as the true soul mate she had considered herself to be. She had been judged and found lacking without even knowing she was on trial, still less on what charges. What hurt, her friend said, was discovering that her husband maintained a complete, separate life from which she had been excluded, a deep secret kept hidden by all the tawdry mechanics of deception—the coded phone calls and the separate room bookings in out-of-the-way hostelries, the flimsy excuses made credible only by her trust, which now seemed the most painful gullibility.

At least no one could accuse Eva Kimberly of such furtive conspiracy in the way she had treated Jeremy Davenport: she had abandoned him in the full glare of gossip and malice, magnified a million times over in the retelling throughout their incestuous, fishbowl, settler society where word of white mischief traveled faster than the bush telegraph, relayed through the way stations of hairdressing salons and afternoon tea parties, cocktail chatter and illicit pillow talk. Jeremy Davenport's shame was hidden from no one. There was no pretense on her part of a platonic relationship: this was raw lust, all the more shocking for the presumption of demure fidelity that people attached to her. He may as well have walked around Nairobi with one of those "end-of-the-world-is-nigh" billboards proclaiming: cuckold, fool. And yet he had come now to seek her out, while Joe Shelby had repaid her in kind, broadcasting his liaison with the Frenchwoman on global television. When she first saw the two of them together at Naivasha—Mata Hari and Captain Wilderness—she had cast the Frenchwoman as the loose cannon, the spoiler. But, in fact, it was Joe Shelby who had entered their settled, settler lives like a free radical, bouncing around an entire organism, spreading infection, wreaking havoc. And in return for what? He had not offered marriage, or even a ring, let alone children or permanency. Barely had they established a home together than he resumed his travels, chronicled in the publication which he called the comic—and which she no longer read—alongside photographs bearing the Frenchwoman's byline. There had been no gentle honeymoon, only the assumption that his work came first. And when his work ceased to come first, it was purely because his condition came first, forcing itself on both of them, an ugly, brutal gate-crasher refusing all entreaties to leave. In the end, all he had offered was a wild, crazy throw of the dice, a lurching switchback ride. She had loved him and betrayed for him and might now be on the point of completing the cycle of treachery—with complete justification considering his behavior. But how could she be even thinking this way? What had changed since he left for the mountains? Only the arrival of the other man, only the offer of a safety line, thrown to a foundering vessel. Yet how could you justify betraying a cripple, no matter how much he had wronged you?

She had said it now, if only to herself. Cripple. Disabled. Handicapped. She felt as if she had released a genie, and could no longer be sure where it might lead.

On the writing desk in the sitting room of the suite he had booked for them as advanced base, she caught sight of the telephone number given to her by the leader of the Keswick Mountain Rescue, and resolved to program it into her mobile. In case. Even betrayal did not have to imply abandoning a weakened man to a cruel fate on a mountain. And, helping a man in trouble might just assuage the guilt of treachery, especially if the man turned out to be less afflicted than initially assumed. Had not the message from his specialist—hold the Mayo!—suggested that the curse was not as dire as first thought, that she would not be abandoning a dying man in his very moment of need? If, after all, Joe Shelby could be helped, then, surely, he could help himself.

She thought the bracer a pathetic idea, a token of all the modern definitions of loser—sad, naff—but she topped it up to a decent level and drank anyway, wishing she had not as soon as the unchilled spirit burned in the back of her throat.

He showered and wrapped a towel around his waist. He pulled back the drapes, opening a sash window to allow the fierce cold to rush into the stuffiness of his centrally heated room, scouring trails of goosebump flesh across his tanned chest and upper arms. He lit a cigarette from a gold lighter, cupping the flame against the buffeting wind that howled from a wilderness he did not understand. In his own lands, in the far-flung emptinesses of scrub and savanna, he could read the signs as clearly as if they had been spelled out in giant letters: a poacher passed this way, an elephant too; a hyena killed; a kite swooped and snatched its prey. But these lakes and mountains were a volume in a foreign language written in some indecipherable script. He was playing away, on alien ground.

He was not used to thinking in terms of fairness and justice. He had been raised to believe that the only true denominator was power—the power of the chief, the big man, proven through guile and ruthlessness, to dominate the lesser beings, the drones; the inherited power of people from his tribe, expressed in estates and mansions and stables and safaris, extending over all those who craved work and shelter for their families; the power of the young predators, forever testing the resolve of the patriarchs until the balance shifted and the mantle of supremacy slipped over them, leaving the old guard to fade or be hounded away.

Yet, contemplating the brute weather, he asked himself: was it fair, this uneven battle to reclaim what had been lost, when his adversary was so disadvantaged and distant, locked away in his own fantasies and illness, placed in physical peril by his dreams? Was there justice or chivalry, fighting in a theater of cozy rooms and mock log fires and decanted, heady wine while his enemy shivered and struggled somewhere out there, chilled and tossed by the storm, unaware of the challenger's gauntlet? The questions lingered only briefly before he dismissed them. Had it been fair or just to return from the bush with the crazy Frenchwoman to find his Eva stolen? Had it been fair of his enemy to make off with his bride-to-be without so much as a chance to offer his case, press his suit? His memory had already filtered out his dishonorable intentions towards the Frenchwoman, relegated the entire episode to the recycle bin of moments that bore no imprint of guilt. However numerous or furtive, they were undertaken lightly, physical moments responding to simple signals, like sneezing or eating a burger. If one-night dalliance was betrayal, then so was self-stimulation, for they answered the same need, one with more satisfaction and triumph than the other.

If he needed further justification, was it not embedded in the instincts of the male of any species to broadcast his seed, to stalk and hunt and use all available weapons to win the rights of coverage of the female? And it was impossible to avoid the hatred. He had hated her for the betrayal, for the intense hurt of rejection, for the sleepless nights stalked by the image of her impaled on him, for the implication of his inferiority, his inadequacy as a male.

The hate had corroded him. A walking tour in the Mara had to be canceled because he was too drunk to leave his tent. But one morning, he awoke, rough and disheveled, to discover that the hate had burned off, the way the sun cauterized the morning mist on the high, Kenyan uplands, over the far-flung cattle ranches and emerald tea estates, revealing a bright crystalline sky, showing him that, beyond the hurt lay an equally bright and obvious solution—revenge.

The idea did not at first come easily. From his teenage years onwards, his life had been built and guided on the premise that she would be at his side, that, in the fullness of time, they would raise a new generation on the ancestral lands, as the survival of their tribe dictated. Every time he attended a settler wedding at Naivasha, he imagined the moment coming when the pews made of straw bales, the ceremonial boat ride across the lake, the champagne and marquees and spit-roasts and women in crinoline would all be feting them. Visiting the grand Kimberly farmhouse with its long, shaded verandahs and lawns of kikuyu grass encircling stands of bamboo fronds and bougainvillea, he imagined the natural course of progression when her father would move into a well-appointed thatched cottage in the grounds, an old monarch in exile, ceding the master suite to them—the same succession as had always been used to pass the generational baton. They shared the secret codes of their people, the unspoken passwords. You could see it in their breeding: a way of dealing with the staff, of positioning yourself in a land where a cruel history had delivered disproportionate privilege that you learned to handle with grace and a certain style. You could see it in acquired and inherited skills: the ability to play decent tennis, ride a horse with grace, fire a rifle with a degree of accuracy, host a dinner party, show no fear in the face of great adversity. For their kind, some things need never be said out loud, some aspects of privilege need never be challenged. They hailed from an aristocracy that had survived its guillotines and tumbrils to prosper under a new order. They shared a common platform bequeathed by their forebears and on it they would play out their lives from a common script. To avenge himself on Eva would cement the rift within the clan, between two of its great families. But she had initiated the break, and on that bright African morning when he awoke to clarity, those considerations fell away completely. What had been a matter of emotional entanglement became, simply, a question of tactics.

❧

ESK HAUSE, ENGLAND. SEPTEMBER 2000

The tent fought back. Joe Shelby was not exactly sure where he was, but he had arrived wherever he had arrived and could go no further. The descent from his bouldery shelter below the summit of Esk Pike had taken far longer than it should have. He had stumbled, found it hard to balance. On the rougher parts of the trail, he needed to plan his progress, working out where his poles would best counterbalance his infirmity. He paused frequently for breath and to scan the compass, anxious not to stray off course. Without the GPS, the process took longer and the laminated map whipped so furiously in the wind that it tore asunder at precisely the fold where his destination was charted in hairline contour markings. By the time he called a halt, shucking off his rucksack as if shedding a millstone, teetering, as if drunk, on weak legs, the light had gone but the wind and sleet had not. He used a torch on a headband to scan this unfamiliar terrain for a patch of ground that was approximately level, not yet saturated. He unpacked the tent and it immediately unfurled like a crazy banner, lashing and crackling in the horizontal wind, refusing to be pinned down on the ground until he wrestled it there. Kneeling, he shoved the skewer-like pegs into the ground to hold down the built-in ground sheet, but the wind came around unexpectedly and filled the body of the tent like an inflating hot-air balloon and tried to tear the pegs from the damp ground. He fought it, rolled on it, flattened it, wept on it, positioned it with the entrance facing downwind, as he had been taught many years back. Using only his right hand, he took the aluminum poles and inserted them in their moorings, then used more pegs to hold down the guylines, but, in this pugilistic weather, they would not be enough. He rose with difficulty, leaning heavily on a walking pole. With his headlamp showing the way he scouted for rocks to weight the lines against the most fierce winds and almost lost the way back to the tent. The headlamp beam picked out the oncoming white rush of snow, the glisten of its wetness against the darkness, a narrow tunnel of light that scanned frantically back and forth over the uneven, tufted fellside until it picked out the alien, blue and yellow beacon: home for this night and no more. He held each rock with an almost-strong right hand and a hanging, swinging left hand that could only just curl fingers around the damp, mossy boulders he found. Twice he returned to find the tent loose and flapping and on the point of takeoff, and cursed, pushing the pegs back into the ground and tightening the lines and lashing them to rocks while the wind and cold crept through all the wrappings of clothing, locating clammy skin. He had water in one bottle from a thin spring. In another, he had whisky, and craved it. He had tobacco and papers, but, at his last halt, where he had brewed tea, the stove had been lost. He had bars of mint-cake and chocolate, but no means of boiling water for hot drinks to nurture and warm him. He had his sleeping bag and tape recorder and self-inflating mattress. He had a night ahead of him where the only solace and shelter was provided by the thin nylon wall of the tent that held back the probing wind and retained whatever heat his body allowed to escape from his balaclava hat and thick, downy sleeping bag. He prayed that the cramps that were part of his condition would ease their grip on his residual calf muscles. He prayed that his shelter would survive the night and dawn would bring bright skies and what passed for a spring to his step.

Crawling into the tent, he made his dispositions, removing his gaiters and boots to form part of his pillow, rolling out the slender mattress that would provide insulation but no real comfort, unfurling the sleeping bag and struggling to insert himself into it without collapsing the tent. He thought of Eva and smiled. He thought of her at advanced base, probably, by now, partaking of a predinner drink, choosing a light meal. He thought of her bathing and naked. He thought of her warmth under a comforter. He pictured her alone and waiting and promised himself he would not do this sort of thing again. If he ever got down the hill to tell her so. He thought of her waistline and curves inviting his touch, before a banshee wail of wind across the tent chased the image away and replaced it with the vision of a skinnier frame full of demons demanding appeasement.

Chapter Sixteen

PARIS. SEPTEMBER 2000

Du Plessis had second-guessed her. She *had* flown first to Paris. She *had* scanned her stored wardrobe for something more fetching than a black tee shirt and black jeans and black, scuffed boots. From the old days, from her former life as a model, she could have taken one of several designer items given as gifts after the shows and never discarded. Joe Shelby had never seen her like this, in her haute couture mode, and she laughed out loud at the idea of tottering towards him on a rocky mountain in strappy, patent leather high heels and a thigh-length tube of flimsy black fabric: Dr. Gucci, I presume. It would not have been out of character. On occasions she had appeared to him in hotel rooms wearing only his bush jacket, or only his high, suede snake boots. She had offered cabaret with Kevlar vest and a clown's mask. She had amused him with Marilyn Monroe lips from the joke shop and a carnival wig in brassy blonde. She had offered him topless tennis on an overgrown court in the suburbs of Kampala. She had been his courtesan, his entertainer, enthralling him with disguises, weaving spells that sometimes

veered too close to the edge, bound him to her as she tracked her obsessions. In the shelling of Sarajevo, in the incessant howl of the incoming
Katyushas, she had danced for him, drawn sniper fire by pushing back
the drapes, then laughed with a witch's cackle. She had insisted on walking through Mogadishu chewing great wads of qat, forcing him to
accompany her, when others sought refuge in armed convoys of technicals—pickups mounted with heavy caliber machine guns. She had won a
photographer's prize for a series of images showing the dying moments
of a stick-bodied, monster-headed child in Uganda but only he knew
she had kissed the infant full on blistered, flyblown lips as the last of life
departed. Surveying her wardrobe, she decided to stick with what would
raise the fewest alarms, offer assurance that she was different now.

She shed the excess baggage that might slow her—the replacement
Kevlar vest, insisted on by the comic but never worn, the tripod and
lights for portrait work, barely used, the scanner and laptop they made
her carry for transmission of celluloid and digital images, the array of
lenses that accumulated on whims. She was pared down now to a single
overnight bag, a single, old Leica with one lens. She would take the earliest Eurostar to London, transit the city by subway, grab the early train
to the nearest point north, a place apparently called Lancaster, and grab
a rental for the last stretch. He would be proud of her because logistics
was a shared passion. She recalled one time, especially, lounging by the
pool at a hotel in Luxor, the story done, the pictures gone, another clash
of faiths—Copts and Muslims this time—packaged and history. The
alarm went up with a sat-phone call that summoned them on to the
next folly, somewhere far away and mysterious, across the Turkish-Azeri
border, uncharted territory for them both. The world, then, was small—
no bigger than the paperback airlines guide that was his constant companion, his Bible, offering commandments enforced by platinum credit
cards and the sheer will to arrive first. They scrambled, throwing pre-
laundry socks and shirts, paperbacks and toothbrushes, film and

notepads into carry-on bags. There was no time to shower, eat. They unhooked laptops, downloaded disks, ignored visa regulations. They stashed raw dollar bills and second passports with incriminating entry stamps from the enemy camp into money belts and hoped for the best. They left their hotel room festooned with wet bathing suits, half-drunk whisky, old notepads, empty film canisters that had once contained cannabis. They checked out faster than the clerks on the desk had ever seen anyone abandon their corner of papyrus and paradise and tombs and tourists. They hopped an EgyptAir schedule to Cairo then, with seconds to spare, headed out from that messy airport, first class on Turkish, to Istanbul, where the trail of likely connections went cold. So onward they hurried in a rental car for the fast Anatolian run, across the Bosphorus bridge and over the high ground at Bolu, swerving past over-loaded taxis, roaring trucks. At Ankara, they dumped the rental, swapped it for a wheezing, prop-driven charter that catapulted them onto Erzurum and a wild, battered ride in a cab with holes in the floor so that their feet froze, and water in the gas so that the engine juddered in the blizzards. Finally, a walk on foot across the old Turkish-Soviet, east-west, badland frontier into Nakchevan for whatever icebound madness was on that day's menu under the shadow of Mount Ararat where Noah's Ark was said to rest. Fast, they went. Down and dirty. Hit the ground running. Harvest—images and soundbites. The soldiers came to the village. As ever. But it was always the civilians who were left to wash and wrap the disfigured bodies, dig the graves in frozen soil, rebuild burned homes, nurse children initiated into barbarity by the sight, scorched onto their retinas, of a father murdered, a mother raped. They told their stories with empty, cried-out eyes, women in head-scarves and men suffused with the rage and shame and relief of having survived when others had not.

Then the turnaround. Another walk. Another cab, the price negoti-ated in zillions of worthless lira. In Erzurum a dingy, low-wattage hotel with a functioning telephone line and photographs of Mustafa Kemal Ataturk, the nation's founder, behind the reception desk and spooks in the lobby. Twenty-four hours out from Luxor's sunlight and palms and camels, and a story of ice and violence was already on its way to the comic. Using a Swiss Army knife, Joe Shelby hacked into the telephone junction box underneath the nightstand, hooking up with alligator clips to the wired world. Laptops hummed, phone lines zinged, compressing and bundling someone else's conflict into byte-sized wads of data for real-time transmission halfway round the planet. The adrenaline carried through to the celebration. Realizing they had not eaten for a day, they devoured tough kebabs and sour wine in a half-lit, heavy-draped dining room, with only the ogling plainclothes men in their clumsy suits and slicked hair for company across the acres of brown velveteen chairs and unlaid tables. Then, just the two of them, crazy with elation in a frayed bedroom with creaking beds and heavy wardrobes. And her revealing that, all the time, throughout that entire passage through international airports, across frontiers, past guards and cops and soldiers and militiamen and spooks, she had been carrying a sacred gram in the false heel of a scuffed black boot and he laughed wildly, offering a platinum card for the ritual chopping and lining. High fives. Whoops. Comic praise: two stories in the same issue, from locations two thousand miles apart, both hot, fresh, exclusive. Praise indeed and the laudatory messages they called herograms. Sex intermittent but intense 'til the gray dawn and the brittle letdown: the airport socked in and the eleven-hour trudge back with barely a word of conversation across the drear, quake-prone reaches of Anatolia in yet another rental with newspapers stuffed down behind the radiator to force the engine to produce warmth. Erzincan. Sivas. A snowy moonscape of sheepdogs with spiked collars to thwart the wolves, and breeze-block cities and truck-stops where men on low stools sipped tea from small, round glasses in the small, cold hours and hunched over backgammon boards in their thick coats and flat caps. And the question, this time by the indoor poolside over burgers at the Ankara Hilton: where next? For you were only as good as your next story and the hunger for it needed constant feeding and renewal.

Mark those days, she thought. Fix them, for they are your shared memory, your common ancestry, your conjugating myth. Where other couples might chart their memories in shared dinners or sunsets, vacations or concerts, their reference points were tragedies and horror stories, their passions magnified by the acts of witnessing and surviving. But it could not be thus again. Not after a farm in Africa finally taught her that death was a transition that offered no replays. Not after his illness showed him how little time he had to stitch a new being from finer cloth. No one could live forever the way they had done, courting burnout or worse. No one could remain on that treadmill of emotion and reward. No one could balance forever on that razor edge between jubilation and destruction. Perhaps that was what his body was telling him and signaling her to explain to him. She thought of a large, remote house with big, high-ceilinged rooms and roaring fires and surf pounding close by: Cornwall, California, Biarritz, Cape Town, wherever. Big rooms and studio lights, studies with books and laptops, solid, steady creation. Words and images as their tools, no longer their masters. No comic, no sat-phones, no last-second self-propulsion through time and space like rogue asteroids. She thought of helping him through wherever the disease led him, until death did them part—a death, finally, without violence. It was clear to her now that he had sought that tranquility, that peace, with his princess, only to find her incapable of delivering. After Rwanda, he had run from her because, deep down, he was crying out for peace, a kind of love that did not need corpses and adrenaline and gunfire to assert itself. And he had thought to find that in Naivasha and Mombasa and in Primrose Hill. But the princess had failed him, neither with him at the front line nor wholeheartedly at his side as he joined the casualties. He had not said it in so many words. But he had come to her, sought her out in Kosovo and Gaza, when the doctors had abandoned him to a destiny whose cruelty the princess could never understand. How could she share the pain of Joe Shelby's descent when she had not been with him on the high peaks, on the summits of passion and risk? How could she understand the depths of his need when she had barely had time to know him at the heights of his power? In his condition, without hope, and quite possibly facing the end, it was natural that Joe Shelby should seek out the one person who had answered his needs in the crazy days and, more than any other, understood death with such clarity and intimacy.

As she packed, she slid the silver gram into the heel of her black, battered boots. On an impulse, surveying her wardrobe, she chose a flimsy, high-ticket, cocktail-hour item that weighed nothing and cost a ransom. And she still had the Marilyn Monroe lips.

Like Du Plessis said: when you've got nothing.

THIRLMERE. SEPTEMBER 2000

Jeremy Davenport led the way to the threshold of the dining room and in to dinner. The hotel seemed to have filled since lunchtime as the fell warriors found their way back in their Swedish and German chariots to their temporary stockade, shedding boots and parkas, swapping rugged outdoor gear for crisp checked country shirts with ties and almost formal, pastel dresses in pink and sky-blue with pearls—a companionable bunch, of a similar, prosperous late middle age, with similar interests in walks and meteorology, scrubbed and ruddy, or prim and powdered after a bracing day. Each table bore its sentry of opened wine commanding an expanse of pink tablecloth and shining cutlery, standing guard between couples whose years together left plenty of room for blank pauses, knowing looks, half-formed sentences started by one, finished by the other.

They traded rueful stories of defeat by weather: couldn't get above the valley today, not in this; visited the Beatrix Potter house, the Pencil Factory, Wordsworth's cottage. Wind was like a knife. And the forecast's no better. What else can you do on a day like this? You'd have to be a lunatic to go up on the High Fells, she heard one of them say. Or a blooming masochist, another said, suddenly hearty in the common admission of failure and frustration. You'd have to have a death wish.

He insinuated himself between the tables with her in pliant tow, heading for a setting for two, placed slightly apart from the rest. Even if he hadn't been wearing an obviously costly sports coat, oozing Savile Row, above his tailored, tight corduroys, he would have exuded authority. The tan and the lithe, stalking movements, the way he held the chair back for his glamorous partner in her fawn silk blouse and understated gold jewelry, the arch to his eyebrows as he cast a falcon's eye over his fellow diners, but smiled anyhow—noblesse oblige—all those elements combined to bring a short, deferential silence that gave way to whispers: aren't they famous? Are they on TV? One of those breakfast talk shows? Celebrities, in any event. On furlough. Or something. Would the headlines say: Talk-show stars in secret love nest?

"Who chose this place? Isn't it somewhat . . . you know . . . geriatric?"

"He chose it because he thought his parents might have liked it, because he wanted to see their kind of people, his kind. He said he thought it would be easy and convenient for me. He wasn't booking it for you." Her voice had risen sharply and he stretched his hand across the table to hers.

"Sorry. Sorry." He had started his campaign badly and regretted it. Tread carefully.

"No. But you're right of course, Jeremy. It's not exactly St. Tropez. How's Nairobi?"

"Nairobi's Nairobi, I'm afraid. Carjackings and gun battles on the Ngong Road. But still fantastic for all that."

"That's not quite what I meant."

"I know. OK. Well, everyone's still very impressed with your *Forbes* cover. And your Pop is still full of plans for this year's Naivasha and a new line of mange-tout he's made some deal with with Sainsbury's or Safeway. And . . ."

"Did he see it? On CNN?"

The waitress intruded. A drinks order, perhaps? Before the meal? He plunged in with a fancy Sancerre, requesting her approval with an arched eyebrow. They ordered starters and mains. She drew another raised eyebrow from him with a request for a vodka and tonic. Double. Plenty of ice. Slice of lemon. He countered with Talisker. Straight. No ice under any circumstances.

"Big spender," she said. "I remember when you thought two chilled Tuskers and a stick of biltong was enough to turn a girl's head."

"Not yours."

"No. I think you saw me more in the candlelight-at-Main-Camp category."

"You were never in any category. You were a one-off. Are."

"And then I expect you'll say they threw away the mold. Your chat-up lines are atrocious."

"Who said I was chatting anybody up?"

"Touché. But you didn't answer the question."

"About?"

"About CNN. Oh. Never mind. It's history. Let's just try and have a nice time."

The drinks arrived with fanfare. The same waitress as served coffee in the afternoon brought vodka and single malt whisky in appropriate crystal. The proprietor in dark suit and regimental-looking striped tie delivered wine in a silver ice bucket, displaying the label before opening it, presenting the cork for approval, insisting on a tasting.

"You know what Pop's like, Eva. Of course he saw it. But he

wouldn't mention it. Least of all to me. He wouldn't want to have it on the agenda. For your sake. And as for the rest of them, it's just small-time gossip, hair-salon stuff."

"That's sweet of you. But I know what you're saying. And you. What about you? How's business?"

"Booming, but that's not why I came here." He paused and she looked at him inquiringly, not sure whether he had finished speaking, wrong-footed by the uncharacteristic lapse into silence. He was thinking: do I dare? There is still time to back off, run for cover, leave her without the scars that I bear. But if you want the Big Victory, then you must deploy the Big Lie. The plan does not work without it.

"I came here because I wanted to ask you to come back with me to Nairobi. For good. For ever and ever. Tonight, if you like. Or tomorrow. But just come back."

She almost choked on her vodka.

They ate slowly, soup and something called organic salmon, guaranteed free of chemicals.

They toyed with the idea of sticky toffee pudding as dessert, and decided on one order, two spoons. Intimate food. Love food. But not yet because there was too much to be said if it was ever to be said. Sometimes, thoughts build as rehearsals for speech, the lines honed and repeated, readied for utterance at some unspecified moment that would reveal itself, as now. And in her rehearsing lay a resolve to be honest, to spare no feelings, to cleave to the notion that only truth will bring healing—although that is rarely the case. She would be just as honest with both of them.

"I felt bad, Jeremy." He thought: not as bad as I did, but kept his silence. "I treated you terribly. I deserved what I got."

"No. That's not true. No one deserved that TV fiasco. And don't think I haven't realized that I got my comeuppance too." But she did not want his confession: she knew most of it, anyhow—for all its vast reaches, Africa was a village, where his transgressions were tallied in a currency devalued by an oversupply of misdeeds among the settlers and expatriates. She wanted just to talk to someone who knew her, a familiar shoulder. She had gone over her lines many times in the quiet evenings of Joe Shelby's absences and decline, but, until now, there had been no stage, no audience.

"Would it be offensive to you if I told you? I mean. I don't want to open closed chapters for you. Really I don't. We can talk about lots of other things." She almost added: before you leave. But did not.

"As far as I'm concerned, the plot's still unfolding. Your story. Tell me your story. Mine you know. And what about his story?"

"That's the hard part. I shouldn't be talking like this. But it's so difficult. I mean it's one thing to try and work out your things with a healthy person. That's bad enough."

"But there shouldn't be guilt. You didn't bring on this illness."

"I know, but if it weren't for his illness, we wouldn't be sitting here."

"The question is, as far as I can see, Evie, is whether, if it weren't for his illness, you'd have put up with all this for so long," he said.

"Forget the illness, Evie. Just for a moment. Put it to one side. Say: this is something I am not responsible for. Just ask yourself: is this what I signed up for? Is this what was promised? And the answer has to be: no. Every relationship has some kind of contract to it, whether it's spoken out loud or not. And if the contract is breached, then the other party isn't bound to it. God. I sound like a lawyer. Hiding behind words. But you know what I'm trying to say. Whatever happened has happened. Finished. Period. Draw a line in the sand. Whatever. But on the other side of that line, you don't have to go on suffering. You don't have to live with broken promises. You have a life of your own. You have a right to be happy."

"We shouldn't be talking like this, Jeremy. Least of all when he's up that stupid, bloody mountain in this stupid bloody weather. You heard what the mountain rescue people said. And the others in here. It's craziness. And probably least of all should I be talking to you."

"No. Most of all to me."

His hand had taken hers across the table. Most of the other diners had finished their meals and repaired to one of the warm, firelit lounges for coffee. The few who lingered, and the waitress, watched them furtively, drawn as if the two of them were bathed in a spotlight, immune to their audience, bound together through their fingertips in a closed world.

"I know it's not what I signed up for. I know I'm not Florence Nightingale. I know I can manage my AIDS orphans like a nice liberal white woman in Africa is supposed to do. I can manage the TB and the malaria and the sleeping sickness. I can handle all the poverty and sickness and everything else. But I can't manage it in my own home. My own bed."

The words were coming fast, unleashed from the rehearsals where she had tried to cast herself in a more noble light. The waitress thought there'd be tears before bedtime, and she thought she could guess which bed that might be in.

"I know I shouldn't have done it. It was wrong to you. It was probably wrong for me. But I made my choice. Maybe I was confused. Certainly I'm confused now. I ran off with someone who offered me a different world. I wasn't satisfied with all the wonderful things I had. I couldn't see that love isn't always about champagne and roses and what did he call it—nights of magic." The wine bottle was empty. But Eva Kimberly did not seem inebriated. Her words were clear and forceful. Her eyes glistened. He was not sure whether she was looking at him when she spoke, or beyond him, at some point where the jigsaw finally fell into place.

"And, by God, it turned out a lot more different than I expected. I thought I wanted his mad adventures, and look where that got me. I thought I'd enjoy the life in the fast lane and now he's looking death in the face in a very slow lane indeed and I don't know where to look at all. He said he loved me. He still says he loves me. But what he really loves is an image, a mirage, an antidote to the Frenchwoman. He takes in the way I speak, the way I look, the way I have a home and roots. He sees me all neat and logical and presentable. But he's seeing something he wants to create for himself. He sees something that you would aspire to if you hadn't had it—a person who knows where they come from while he's completely confused about whether he's a cripple or a hero. He doesn't know, deep down, if he belongs here or nowhere. He wants me to be his anchor and he thinks that because I know where I come from, he can cling to that. He's like someone who's cast off so often they don't have a home port anymore. Sometimes I think I was tricked, then I think I fooled myself into thinking he was what he seemed to be. I was in love. Am. Don't look away, Jeremy. You wanted to hear it all and I'm telling you. It's not nice, is it? It's not the old Eva, always knowing the right thing to do at the right time, how to arrange Pop's Naivasha parties and how to run Home Farm and how to manage the clinics in the Rift Valley. Everything the memsahib is supposed to do. And now I'm all adrift. Like him. He's got us both confused. I don't know what to do. I'm in a situation I can't control. No one showed me the script. I don't know my lines. Look at me, Jeremy. Look at the bags under my eyes. Look at the wine bottle and ask who drank it. I'm not your old Eva. Old faithful. I made a choice and it went wrong and I have to stick with it now because he needs me. Forget the crazy Frenchwoman. He's doing this ridiculous expedition to prove something to himself and to me. Not to her. Whatever there was with her was in Israel. This is England. His home base, if there is such a thing. His damp, cold, icy roots. Before he left he was very sweet. He wasn't the person you saw at Naivasha, all blood and guts and Captain Wilderness. He was a frightened and quite brave man doing something scary that was like his farewell. Like shaking off an old skin. An old life. When I met him he always knew exactly what he wanted to do and he had this total lack of self-doubt about getting there. When he set off on this expedition, he didn't know whether he'd make it past the first farmhouse. He didn't know if he'd get down. I don't even know where he is. But I do know he needs me to be there for him for that, no matter what happened in Israel. We don't know what happened there, anyhow. We don't know if they got together again in the way you think. Oh, I know you think I'm naïve. You think: of course they had a screw or a bonk or a rumpy-pumpy or whatever you want to call it—don't smirk like that or I'll use another word very loudly, like fuck or shag. OK? You think they did because you would have done. Right, Jeremy? Isn't that what you always did on your safaris? If it moves, screw it. Shag it. Fuck it. Client's wives. Friend's lovers. Did you think I didn't know? Of course I knew. Didn't you think you made it easy for me to try someone else? Especially after your photo-safari stunt with the Frenchwoman. Funny, really, that she's messed around with all of us and here we are wondering just what he did with her. Hilarious. But it's not so funny now, is it? Sorry. Sorry. I shouldn't have said that. But it's true all the same. When you went off into the bush with her, you left me alone and you just took it for granted that I'd be waiting when you'd had your fun. How long did you think I could take that before I started thinking that sauce for the goose was sauce for the gander. Except that I couldn't just do the one-night-stand thing, like you always did. No. I was a one-guy-gal. I had to go the whole hog and it all went wrong. Or right. But at least I could hide my conscience. I could say to myself: well, Jeremy won't mind because he's always got his clients or whatever he calls them. He did it first. And even as Joe was coming knocking on my door, you were off with his floozy in the bush. You're thinking I've turned into a shrew, a lush, aren't you? You're thinking: where did this tirade come from, aren't you?"

The restaurant had emptied and the kitchen staff had adopted that look of impatience that is designed to hurry the stragglers away. They had begun setting tables for the morning's breakfast. There were yawns and furtive glances at wristwatches. But she was not finished.

"And then there they are on TV, the same woman for both of you. One size fits all. Is that it? And, no, I don't know what they did after their prime time heroics, and perhaps it doesn't matter because the worst betrayal isn't the bedtime kind, it's the feeling that you aren't needed anymore, that you're inadequate. It's the if onlys. If only I'd done X then there wouldn't have been a Y and then there wouldn't be a Z, a betrayal. But one day, maybe soon for all I know, I'll find out and there won't be so many ifs: if he survives, if he tells me, if it's true. If they did screw or shag or fuck or whatever, if it turns out that way, well, that's a new script and I'll know my lines. And I'll walk away. Probably alone. But, until then, he needs me to be there when he comes back down that hill to tell me he did something good. He'll probably, if he survives at all, tell me he doesn't want to drag me down with him. But until he makes that choice, I have no choice either."

"You do, Eva. You do have a choice. You've opened up, cleared the air. You've said all you need to say. You're right about me in the past. But that's past. I'm different. I'm all yours if you want me. You have a choice right now. Tonight. You can choose me—no commitments, if you like, no promises. You can choose me and tell the mountain rescue to go find him and they will. You will have acquitted yourself. And it is not you who has a debt. It's him. He owes you and you can call that debt by coming with me. Not for revenge but to come back to where you belong, where you're happy, where your work is, your family, your friends. People like you and me, we just don't transplant. We look across the ocean and see the world and it looks exciting, but when we get there, all we do is hanker for Africa. We want to go home. Look, his doctor says he's not as sick as he thinks. Hold the Mayo, or whatever. He has a life. He has the crazy Frenchwoman. You don't have to be alone. You don't have to be messed about like this. You can choose."

A particularly ferocious gust of wind rattled at the dining room windows behind heavy, velvet drapes, wrenching them open and blowing the curtains apart with a blast of cold and snow that came straight from the heights beyond.

GREAT GABLE

from Lingmell

Chapter Seventeen

No GPS to tell me where I am or how far I went. No watch either because I was using the one in the GPS. And no mobile. Ground control to Major Tom. Floating off, outside the gravitational pull. Beyond hope of return or rescue. Camp Two blues. The summit is everything. Everything that has been building up, every small step accumulating. Left, right. Stumble, slip. But progress. Without the summit, everything that went before has no logic.

You can't control the way people perceive you. You can't control the surreptitious glance to see if your foot's been caught in a mangle. You can't run, flex muscle, swim, kick sand and do all those other things that mark out your territory. You can't say: don't mess with me because it's pretty obvious that people can mess with you with impunity and you have no reprisals to threaten. And so, back to the summit. The summit, the lonely, conquered, obliging summit redeems all that. On the summit, you send your signals again. You are whole.

Think, though: you're alive to do this. You can still get up onto these hills,

215

and feel your nostrils freeze and swallow the icy fog, the foggy dew. You can feel the snow on your lips and hear the wind screech and watch the gray veils of mist rolling over the rocks and the lichen and the peat moss. All this says: I'm alive and life is very very sweet indeed and when they take all this away from me, when IT takes everything away from me, then I'll know what it was to be here and to have beaten IT one last time. The microphone is clipped to my collar and it voice activates. Because of the wind and the sound of the tent flapping in this appalling gale, I've set the voice activation at a fairly high threshold, which is quite technologically smart of me. But the reason I did it is so that I have my good hand free for Johnnie. Mix this one with a little spring water. Perfect. Except for the wind. Really howling. And the nylon flapping like a loose sail, rippling and crackling. Nothing I can do now. Rocks on the guylines. Pegs hammered in as deep as they'll go. No cooking because no stove. Evening meal: peanuts and Kendal Mint Cake and (voice activation off).

Gaza, then Jerusalem. Room 5 at the American Colony, with its big, high, wood-carved Ottoman ceiling, and cool, stone floors and the big double bed. Just outside the window, there's the minaret of the local mosque. It's only a stunted little minaret, not one of those great soaring spires you see in Cairo or Damascus or Istanbul—all those places where the sultans and the mullahs and the muftis built their huge tributes to Allah and his prophet untrammeled by anyone else's notion of faith, or perhaps, like medieval cathedrals in Europe, to say: there really is only one God and we've got the exclusive rights of access, whatever you Buddhists or Hindus or Jews or Animists might have to say about it. But the thing about this little minaret in Jerusalem is that the muezzin turns up the volume of his morning prayer call during Jewish holidays so that in Yom Kippur it nearly blows you out of bed. Allah-uh akhbar, o yes. And don't you forget it. The rest of the time it's not so loud and you get used to the muezzin's call and even look forward to it because it's actually telling you that you are in an exotic, alien place where you don't really belong and which cannot therefore impose any standards or norms on you. Cloud cuckoo land. Charlie charlie lima, as F called it—that hack sense of floating above other people's rules and moving on, never being bound and *immune to any consequences of any actions because the next plane out will take you to another country where the wench is not yet dead. The room's big and airy, with cool stone floors in the summer and a big warm bed in the winter. The walls are immensely thick, in pale honey stone, protective and reassuring. Room 5 always was my favorite. Something about it. And special with F because after that time in Gaza, right at the beginning, with the sniper, that was where . . . no second prizes for guessing. But even then, especially then you had to have a special quality of trust—she demanded trust—she said: this is how I am. And when you said: but how can I know that I can trust this, place my faith in it, somehow, one day, feel secure with it, she said: well, no one can ever be sure that one day things won't change, or something like that. She said, precisely, exactly: no one can guarantee that one of us won't be tempted. And when I heard that, I knew I'd reach my limit with her at some stage when the sacrifice just got too big, the craziness too overwhelming to justify my trust in her.*

But when you love with that kind of intensity, you can never expunge the traces. The first real love never dies. It's like some addiction just waiting to be reactivated, a DNA transplant so that you become part of another person and they become part of you and you can't just shake that. You imagine all these little closed boxes from your past, all with their little locked doors and you know that, in most of them, there's nothing. A memory, maybe. A liaison. An episode crumbled to dust. Motes. Nothing more. But in one box, with the door straining and cracking, there's a demon, a monster, a great massive Love with a capital L, and you can't keep the door closed. You try but you know that as soon as you open that door just the tiniest chink, you unleash the madness you were trying to lock away. The door bursts open, flies off the hinges, crack, kerpow, and you're wrestling with feelings you shouldn't be having because there's someone else in your life you owe things to, but you can't just shove this great raving beast back into its box and nail down the lid because—and this is the crux of the matter, Johnnie, me old mate—because you don't want to. Like giving up smokes. You say you want to but you don't. You don't want to abandon that sweet, heady rush with your coffee, or after sex, and when you've filed your story or when you've just got back to cover from some exposed bit of highway in Tetovo, some place where the mortars and the snipers can't reach you. You say: I wish I didn't need these things. But you light up your Marlboro and take the smoke deep into your lungs and you know it's self-destruction but you can't resist because you won't resist. And that was Room 5. I guess. In Room 5, we opened the box again and now we both know what's inside.

OK, I shouldn't have called her from the Mayo. But I was scared after what they told me. I didn't want to tell Eva because I wanted to protect her and I thought—I admit it—I thought that she might not hack it like F would, that she'd think: shit where does that diagnosis leave me, not where does that leave old Joe Shelby? And I wanted 100 percent TLC because it shocked me, more than hearing my first bullet or seeing the first corpse. It shocked me because right up until then I'd been hoping that some wizard would weave a spell—or lift one—and it would be your standard third-grade-story ending: and it had all been a dream. But it wasn't like that. The ending was: it's not a dream, it's actually a nightmare, and it's only just starting. So I called F because I thought she would understand nightmares better than dreams and you were only deluding yourself if you thought that there could ever be any kind of script with her. When was there ever a script? Wasn't that the whole point about it? Wasn't it that vortex of chaos that drew you to her in the first place? When you went with F you tore up the script, the norms, the standards. But even by those standards, things went awry. For a start, it wasn't in the script for her to rescue me like that, in front of the cameras and all. Was that in the script, Johnnie? No, sir, it was not. And it sure as shit was not in the script to go back to the Colony with her. And it was just a chance that they had given me Room 5, but she always did like her omens. She traveled with a black juju doll from the Congo in her camera bag and some talisman on the cord round her neck next to her coke spoon. So she thought it was an augury, I guess, that the Colony had put me back in the room where it all started. I could have said: no entry. I could have said: look, Faria, it's different now, I'm with Eva, I have an illness and responsibilities and there shouldn't be any treachery. But what the hell. It'd been on TV. Sheep as a lamb—the old cock-driven logic of many a male—it's come this far, my guilt is already assumed, so why not go for it. Why not be hung for the whole goddam flock of animals instead of just the lamb. So I said: come into Room 5, Faria. Hold my hand. Hold me. I need to talk. I need.

She had changed. I had changed. The mystery of Room 5. All confession, intimacies, talk. Very late, sometimes drunken, or stoned. Sometimes with hugs.

And was there sex? I suppose there was.

Joe Shelby paused for a long time, thinking back from tent to hotel room, from chill solitude to warm companionship. The tape recorder switched itself off as he had programmed it to do in response to silences and lacunae. But when he restarted his monologue, technology betrayed him for the machine did not reactivate itself as he had instructed it to, and his concluding words were lost to the wind that zinged in the guy-lines of his tent:

Yes, there was sex only in the sense that we were two people of opposing gender who had shared a lot and survived a lot and could snuggle and feel the horniness stirring. And that was it. Really. It went no further because there was too much baggage on both sides for consummation. Just hugs, cuddles, babes in the wood stuff. But that's infidelity, isn't it, Johnnie? The breach of trust is partly in the intention and partly in the admission that you are looking beyond your one chosen person for something they offer you and you reject implicitly as inadequate. Betrayal is when you take the absolute core, the essence of the secret bestowed upon you by person A and give it to person B. Real treachery is when you take the soul with which you have been entrusted and expose it to an event or events that you know with 100 percent certainty would destroy it completely.

So ask yourself two questions: did you betray—or have you ever betrayed—E in Jerusalem by any definition whatever? And, irrespective of the answer to that, you ask the second question: if you were given a reprieve, if Nigel Lampton called and said the Mayo was wrong, who would you call first to tell the news to? And the answer would be impossible because you were not biologically unfaithful and if you had to say who will I spend my life with you'd say Eva but if the question was: who will you hanker after for the rest of your days, whose will be the name on your lips when the Dutch doctor slides home the needle, whose face will be on your mind when you awake in any bed in any place in any gin joint in all the world then the answer to that you've known since the very first dawn in Gaza.

❧

She knew there would be a light tapping on the door. She knew she had not locked the door. She knew she would not sleep and despaired of thinking matters further through than that.

❧

TAPE THREE, SEGMENT THREE
SEPTEMBER 16, 2000
MONITORED SEPTEMBER 17

. . . *cking tape switch off? Weather foul. Johnnie gone. All gone.*

❧

On the first Eurostar train before a new day's dawn, there were no asylum seekers clinging to the axles, no sudden rush of Afghans or Kurds at Calais trying to hide in its crevices. In the absence of such hindrances, the train made good time, benefiting from the hour that accrued in its favor as it passed through the thirty-mile tunnel under the sloshing, gray wilderness of the Channel. The woman in black, curled in a first class seat, slept for most of the journey, clutching a worn canvas shoulder bag. When the train arrived at London's Waterloo, she pulled on a down vest and a woolen hat—also in black—and walked resolutely through immigration control waving her French passport. The immigration officers took her for some minor celebrity or fashion model roughing it by traveling without an entourage. She had a clear route map in her mind and hurried to catch the morning West Coast express from Euston to a town she had never visited called Lancaster. She found it amusing to think that, though she had travelled in a burqa on a donkey across Afghanistan to seek out the mujahideen in the old days and had meandered across Africa from the Sudan to Rwanda to Zimbabwe, though she had been with the 101st Airborne Division in southern Iraq and with the rump Spesnatz in Grozny, she had never experienced quite the same quality of voyager's apprehension as she did contemplating the markers of her day's planned route—Kendal and Shap, Penrith, Keswick, Borrowdale. Was that not the name he had given? A village, where his journey would end? And the name of a hotel. Who could guess what situation she would find there, anymore than they had ever known for sure in Rwanda or Gaza what their destination for the day would bring?

Chapter Eighteen

THIRLMERE, ESK HAUSE, ENGLAND.
SEPTEMBER 2000

They awoke separated by distance, altitude, commissions, omissions.

With no device to chart time's crawl through the cold and dark, he was aware of a barely perceptible lightening of the sky and an inexplicable weight on the nylon walls of the tent. It was very cold, far below zero. Condensation had frozen into the inner lining of the tent above his head, as if he were looking at the chill sails of some ghostly vessel on icy seas. He was wearing gloves, socks, a woolen hat, fleece and trousers—all inside the down sleeping bag—but he shivered nonetheless. Whether it was the half-felt shift in the light or the predawn swoon of the temperature he was not sure.

She awoke behind the dark, lined drapes of her room. The tangled sheets wrapped around her like hot towels in an old-fashioned barber shop. She was surprised to find herself alone. Casting aside the curtains and sliding open the sash window, she saw the ground transformed into a white, frozen landscape where snow was still falling. She reached for her cellular phone and the number of the mountain rescue team. She switched on the kettle in her room to make coffee. The mountain rescue number did not respond. It was 5:00 A.M.

Without the stove, he had only water in his aluminum water bottle, which rattled like a drinks mixer with the ice that had formed overnight. His headlight torch cast light and shadow around the mess of the tent. He figured that the walls bellied in because snow had fallen on them— a conclusion confirmed when he opened the door zipper and a cascade of cold white powder fell onto his sleeping bag. The wind moaned then ceased. In the stillness, he tried to recall what the experts said about such conditions: did you stay put and keep warm, or did you move out before your shelter collapsed onto you? Did you sit it out or look for help, fire flares, send messages? He had no flares, no messaging device, no means of creating heat. He thought the wise move would be to shovel away the snow and await the light of day. But his left arm had no strength and he had no shovel. He had no stove to melt ice, brew tea. He was shivering. The lighter he used to fire up a clumsily rolled cigarette guttered and went out.

The kettle boiled and she busied herself with two sachets of instant coffee, sugar and cream. There was still no answer from the mountain rescue number. She cast around in case he had left a note and wondered why he had stolen away like a thief in the night. Unless he was a thief in the night.

If there had been a view, it would have been magnificent, one of those vistas that people treasure. Somewhere, in his stored or half-unpacked belongings, he had a tinted photograph entitled Great Gable from Esk

Hause. It showed the crossing of the pathways located deceptively short of the watershed between the valleys. The terrain was furrowed with streams, crevices, gullies, treachery. It led the eye on to the blunt flank of Great Gable with the impossibly steep rocky path that scarred it—the wall of mountain that gave the peak its name. To the right, the north, of Great Gable was the lesser summit of Green Gable and another steep cleft that ran to the col between them. The colors were washed green and blushed pink, giving way to the gray granite of the Gable Crags with their renowned landmark of Nape's Needle. He knew it all intimately but could not see it now and did not trust memory as a guide. Without the GPS device, he figured he would need his compass and maps and thanked his deity that he had brought such old fashioned devices. From Esk Hause the pathway lay almost exactly due west to the 2,600 foot line, where it turned 15 or 20 degrees south towards Broad Crag, following the summit ridge with its celebrated obstacle course of boulder fields. It was possible—easy—to err here, to stray onto the steep, broken ramparts and fissured gullies of Great End where people had died, or across the ridge, descending by mistake into the jaws of Greta Gill or Piers Gill, the twin ravines that cut jagged grooves through the mountain's breast. Yet, many others had come this way, left their imprints, their cairns of piled rocks, their scratchings and gougings on the trail that drew a pale ribbon running to the summit of England's highest mountain. No giant. No monster. No Everest. The distance was risible, barely more than a mile. But in this half-light, in the stillness, balancing uncertainly on his walking poles outside the half-buried tent, the prospect was unsettling, nerve-wracking. There was an option, of course. There were always options, but they seemed to narrow as you advanced. And his option, now, was defeat, retreat, failure. He could simply cast around for the trail that led down, not up, towards Styhead Pass to the northwest, at around 1,500 feet, then, on a heading north-northeast, the slow descent alongside the stream called

Styhead Gill to the valley, and safety, and Eva, of course. Eva who was waiting. Eva to whom his tape pledged loyalty whatever the secrets of Room 5. Eva to whom he owed a duty to stay alive for long enough to put things in order, provide the decent exit.

She hated instant coffee but there was no option. The kitchen staff had not yet arrived, the way they do in fancier hotels that, in the very early hours, sound like ocean liners making ready to cast off, slowly filling with indistinct clatters and offstage clutter of pans and cutlery. The coffee, at least, was hot and sweet. There were digestive biscuits in bright packaging. She was tired, though she must have slept. But before she slept, she recalled, there had been a struggle, a wrestle—not so much physical, although there was something of that—but more with conscience. She should not have had the nightcap, not on top of the predinner vodka, the wine. She should not have allowed him into her room—this very room where she was supposedly awaiting her crazy man of the mountains. As if she were some virgin bride, bedecked and bespangled with jewels and geegaws, in some remote yurt or hut or apartment filled with quarter-tones and incense. She was none of that. None. Neither virgin nor bride. Unless she had said differently to Jeremy Davenport in the close time they had spent, clinched and squirming.

The snow left only the bright ridge of the tent exposed as if it were a miniature replica of the real thing. As he had been taught, he had pitched it with its entrance door facing downwind. Otherwise he would not have been able to clamber out. As it was, the snow had gusted and drifted to form a cozy hollow around the tent's round door so that he could exit from it. But there was no way he could break camp. This option, at least, was clear. The tent would be abandoned along with just about everything else. Apart from his water bottle and compass—and the Vestpocket camera, of course, and the tape recorder, naturally, for a reporter—there was no point at all in even attempting to load his gear onto his back. The dehydrated food could not be rehydrated because he had no stove to make water. The GPS was broken. The tent was snowed in. He had come to the last page of the walking guide and must now find his own way, down or up. The page itself was blank, as featureless as the snowfield in which he now found himself.

❧

The early train from London's Euston station was pulling out of the platform and the attendant was asking whether she required English or continental and Faria Duclos was thinking: both.

❧

TAPE FOUR, SEGMENT ONE
SEPTEMBER 16, 2000
MONITORED SEPTEMBER 17

Snow came in by stealth, layer upon layer in the night, followed by a dense freezing mist that cuts the visibility to a matter of yards. From here I should be getting that great view of Great Gable and the gullies on Great End where we used to do the winter climbs and pretend we were in the Alps or the Himalayas, with crampon points biting into frozen waterfalls and temperatures low enough to do serious damage. But none of that today. Just a wall. I left my headlight on because it's still not light and I want to follow a westbound heading on the compass because the problem is that you can't really see the trails at all under the snow and it's treacherous with the rocks and little streams and stuff. What I have to do is head west without descending because if I start descending it'll mean I'm too far south towards Eskdale and I'll miss the way. The headlight battles. It cuts a vague tunnel

into the fog so that you can see the beginnings of wind stirring the mist around like
a witch's brew. But the beam isn't strong enough to go too far so it seems to create a
gray impenetrable wall about ten yards ahead and that's what you get for visibility.
They say Mallory and Irvine started late and that was their mistake because they
ran out of time somewhere up there on the ridge, but early starts don't seem to be
all that great either because you can't see. It looks as if I have about five hundred
yards to go on this heading and then I should reach the col at Calf Cove and turn
a few degrees south to get on the summit ridge. But at least Esk Hause is behind
me and if I turn round now and shine my beam back I can't see the tent at all and
even my footsteps are lost in this white-out. Gray-out really. So I suppose I'm
committed. More than ever. Going with some clumsiness for the summit.

The man answered the phone with the slow thickness of disturbed
sleep. She cajoled, begged. Do you remember me? In the street yesterday? Well, he's still not back. No sign. And this weather. He's not
equipped. He's ill. Weak. He has a neurological condition that makes
him that way. Of course, I know he should not have gone. But he's stubborn, headstrong. He felt he had to do it. And nobody forecast weather
like this did they?

She read from the copy of his route card that he had left with her.
Camp Two at Esk Hause, she said. She pronounced it: Esk House? OK,
the man said, we'll scramble. We'll head for Esk Hause. It sounded like:
Esk Hawse. But it's a vile day for it. No chance of a chopper. And we
might have to wait out the weather once we're assembled.

Joe Shelby found it hard to pinpoint his mood at that moment when, by
his calculations and his sense of terrain, he arrived panting and tiring on

the col that brought him to the summit ridge. His feelings reminded him a little of the very early days of his life of danger when he would propel himself in a rental car or on foot towards the start of a particularly exposed section of crackling, fired-up, bullet-zipped urban war zone and have to make the call of advance or retreat. As he reached the summit ridge and turned 15 degrees south he felt that same elation—the excitement of survival, the false summit of hope that came when you passed one obstacle only to realize that you faced another, even greater hurdle and had cut off easy retreat by overcoming the first one. It was fear but not simply fear. It was fear with a rictus of thrilling danger. It was the sense of burned bridges and a long haul to reach safety and rest. It was, of course, ultimately the fear that this time there would be no second chance, no guardian angel, no zephyr of wind to nudge the sniper's bullet the merest fraction off course. But he was here, he told himself. And if he had to go, where would he rather that be? Here, of course. At this point of fusion between dream and history, along this rumpled spine of granite in the land that bore him, where his ancestors' spirits rested in their urns and caskets, captured in framed photographs in black and white that showed them reclining against a Ford Popular or Riley Nine, with Blackpool tower or the flat, endless beach and donkey rides of Southport in the fuzzy background. In the end, for all his journeyings and visas and wars, he was no different from those he chronicled, who played out their lives on less-traveled stages, held to the ancestral soil by forces they understood as their destiny. So he would fall and be mummified in this bitter cold and come spring they might find him if the winter was particularly harsh and there would be no need for awkward farewells. Those he cared about would interpret his passing kindly, saying it was how he would have wished, though they would be wrong. He would not be called upon to explain himself, or make decisions, or draw up his testament. Or he would not fail. He would reach the summit and achieve the descent and take it from there. He would kneel in chapels and cathedrals and pray to his God for mercy and deliverance and rescue from his blighted limbs, his exhausted nerves. Putting one aluminum pole before the other, swinging his body to compensate for the weakness on his left side, he advanced and crabbed forward and upward, with a pure pain burning in his thighs as the muscles there took unfamiliar strain and the going underfoot became deceitful because, under the snow, there were boulders cloaked in ice.

He wore gloves over his hands and two fleeces over his silk vest and thermal shirt. He covered himself in an expensive parka made of a scientific material that people used in the Himalayas. He wore snow gaiters over the waterproof overtrousers that covered his jeans and long underwear and thick socks. He had pulled his fleece helmet so that it covered most of his face under the hood of his parka. He was still cold. His breath came in white clouds. When he paused, he heard nothing at all. No voices. No whistles. No evidence that anyone else was on the mountain on a day like that. anymore than Mallory and Irvine expected company on the North Ridge. But they had each other and they were climbing Everest. Joe Shelby was alone on Scafell Pike, a mountain conquered by parties of schoolchildren and pensioners, droves of them, caravans of walkers who traipsed in great gaggles across these mountains in the summer and on bright days, but did not see them like this in their most barren and heartless moments when all life seemed denied. A radio might have helped. A radio might have told him whether the forecast said it would get better or worse. But he had run out of options now. Retreat would be as difficult as advance, without the faint lure of triumph to sustain him.

Chapter Nineteen

The messages went out early, spreading along a prearranged sequence of onward calls and crackling radios until the rescue team members were all apprised of the call-out and, part grumbling, drove their cars and Land Rovers to the assembly point at Seathwaite to which they had been summoned. The drill had been established and practiced in many exercises and real emergencies over the years.

In the village of Rosthwaite, the team leader, Ken Gill, had risen and was drinking tea in the warm kitchen of his granite-and-slate cottage. The radio was burbling news noise—the litany of England rising—and the local weekly newspaper carried a leading article asking sternly when the use of speedboats on Windermere would be outlawed once and for all. The team leader had stepped outside into the darkness beyond his back door and hastily retreated. The snow lay thick on his gravel driveway and sat on the hood of his Land Rover like a bright, white foam mattress. The sky that should have been lightening was hidden by a low wall of dense fog that seemed to have settled almost on the valley floor. It was one of those days when people familiar with the mountains did everything they could to persuade unfamiliar offcomers to stay down in the valleys. It was one of those days when the extreme weather would make a search difficult and a rescue challenging or even impossible. For most people, the Lake District was either rainy days in tea shops or benevolent strolls on worn trails. But for people here year round, or caught out by a fluke of meteorology, the hills could turn into something completely different—vicious and unforgiving, merciless. And now the word was that some fool walker—a cripple, no less—had chosen this day to get himself stranded in some of the least hospitable terrain the mountains had to offer.

Ken Gill dressed quickly in his warmest gear, topped by the distinctive red parka of the rescue team. The big rucksack carrying medical equipment was already packed. The physical preparations for a search and rescue—SAR as they called it—were reflexive. They would assemble at Seathwaite, probably forty of them at this time of year. All were volunteers and supremely fit, trained to traverse these mountains in all conditions, carrying loads designed to meet all eventualities. They would have ropes and space blankets. Stoves. Bivouac shelter. Crampons. Ice axes. Emergency rations. Medication for hypothermia and frostbite. Radios for communications. That much was all automatic. That was what they did, what they practiced for on the Keswick Mountain Rescue Team. What concerned him was the location. Esk Hause was a broad, tilted plateau. It could be reached from Borrowdale either from the Grains Gill path or via Styhead, where the Mountain Rescue Service had a prepositioned stretcher and other equipment in a container. Technically, two other teams—in Langdale and Wasdale—would need to be alerted because Esk Hause was equidistant from all of them. And if Esk Hause was the last known—or, at least, suspected—whereabouts for the walker, then the team would best split into two, one group heading directly via Grains Gill, the other via Styhead. It had to be assumed that, if the walker had camped on Esk Hause, he would either remain in his camp or seek a descent to Borrowdale, which he had given as his ultimate destination. So the search would focus on Esk Hause and its approaches. No one in his right mind would consider for one moment going higher—for instance, to the Scafell Pike summit which he was apparently aiming for—not in this weather. For that would be the height of folly.

☙

TAPE FOUR, SEGMENT TWO
SEPTEMBER 16, 2000
MONITORED SEPTEMBER 17

... Summit close. Feel it, sense it. Fall didn't help. Slipped on boulders and my leg hurts. Bad leg, of course ...

... Sitting, see ice form on rocks. September, for Chrissakes. Know it's there, the summit—only have to get up and push on and I'll get there. Started from Camp Two—haa haa—at first light. Weather awful. Big wind coming up over the col. Horizontal sleet. Barely drag myself out of the sleeping bag. But soldier on. Right? What we do. Soldier on, take it on the chin. So out of the tent. Compass bearing from the map. Tricky, because I wasn't sure I'd camped in the right place. Weather indescribable. Freak storm. If I hadn't fallen, it would have knocked me over. But I fell. I did. Just when I needed my leg to work, it didn't. And it's cold.

... No one else around. But I wanted it that way. Solo bid. Dawn start. Summit alone. And there won't be anyone else around. Not up here. Not in weather like this. Color note: gray rock, encrusted with ice like salt deposits. No. Like crystals. Visibility zero. The cloud has descended like a blanket. No, scrub that. The cloud has fallen here and come to rest, wrapping my world in its frigid grayness. Even worse.

. . . *In the middle of the boulder field. Ice Fall. Khumbu Glacier. The ice crystals look as if they have been here forever. But I have to move . . . get frost-bite. Or hypothermia. You slip away in a dream world, feel warm and happy and your eyes start to close. Want to sleep. Should sleep. In the cradle of the angels.*

. . . *More scared than I ever was. More scared than Beirut, Sarajevo, Grozny, Gaza . . . in the war zones, you could hide in a cellar or a bunker or behind a wall. You could call in on the sat-phone and hear a voice at the comic back in New York. But there's nowhere to hide up here. No one to talk to. Wind always finds you. And cold.*

. . . *don't want outsiders coming to the rescue. Want to rescue myself. Want power to flow from within that will enable me to stand up on these treacherous, snow-gray, white-out, gray-out boulders and move myself into the right direc-tion to that great round cairn that I remember as the summit. You pray for many things. Forgiveness. Help. You pray on behalf of other people. You pray so that you can imagine you are communicating with those in the parallel life. The ancestors. The spirits. But you pray for specific things, too. Strength. Fortitude. And you never know whether you will be heard until you have been heard. Goodness is the base line and evil is an aberration—that is the core of faith. And anyone who says they cannot believe in good because of the existence of evil is missing the point. The only weapon against evil is belief in good. And goodness is what will certainly not get me up onto my feet again. Dear Lord, if there is one prayer now in this cold, dead core of where I came from, it is this: please help me to get up, to grit my teeth, to stop myself drifting away in thoughts and dreams and half-sleep to walk and reach the summit without which all these efforts and preparations will be in vain. Just now I know I think I slept. My eyes closed and then opened and I don't know how long they were closed and isn't that the danger sign—when you start drifting off and in that sleep of death, what dreams? None, or sweet ones. Warm days and friends and no hard choices and E and F redeemed and reconciled. And perhaps this is what they mean when they say: your number is up. This is the appointed moment for the transition to the par-allel world so maybe this is my day. But, dear Lord, Our Father who art, I do not wish to die here so close to the summit but not yet on it, and if it is your will that this day should be my last, allow me the one final single grace of reaching that place higher than all others in this realm before I am transported to the next. My eyes opened again so I guess they must have closed. All the time, in the wars, I never really believed—even when I was most terrified—that I wouldn't make it. But now I can see that it's for real because I'm not an observer in all this, I'm a player, a participant, at last. It's for real and in the real world there are no easy ways up, down, out.*

✍

At breakfast there was no sign of him. She had showered, dressed ready for the long wait while the rescuers went to look for Joe Shelby. She had imagined that Jeremy Davenport would be at her side to give her strength, support her and show that—whatever it had been between them—it had been with love. But there was no sign of him and his rental car was gone from the parking lot.

✍

In London the rain in the neon over the black streets reminded her of swarms of insects she had seen in African street lamps, gusting and crowding but never ceasing. The train left in the darkness and it seemed the darkness had vanquished all before it. Even when a technical dawn sought to lighten the sky, it succeeded merely in exchanging the darkness of night for the darkness of low, solid cloud. Faria Duclos had known Joe Shelby in many places. They had snuggled in round clay houses in Zululand, luxurious hotels in the Middle East, tawdry, ex-communist establishments in Tashkent and Samarkand. They had been alcohol-free together in Islamabad and Kuwait, and they had soaked in the stuff in Cape Town and Harare. But she had never associated him before with the places she passed through that provided the route map to his roots. What on earth was Milton Keynes? Maynard Keynes, yes. That she understood. And John Milton. But why a town named for a poet-economist? And Rugby. A game? A school? A town? And all these places were concealed from her, behind the curtain of rain, focusing the view on windswept railway station platforms where commuters shivered for the southbound trains to London but no one headed north from Stafford or Crewe. They called it the western mainline and her ticket told her she was riding first class, but the arm fell off her seat and the rattling trolley of supposed breakfast seemed to bear only tawdry fare. The coffee was a vile, national insult to anyone of French origins. Welcome to Britain, where late dawns and early dusks shouldered aside the half-light, as if, with his condition, the brightness was draining away, leaving him to confront perpetual darkness at his core. And she understood that darkness, so she would remain with him until the end came, and lay him to his final rest and celebrate the final days or weeks or months. It was not just Du Plessis's goading. She owed him the life he had plucked from the brink in Rwanda.

PIERS GILL

looking down from the corridor route

Chapter Twenty

BORROWDALE, ENGLAND. SEPTEMBER 2000

They assembled at Seathwaite, thirty-two of them, all volunteers. Some abandoned jobs as teachers or store managers, handing over their classes and till passes to understanding colleagues. Some jettisoned writing projects, canvasses, drama groups. Many sent children to babysitters or prevailed on partners and spouses to stay home with infants. But all of them responded. The call was not something to be ignored by people who understood the fells.

In the billowing snow that cascaded down the valleys and into the small, gray, invisible village, they shook their heads at the folly of it. They had one clue—a suspected campsite at Esk Hause, almost 2,500 feet above them.

Had the missing walker even made it that far?

He—or was it she?—might never have crossed Crinkle Crags and Bowfell. For all they knew, he—yes, it was he—might well have slipped somewhere on that treacherous, knuckle ridge long before reaching his projected campsite. For all they knew, he might at this moment be lying, quite still, beyond any help they could give, at the base of some precipice crossed in error. And even if he had reached Esk Hause, was he still there? At the back of everyone's minds, men and women, young and older, was the unspoken thought: was he still alive? Were they risking their own necks for the sake of a corpse, as stiff and lifeless as Mallory's, but with no significance at all other than as a statistic?

Ken Gill, their leader, placed calls to the other mountain rescue teams in Langdale and Wasdale, requesting them to be on alert as backup, in case the first sweep over Esk Hause and Styhead turned up nothing. The Langdale team could strike easily up The Band, or via Red Tarn, to reach the Crinkle Crags–Bowfell–Esk Pike axis. Wasdale lay directly below the summit of Scafell Pike and, from the valley formed by Wastwater, the deepest of the district's lakes, rescuers could strike up by the steep, short tourists' route via Brown Tongue and Lingmell Col if it came to that, if the first search of Esk Hause and Styhead failed to turn up the cripple—dead or alive. Of course, they had no beacon, no locator number, no code or satellite bearings to home in on. When Ken Gill called the RAF commander to inquire about the chances of a helicopter, the duty sergeant simply laughed and told him to look out of the window, laddie, and tell him what he could see. Nothing. Right? Nothing. So if there was zero visibility what miracles did he expect from the pilots?

It would be the old-fashioned kind of search, the establishment of a central command post and the quartering from there on very definite grid references to ensure that the rescuers themselves did not become the rescued. They would establish temporary camp at Esk Hause and Styhead, radiating the search out from those points, maintaining a forward headquarters for the rescuers to work in relays, resting between forays, maintaining adequate levels of hot liquids, sugars, soup. No general likes splitting armies, but here there was no choice. Ken Gill would divide his team into two, sending one to Styhead and the other, via

Grains Gill and the ravine of Ruddy Gill, direct to Esk Hause. They would search those areas, hoping to find the man at or near his camp-site, or already descending on one of the two available routes. They would not search the summit ridge of Scafell Pike. In this weather, that was lunacy, an unlikely location for the lost man, the target, and an unacceptable risk for the team. They would leave three men—older men, not likely to grumble beyond token complaints at being spared the blizzard—to run the radio base station at Seathwaite. Operating from inside a farmer's barn, out of the worst of the weather, it would be their job to maintain communication with other emergency services, anchor the operation. They would be responsible for arranging backup—ambulance, a chopper if the weather lifted, press liaison with Cumbria newspapers and broadcasters, nationals, too, if the drama merited. Then there would be liaison with the mortuary services and the coroner and the next of kin if the worst came to the worst. They had one contact name on that list—Eva Kimberly, lodging at one of the fancy hotels. Wife? Girlfriend? Not clear. Just a mobile phone number and a hotel room number. She had been responsible for the call-out. She had insisted that the man was not safe, that he was a cripple playing out crazy dreams. The coroner was already on alert, just in case someone had to make the call between accidental death and suicide—a narrow distinction sometimes among the romantics who came here to die and succeeded in spite of themselves. The rest of the team would be SAR: search and rescue.

Ken Gill inspected their kit. Each was clad for maximum warmth, with down jackets in their rucksacks. They carried GPS devices, lami-nated maps and old fashioned compasses, even though all of them knew these hills and mountains with the familiarity of frequent encounters in most kinds of weather, on the trails and on the rock faces, along the streambeds and high on the fellsides. They wore snow gaiters over waterproof, padded trousers and, in addition to the extending walking poles, they carried ice axes and crampons strapped to their packs. They were trained, fit, not quite certain of the timing.

"I don't like it much either," Ken Gill told the team, assembled behind a high barn wall made of Lakeland slate that sheltered them from the wind and snow. "The timing's not perfect. But we have to remember what we're here for—to save lives. We're all trained. We know what we're doing. We've rehearsed this a hundred times. We can do it and if we stick to what we've learned we'll come out of this fine. But just remember. The two teams stay in radio contact at all times. Within the teams, we maintain visual contact whilst on the move. We report our whereabouts to Seathwaite base on a fifteen-minute basis. We don't stray. We don't do unilaterals. And we don't do heroics. But if we don't try now, in these conditions, our chances of a successful outcome reduce very quickly. And you all know what I mean by that."

They nodded and moved out, swallowed up by the gusts so that the bright colors of their parkas and gaiters and rucksacks were soon drained and absorbed, leached into the storm. For less than one mile, they moved in one single file, thirty-two of them, following the path along the broad valley where the beginnings of the River Derwent sluiced and cascaded through the glacial moraines. Then, at Stockley Bridge, they broke into two teams of sixteen each, one, led by Ken Gill, heading west and then southwest to Styhead, the pass leading from Wasdale to Borrowdale.

Technically, the path to Styhead was called a bridleway and the stone bridge suggested that it had been designed for use by packhorse. Now the trail was a walkers' gateway to the high ground, striking obliquely across a rough hillside, passing through a gate in a drystone wall before penetrating an upland valley where travelers picked their way across awkward fields of rocks strewn arbitrarily alongside a rushing stream.

The other group, led by Angie Cartwright, kept on almost dead south, following the streambed of Grains Gill that led to the steep, zigzag pull up a rocky flank of fellside below Esk Hause. If the weather had been clear, their route would have been dominated by the gullies and broken buttresses of Great End—the northernmost abutment of the Scafell summit ridge. But, with the storm gathering in intensity, it was all they could do to keep track of the rescuer directly ahead. As the path steepened, desultory conversation and the occasional gallows quip about who'd rescue the rescuers gave way to the silence of concentration and exertion. It was not quite 10:00 A.M. and they were already beyond the snow line.

✍

He had not quite risen. Risen would definitely be too strong a word for it. Using both aluminum poles he had more or less cranked himself to half height, then subsided into a baby crawl, using his gloved hands— now cold and soaked—to feel a way across the boulder field, dragging the poles behind him. It was not comfortable or elegant, and he would not have even attempted it had there been the slightest prospect of encountering another human being. In fact, if he had encountered another human being he would probably have wept for joy and relief and begged for help. But there was no one else, and when he tried to walk across the boulder field at full or half height, his balance betrayed him and his feet found no purchase on the boulders, hidden and glazed, that lay below the powdering of snow. Being on the boulder field—and this was the only, faint consolation—meant he had reached the southern flank of Broad Crag, at around 3,000 feet, as much a marker of the summit's proximity—and deceptive distance—as the notches on the ridge before the summit pyramid of Everest. The heading now would be almost directly southwest and it was essential not to stray north or south into the ravine of Piers Ghyll or the steep trail to Little Narrow-cove that would lead him far from his destination, down toward

Eskdale and a long, long hike for any salvation, far beyond his physical resources.

Up until now, the idea of losing his way had not been so terrifying for, with his checklists and his kit, he had been equipped to survive unscheduled delays on the mountains. But he no longer had that luxury. He had jettisoned most of the survival gear at Esk Hause as he prepared this crazy dash for the summit—if dash was not perhaps something of an overstatement. And he had not factored in weather like this dense, sightless, frozen murk that iced his two-day stubble and clogged his nostrils within the cowl of his parka pulled tight over his balaclava. So the imperative was to remain on course. To head for the summit. To ensure that one breath followed another.

He had left no trace, no spoor. His disappearance bore no relation to the effusive protestations that preceded the tapping on her bedroom door, the fleet-foot tread of the villain on the deep-pile carpet of the boudoir. As the vodka-wine-cognac haze began to thin, the sequence of subsequent events began to reemerge in spectral outline. He had entered the suite, Joe Shelby's unguarded citadel. They had spoken little. They had clinched and hugged and the outcome seemed predictable, certainly from her perspective. Somewhere, over dinner, a decision had been taken, a switch had been thrown. Her year's error with Joe Shelby seemed no more than that—an aberration from which recovery was still possible provided she committed herself now through this sacrificial act of treachery. Whatever the outcome of Joe Shelby's expedition—success or failure, life or death—she had made the decision for all of them.

Then the frame slipped. At some advanced fumbling stage, the preordained sequences had been suspended. The event that should have happened had not, not because she had balked, but because Jeremy

Davenport had begun muttering about having made his point, achieved his goal, scored enough of a victory bringing her to this point. Yet, she knew, that was not the true reason for this failed consummation. One probing brush of her fingers told her what had happened. Her harsh laughter had been involuntary, directed at her own stupidity in thinking that this single act of joining could erase all the pains and hurts and traumas. But he took it as directed at him, at his failure, his collapse in the final moment of his campaign. His departure had been raging, incoherent. She remembered it all quite clearly now as she drove to make contact with the rescue base station, feeling besmirched by failure, acknowledging to herself that Joe Shelby might be right, that truth could contain its own opposite, a mirror of appearance and reality.

❧

For much of her daily life, Angie Cartwright was a high-school math teacher and parent of a four-year-old daughter, Jemima, whose father had died in a rock-climbing accident three years earlier. For a very important portion of her life she was also deputy leader of the mountain rescue and team leader of one of its main rock and fell units. She had paramedic training to offer initial assistance in the event of trauma, hypothermia, frostbite, fractures, spinal and skull injuries. As a walker she had long since completed the Munros—the Scottish peaks over 3,000 feet. As a rock climber she had conquered classics on El Cap in Yosemite and on the Tre Cime di Lavaredo in the Italian Dolomites— until, of course, her husband's death, after which she concluded that Jemima did not deserve two dead parents. But she had not given up the mountains and she had not given up the mountain rescue. When her husband died, he had been climbing solo in bad weather on the Central Buttress of Scafell Crag, opposite the summit of Scafell Pike across the broad, barren col known as Mickeldore. If a mountain rescue team had reached him, he might well have survived. But he had been foolish, over-confident, a supreme cragsman and brilliant technical climber, but a poor mountaineer who had never learned to guess the mood of the high ground or respect its caprices. He had told no one where he was going, probably because he knew people would have tried to dissuade him. As a result, the rescuers were not even alerted until the following day. By then, it was too late. He had died of exposure with both legs, three ribs and one arm broken, internal bleeding and severe lacerations to the skull. Angie Cartwright had led the team that found him, following her instinct to the boulders below Central Buttress.

She did not know the man at Esk Hause, but she knew that men are foolish and put their egos and whims ahead of their families. She did not know whether this man had a family or not but she did know that, unless they looked for him on this day, the weather would take him as surely as a slip had slain her own husband. She was a short, wiry woman, perfectly proportioned, who looked faintly silly in her Michelin-man down jacket, but no one laughed at her. On the steep grind up to Esk Hause through Grains Gill she set a grueling pace that even the fittest of her team found hard to follow. She located the route unerringly despite the snow and the flurries that cut visibility to a matter of yards and hid the cairns that marked the route. At around the 1,700 foot contour, the trail narrowed, entering a sharp vee of ravine, becoming no more than a slender shelf on the steep hillside. She contemplated urging the team to rope up, but decided they were nimble and fit enough to negotiate this steep and hazardous stretch without extra safety precautions. Above her, the cloud broke for a fleeting second to reveal the ramparts of Great End, covered in a wedding-cake crust of snow and ice, white against the deep, black strips of the crag's gullies that plummeted six hundred sheer feet from summit to base. Over the years, the trails in this region had become first eroded, then—as in many other places—repaired using flat rocks and boulders to create steep, uneven staircases winding to the heights, bearing aloft legions of fell walkers. Today they saw no one. Even late in the year, in normal weather, there would be enthusiasts—hardy spindly aficionados, sprightly grannies in bright fleeces—criss-crossing the mountains of the central massif, hailing one another, carrying sandwiches and thermos flasks of sweet, milky tea. Eerily, on this September morning, the fells were as bleak and deserted as they had ever been. In weather such as this, only the foolish or the ignorant would venture forth and she wondered which category best defined her team.

Breasting the high point of Ruddy Gill, she barely paused to check the GPS before finding a bearing south-southeast that would take her surefootedly to the confusing plateau of Esk Hause at the junction of north-south and east-west trails over the high ground. She knew she was making for the wall shelter at 2,400 feet just below the top of the pass, but saw beyond it in a gap of cloud a brighter dash of color and broke into a stumbling jog, ploughing through the drifts with her team calling to her to slow down.

"Hello! Hello, anybody there?" she was shouting at the bright ridge of Joe Shelby's tent.

Her team clustered round her. Obviously enough, it had simply been abandoned. The sleeping bag was inside out in a pile of other gear, a new-looking rucksack and packets of dehydrated food, a GPS satellite navigation aid that looked broken but needed only a new battery. There were spare socks, a toothbrush, bandages and liniment, a small notebook bound with elastic and laminated maps cut into squares. There was no stove, no warmth, no smell of human that might have suggested recent residence. She checked the name inside the notebook, just to be sure that it tallied with the name of her target, and it did.

"Dead man's kit," one of the team muttered.

"Don't say that. We'll make this base."

On a northwest heading, a little over one mile distant, Ken Gill and his team had settled around the prepositioned rescue trunk, throwing up bivouac shelters to keep the wind off stoves where they were making sugary tea to maintain their glucose and liquid levels. The rescue equipment, in a long coffin-like container emblazoned with the words "Stretcher Box," offered a windbreak, diverting the gusts that rose on the breath of the clouds, up from Wasdale and over the summit of the pass, down, past the black triangle of Styhead Tarn where ice had begun to fringe the shoreline.

"They found his tent," he called to his team, crouching over his radio, out of the wind behind the rescue container.

"Angie. Is the search target there? I repeat. Is the search target there?"

"Negative, Ken. Repeat. Negative."

At Seathwaite, the older men clustered around the base station tuned to the same frequency, intercepting the traffic between the two rescue teams. At first, they did not notice the woman in the heavy, black shearling coat. She had been standing at the door of the slate-and-granite barn where they had set up their station. They had erected a high radio mast and a portable satellite dish for backup. Across the way from the barn, twists of coal smoke trickled from the chimneys of a terrace of cottages behind low garden walls that made up most of the village. Everything was gray—the slate of the barn walls and the roofs, the cloud that fell down from the invisible mountains. Even the snowflakes seemed gray when she looked up to search for even a glimmer of brightness. Eva Kimberly had parked her car on the last stretch of the narrow lane leading into the hamlet. She had listened in to the radio exchange between Angie Cartwright and Ken Gill, then turned away, gnawing at bunched knuckles. Then, one of the base team saw her and went over to her.

"You must be the wife," he said, looking into red-rimmed hazel eyes set in a blanched face.

"Sort of."

"We'll be brewing a cuppa now."

"You're very kind."

The discovery of the tent made the planning easier. Its presence, combined with what they knew of his schedule, meant that he had presumably been alive that morning. He had not been sighted by either of the two search teams heading up from Borrowdale, and Ken Gill radioed Langdale and Eskdale to inquire whether teams from either of those valleys could cover their approaches to Esk Hause. That left two principal options in the main search area. The man could be somewhere between the two search teams, between Esk Hause and Styhead. Or he could be somewhere on the Scafell massif itself. That was the tricky one. Ken Gill had no qualms about sending teams of four to reconnoiter the lower pathways. But he felt an instinctive aversion to the idea of risking his people on Scafell without at least some indication that they were not searching in vain.

At Esk Hause, Angie Cartwright cast about for anything that might indicate the route the man had taken. She knew his itinerary would take him to Scafell Pike by the main, rocky ridge—a tricky assignment in these conditions, even for a trained climber. But since the morning, the snow had been falling steadily and there were no signs of footsteps, or the distinctive marks left by walking poles, to tell them whether he had decided to proceed according to plan or retreat, somehow. They did not know what kind of person he was, this Shelby, or whether he was in any way familiar with the terrain. Her radio crackled.

"Base to Angie. Over."

"Base. This is Angie."

"Someone to talk to you. Stand by."

There was a pause. She thought it might be Jemima with a story about her drawing class. Or her mother just to let her know that her daughter was fine and not to worry. Instead it was a voice she did not know, a woman who said she was the lost man's partner. Even over the radio, the woman spoke with the kind of upper-crusty tones that set Angie Cartwright's nerves on edge—posh, privileged, self-aware, the kind of woman who drove a late-model car and, if she deigned to have children, would have nannies, too. But it was a voice that caught on the question of whether there was any sign of a man called Joe and that set Angie Cartwright to recalling what it was like to lose a man on the mountains.

"I need to know more about him so I can try and work out where to look."

"Stubborn," the voice on the radio said. "He never retreated in his job. He's very brave. He knows the hills. He was a climber. He's been over all of them before. They're his history, in a way. He wants to write his own history. But you should know that he has a progressive illness. He desperately wants to get to the top before the illness makes it physically impossible. I think he'd rather die than fail at this stage."

"Thank you. That has been a great help," Angie Cartwright said. What she was thinking was: so we can conclude that he went for broke, and now we have to find a cripple in a blizzard. There had been something else before she closed down the transmission, something about telling him if she found him that someone had said something that sounded like hold the mayo. But she put that down to atmospheric interference with the wireless signal.

From Styhead, Ken Gill resolved to send one team straight for the summit via what they call the Corridor Route from Styhead to Lingmell Col, past the treacherous caverns of Piers Gill and Greta Gill, long ravines that scarred the mountainside like unhealed wounds. Angie would take another team—her best people on ice and snow with ropes and crampons and the full kit—across the main ridge. A third team would quarter the lumpy ground around Sprinkling Tarn, under the shadow of Great End, between Styhead and Esk Hause. And if they did not find him like that, then God help him.

Barely north of Lancaster, Faria Duclos discovered that the rain had turned first to sleet and then to snow. In September? What kind of weather did the English have? Before driving out onto the A6 and then the A591, she had checked her route on a road map from the car rental agency. Kendal. Grasmere. Keswick. Borrowdale. Those were all places she recalled Joe Shelby talking about when he discussed his expedition with her. Borrowdale, he had said, was the final point of the journey, the point of arrival, triumph. If he reached Borrowdale, he would have achieved his goal. And how big could Borrowdale be? If she had been able to locate the hidden famines of Ethiopia and the great warrior of the Panjshir Valley in Afghanistan, then surely she could locate one single lover in one single, short English vale. The local news radio station was carrying a lead, breaking story that the mountain rescue had been called out following reports that a man was thought to have gone missing in the worst September weather on record. Faria Duclos thought that search might narrow hers too.

She was driving on a winding road, through small settlements of bungalows and old cottages and cemeteries. The sandstone of the oldest houses had been weathered to a dark, grimy texture and the windows were narrow, set in thick walls to keep off weather and marauders. It was not her open, fecund Mediterranean environment, but there was a warmth to the kitchens espied through the snow flurries and the hearths where people drank tea. It was his land, his combination of closure and welcome, rejection and embrace.

Chapter Twenty-One

Switched tapes, took photograph. Oh, yes. No making that mistake with the Kodak Vestpocket. Lost a glove. But got the photo. The summit photo, with the camera balanced on a rock and on self-timer and me standing there and on the summit and feeling deflated somehow because this was it and all I could imagine was getting down again. Because it's the descent that gets you, really, in the knees and thighs, and most of all it's balance. In this condition, balance is what trips you up. Of course. But like now when you are descending and I think I'm going the right way because the compass says northwest before you loop around, which is the route I'm on. But with one pole—did I mention that I lost the other, that and one glove? Well I did, lose them, that is—you can't quite get the balance on these steep tricky narrow bits where there's no going round the side or making your own way and you have to put the pole out like a blind man testing the ground and find some kind of purchase so you can use the pole as an extra limb. Easier with two. But I lost one. And it's balance that's the issue, not so much

*weakness per se. Because if you lose your balance you're going to fall like I did
back there on the boulder field and it's only a matter of sheer chance or good fortune that I didn't break a bone. On these limbs where the muscles are wasted you
feel the bones too close to the skin. You feel they don't have the covering and support you'd like them to have. So they'll crack, like a whip. Crack and you're down,
gone finished because no one's going to find you up here in this awful murk where
you can't see a damn thing. I mean there I was at the summit of Scafell Pike, at
the highest point in England, and I couldn't even see the summit cairn, which is
as big as a house. But I knew I was there because there was no way up anymore.
All paths led down and that was the miracle. Finally to have achieved it. Praise
God. Thank you, Lord. And no complaints. Take me now if you want me. Because I made it and that's all.*

*Trying now very hard to keep the left hand without the glove in a pocket but
the arm is getting too weak to raise it and stick it into the pocket of the parka
which thank the Lord is the top-of-the-range Arctic Everest model or otherwise
I'd be frozen solid. And that leaves me with the right hand to hold the remaining
pole and sort of crab with the extra limb on the right side but no support on the
left. When I come to a junction in the paths I know I should turn right for Lingmell Col. Corridor Route. Styhead. But I did it and now that I have got my left
hand in my pocket I find it's empty which is very odd as this is the same left
pocket as I put the camera in after the famous summit shots.*

At Esk Hause Angie Cartwright had established an advanced base around
the missing walker's effects, which had been packed with the exception of
his bivouac tent, now in use as a temporary shelter for as many of her team
as could squeeze in out of the blizzard. Then Angie herself with three
other climbers, one radio and two emergency packs had struck out from
Esk Hause onto the ridge, ready with ropes and ice gear and in constant
radio contact. The comms loop now linked base station in Seathwaite to
Esk Hause and Styhead fixed positions and the mobile searchers making
their initial probes. Ken Gill left just four members of his team at the

Stretcher Box. Four would be enough to cope if the man somehow materialized. That left two units of six, one moving cautiously along and parallel to the Corridor Route—except of course for those stretches where it crossed ravines. The other he was leading up the main path heading southeast to Esk Hause in the gusting wind that turned the mini-waterfalls in the stream alongside the track into little maelstroms, blowing back up against themselves in defiance of the laws of gravity and the character of water. On a good day, he knew from many, many visits, his back would be to the huge, stalwart, broad flank of Great Gable with its pink-tinted scree runs and steep, frontal path. And above him, omnipresent, would be the dome of Great End. But this was not a good day. The trail made of boulders was icy and treacherous, slowing their pace. And where it was possible, they spread out—causing further delays—blowing whistles in the vain hope of hearing an answering blast. Past Sprinkling Tarn, he dispatched four searchers to circumvent the small sheet of dark water to look for any signs of a stray walker, a cripple, a man said to be determined but also sick. It was conceivable that, from Esk Hause, he might have chosen this route to descend towards Sty Head and safety. But it was equally possible that, having made that choice, he might have strayed over Seathwaite Fell and Aaron Crags. If Ken Gill admitted it to himself, many other things were possible, too—a fall on Great End, a slip into the abyss of Ruddy Gill. His team made slow progress because they were careful, because they did not want to have to revisit places unnecessarily when the search dug in for the long haul. Once he and his team met up with Angie Cartwright's advance base in the abandoned tent at Esk Hause, they would take stock, reappraise the situation, consider their own options as the day wore on and the afternoon light began to weaken and falter. With ice forming already, the temperatures would only fall to some hideous depth, and with a wind buffeting the murk around them, sending the cloud hurrying like desperate legions, the chill factor would increase as the day wound towards night. This was not a place he wanted his team split and benighted.

The mountains have always said: this is the point beyond which you cannot go. This is your limit. The moral is that your limits narrow and you don't realize until it's much too late. I wanted the walking guide and there it was right in front of me all the time and all I had to do was make the realization that, at some point—same for everybody, really—your horizons begin to narrow, your route is shorter and you move along it with ever-decreasing speed so the point is to set the destination someplace within reach or you finish up like this, beyond your limits. And then you say: but that's how it always was. That's what I always wanted to do. I wanted to set my limits far and wide and I did. I ignored limits. I repudiated limits. I denied their existence. So that, now, just when you needed a walking guide, you ignored what it was telling you. It was telling you to go peck shit with the chickens and you wanted one more chance to soar with the eagles. And you did. You soared to the very summit of England.

Angie Cartwright was pushing them too hard for absolute safety but it was a calculated decision. Her radio told her that Ken Gill had reached Esk Hause without locating the errant walker. So the teams had reunited there, at his camp, and would begin moving back in relays now down towards Styhead, searching and whistling as they went, but primarily with the intention of regrouping. In the comms loop, she heard Ken Gill asking the team on the Corridor Route for a progress report but of course it was negative because, Angie Cartwright knew, the man would either be up here, on the high ridge, or not too far below it. At some stage his energy would run out and that often happened just after summiting with the grim realization that it was all downhill from there on out. If he had summited.

She would like to think he had, just as she always thought that her husband knew when he fell that he had achieved what he set out to do in some more abstruse way that the people who condemned him never understood. There were some people, she believed, who were destined to strive for excellence, to shun mediocrity, and for them the attempt was almost as important as its outcome. So if her husband had fallen and died because he was climbing solo and unroped, then the truth of his demise—the truth to be cherished for Jemima—was that her father had perished knowing that he might well perish as he pushed himself to overcome that risk, to overcome fear. He had died because he was striving for a goal beyond that of normal mortals and that was good and essential, because if no one made those efforts, if no one set courage before humdrum concerns, then the world would be a tawdry place, robbed of ideals, of goals, of purity of spirit.

They had reached Broad Crag col when the omens began to look bad. Close to one another, lying in the snow, were a walking pole and a glove. This was two hundred feet below the summit. Why had he removed a glove at this stage? How could he have lost so vital a piece of equipment as his pole? To her right, slightly to the northwest, she saw a potential answer—a bright dash of blue and yellow, the packaging of a disposable camera. What did they tell her? Was there anything more to them than the Irvine ice ax she had seen in an exhibit, an abandoned oxygen tank on the north ridge, the detritus of a broken altimeter found in Mallory's pocket? What did forensic evidence say about the striving that claimed her husband, or Mallory or Irvine or even this poor deluded cripple she was searching for? Did her findings mean he had or had not been to the summit? And how did you define summit? She ordered a halt. She radioed her findings to Ken Gill. She made her arrangements. She thought that from the way his lost equipment was strewn about it was impossible to conclude whether he had been to the top of Scafell Pike, or summited Broad Crag, or achieved neither. But the main thing, she figured, was to find him.

Eva Kimberly sat hunched in a folding chair in the barn where the rescuers had set up their base. She had been offered, and had accepted, a mug of tea, sickly and sugary, with condensed milk. The rescuers had set up a gas heater around their equipment of radios and cables. There was no signal for mobile phones, but a satellite phone trilled occasionally as radio stations and newspapers called in for an update and were told: nothing yet; stay in touch. Along the lane outside, an outside broadcast van had pulled up, but the rescuers had kept Eva's presence secret from the television crew. Alongside the dry stone wall, a live camera had been set up on a tripod to run automatically, without the tending of a technician, so that, every half hour or so, the reporter would emerge in a miasma of warmth and cigarette smoke from the outside broadcast van to speak earnestly into the solitary camera, broadcasting live to a nation in warm living rooms from a bleak, cold valley in the Lake District. Sometimes, Eva Kimberly caught the reporter's words. "Day wearing on and rescue still in progress" . . . "no sightings so far and hope must by now be fading" . . . "team close to a decision whether to call off before nightfall." She was disturbed by another voice, crackling on the rescue radio, as Angie Cartwright reported finding a walking pole and a glove, a throwaway camera. But no Joe Shelby. And the drifting snow had made his tracks difficult to follow. Eva Kimberly drew her coat closer around her.

"Don't you worry," one of the rescuers told her. "If anyone can find him, Angie Cartwright can." It struck Eva Kimberly that there always seemed to be another woman ready to find a man she did not realize she had lost.

Ken Gill wanted them reunited before nightfall and radioed Angie Cartwright's team to retrace their footsteps to Esk Hause so that the rescuers could begin to regroup. He ordered the Corridor Route team to pull back to Styhead. The emphasis now was on the safety of the team. With only two hours of daylight left, they would be hard-pressed to cover the ground, at least as far as Stockley Bridge, before dusk made the going treacherous. The immediate weather forecast, relayed from Seathwaite base, suggested that the storm had not blown itself out and would intensify before peaking overnight. That meant they would be able to search the following morning with far better visibility, although they would probably be searching for a frozen corpse by that stage. On an impulse, Ken Gill ordered that the walker's tent be left in place and stocked with a ration of food and water, a stove and fuel. In case the man found his way back there. Just in case.

Angie Cartwright had already struck out to the summit of Scafell Pike and returned to Broad Crag col and made her own point on the radio that it made more sense for at least some of her team to descend via the Corridor Route to check out its upper reaches. Ken Gill said he was not sure that wasn't risky. Angie Cartwright said it was risky whichever way she went, but it would be plain wrong to avoid ground where the lost walker might still be. Eva Kimberly heard the disagreement from Seathwaite base and prayed that the woman up there on the mountain would prevail. But she could tell that the signs were looking bad. The old-timers had lost their jollity and their jokes and had taken to standing outside the barn, in the swirl of snowflakes, peering up towards the mountains, smoking their cigarettes with a slight bitterness. After a conversation with one of them, the TV reporter broadcast live to say it was now increasingly likely that the search would be called off in the failing light and terrible weather. And, after apparently listening to a question from the studio, the reporter said: "Exactly. It would indeed take a miracle for anyone to survive the night out there." Spoiling the broadcast, a brown hen pecked a way across the road and a small dog yapped somewhere off-camera.

TAPE FIVE, SEGMENT THREE
SEPTEMBER 16, 2000
MONITORED SEPTEMBER 17

So that's it, I guess, my story. The last chapter. I can't quite believe this is really it, but it must be. I just can't go on anymore. I have given of my best and it's time.

Not just balance you need, but a certain elan, flexibility, the ability to hop and maneuver. And I've got neither now. So just sit down for a moment. Like to roll one and difficult because left hand white and feel a bit sleepy. Kill for a hit of Johnnie. Prisoner's last request. Death Row. Didn't think it would necessarily come to this, but there was always the chance. Followed the route down from the summit heading northwest then found a trail going north-northeast so must be on the right route. But it's difficult to see because of the snow and the cold makes my eyelids feel as if they've iced up. Getting darker now and the storm is quite strong but it's odd that I feel so warm considering that everything else is frozen. Found this flat rock and when the snow recedes I can see a big black hole in the mountain side and I suppose that is the gateway we all fear and in the end all welcome when the struggling is over. Like now. I think of them, Eva and Faria, and I want to say goodbye, farewell and thank you and good night. Thank you for putting up with me. Thank you for loving me and letting me love you. Don't want to weep. But I am weeping and the tears are freezing because I'm sorry, sorry that I let you down, failed you both when you needed me. Betrayed, really, is the word for it. So forgive me if you hear this, forgive my treachery and know that I meant no harm and meant to love properly. I want to be angry. I want to rage against the dying of the light but I have no strength to rage against my broken nerves any longer so if it could be gentle into that good night then that's fine by me. For I see now that the mystery is redeemed and I have been granted my triumph in this

258

realm as a final gift before passing to the next, so the faith is confirmed in my soul and the Lord has guided me and sent an angel to be my guide from this mountain to the parallel universe. Only, I didn't take the moment to take her face in my hands and look the last time into those eyes and say in my way I loved you the best and forgive me, dear Lord, forgive me, all the failings that came with it. And I wanted so badly to have this solemn parade around the paddock but I never realized it would be the last forever and ever amen so there is no chance now to say all those things you store up for the last moment, the final testament you offer to the people you have loved and hurt and damaged. And there's no time or place now to look for the absolution you crave from them when you say to the ones you loved the most: please give me your blessing at this last moment and forgive me my sins and crimes and selfishness, for the ego is a great corrupter, and tell me, please tell me, that I was not all bad and did some good and finally that you were proud of me sometimes and thought me worthy. When I look into your eyes I can read the hurt there, my darling, and I want my tears to wash it all away and I want you to forgive me more than anything or anybody and I want you to draw a cross of tears on my forehead and release me with your benediction. Dearest one. My only love. The temptation to sleep now is quite strong so I guess that must be—

It made the national television news. The camera showed what looked, at first, like a necklace of lights strung out across the snowy, blustery lower slopes. The lights turned out to be the headlamps worn by the thirty-two members of the Mountain Rescue Team as they pulled back from Styhead Pass and down towards Stockley Bridge. Between them— heavy and awkward to manhandle—they carried the stretcher from the wooden box at the summit of the pass. On it, a bundle, a bulky, human form, strapped in as the team descended to prevent it from falling.

The base team, along with Eva Kimberly, had moved up to Stockley Bridge and the TV crew had followed them for this final act of the drama. They waited, now, quietly as the procession descended the last steep section of the Styhead trail and crossed from east to west. Ken Gill led the way and Angie Cartwright kept close to the stretcher, leaning over it as they bore it across the stone bridge.

"Did he make it to the summit?" Eva Kimberly asked.

"Oh yes, certainly," Angie Cartwright replied, thinking, yes, he made it to his summit.

Chapter Twenty-Two

Angie Cartwright told Eva Kimberly that she found Joe Shelby perched above the deep ravine of Piers Ghyll on the Corridor Route. In the old days, she said, it had been called the Guide's Route and that was quite ironic because he had been asleep on a flat rock, sliding towards oblivion, and, when she awoke him with a rough shake, he said to her: are you the walking guide? Are you my guide? Humoring him she said: yes, I'm your walking guide. And he said: good, that's very good.

With the big lads in the team supporting him they managed to grapple him down the steep zigzags and slippery surfaces of the Scafell Pike flank to Styhead where the rest of the team huddled from the weather. There, with water warmed to exactly 40 degrees centigrade, they thawed out his frozen left hand and poured hot drinks full of sugar and cups of soup down his throat until at least the danger of hypothermia had passed. They kept him walking at intervals just to make sure that the worst was over and the medics on the team said he'd be fine so all he'd need now was a hot bath and a week's sleep. They used the stretcher from Styhead pass to get him down the steep and tricky bits towards the valley floor because he was very weak, from exhaustion, not just from his condition. To have reached the point he had, Angie Cartwright reckoned, he must have been running on willpower alone but that, too, had finally fizzled out and he displayed all the signs that usually precede a hypothermia death. Right at the end, as they crossed Stockley Bridge, she said, he had tried to raise himself up from the stretcher to walk the last few yards, but had fallen back.

The team escorted them to the hotel, assuring her that while no bones were broken and while his core temperature had been restored to normal, he was a very tired, very fortunate man. Privately, Ken Gill thought him a very foolish man. Angie Cartwright leavened her assessment of his stupidity with a sprinkling of admiration for his courage: in his condition, to have gone up there, alone, that needed bottle, she said, and didn't mind who knew it.

Arriving back at the suite—advanced base—Eva Kimberly helped him peel off his wet cold boots and gaiters, leaving him with his privacy to struggle free of thermal underclothing, rank from three days' uninterrupted wear. She helped him negotiate the treacherous descent into a hot, drowsy bathtub and the subsequent transfer to the big double bed, underneath the down comforter, where he slept immediately. But she did not sleep at all—not after she found his tapes and tape player in a zipped inner pocket of his parka and began to listen.

At first, she was filled with fondness at his boyish enthusiasms, his keenness. She stirred guiltily at his expressions of faith in her, at his thoughts of abandoning the project in order to return to her. And, she wondered, how might that have changed the course of events if he had returned prematurely to advanced base to find her in wrestled embrace with Jeremy Davenport? He had called out to his Ruth, waiting in the valley below, but she had proved to be his Jezebel. She sipped steadily at her whisky, her chosen confessor, asking herself: where should the forgiveness begin? Who should forgive whom?

Then, as the other disclosures unfolded with that insufferably self-absorbed arrogance of his kind, her mood darkened. The egotism spilling from the little silver machine was monstrous. The use of his malady as a justification and a cover for his failings was obscene. The illness was not simply a set of physical consequences, but the center of the entire universe, placed there for all to gyrate around in a dance of homage. Whatever crime or sin he committed, his condition absolved him.

Over and over again she played back his crude justifications and definitions of betrayal, his gloating over the tryst in Room 5 of the American Colony after his appalling display on the television. If there was a parallel with her own behavior at advanced base, then it eluded her, for he had shown no remorse at all and neither had he behaved as if he meant a clean break with anybody.

He had not for one moment thought of returning home to London, to Eva Kimberly. It had not occurred to him that his televised treachery had wounded her grievously and he should therefore fly forthwith to her side to bring comfort and reassurance, take the consequences of his actions like a man. No. He was far too cowardly for that, far too remote from any kind of nobility of feeling or birth. There was no hint of simple, ordinary kindness or compassion, just the mumbo jumbo worship of the French bitch he had once called crazy and now seemed to be restoring to her pedestal. Yes, he had kissed her in front of the whole world. Yes, he had lied brazenly on the telephone to London that same evening, thrice denying the impostor even as she sat at his side in their disgusting love nest, even as they wove their coy secrets. *"And was there sex? I suppose there was."*

He "supposed."

As if Judas Iscariot "supposed" he had received thirty pieces of silver but could not quite recall the details of the transaction.

. . .

At first light, Eva Kimberly pulled back the heavy, lined drapes. She saw a sky whose rage had gone, cauterized by the same storms as had made the final tapes so indistinct. Outside, the lake mirrored the foothills—indigo water, emerald slopes, sky losing dawn's rose-glow to a hard azure. But there was nothing to stay for, least of all the view.

She opened the small black notebook he had presented to her before he started, and, uncapping a gold-nibbed fountain pen, wrote a single line: "You made me a foolish wife." She wanted to say more but did not trust her rage. She wanted to wake him and break him, pull at his hair and scratch at his body and shout at him: I was ready to screw Jeremy Davenport and would have if he had not failed, do you hear? But, looking at him, stubbled and pale, deep in sleep, she felt suddenly too drained, as if his betrayal had anesthetized her against passion. She wondered if a heart could be broken simply by being tugged hither and thither for too long.

She placed the notebook and the tapes together with the fax from Joe Shelby's neurologist, promising a new diagnosis. Mercifully, after hearing the tapes, that was no longer her problem. He had forfeited her concern. He had freed her of the burden of his illness. Let his crazy French bitch fret for him now. Let them all try to work out if anyone had emerged unscathed from the fission that began unheralded at Naivasha.

She repacked her travel bag with all its vain finery and fripperies and closed the door on him gently so as not to wake him, no longer requiring or wishing for his witness. She switched off her mobile phone so that no man might reach her. As she drove away, she saw a parked car in the hotel forecourt. For a second Eva Kimberly thought the woman at the wheel, behind the misted windows, looked remarkably like a woman who had once gate-crashed her African party—her whole life, really. But she knew that was preposterous, impossible. Surely.

Joe Shelby awoke close to lunchtime. He had slept for more than fifteen hours. His leg muscles ached excruciatingly. The effort of leaving his bed made him dizzy with the exertion. His body felt as though it had been passed involuntarily through gigantic steel rollers. He was enormously weary, drained of energy. He had memories of reaching a summit and then of sleeping. It seemed to him—although he could not confirm the veracity of his impressions—that he had achieved his goal and then readied himself to die, allowing the blackness without exit to fold its warm cloak over him. But an angel had come to him, dressed in fleece and Gore-Tex, a small, round, feisty angel who shook him back to life, chased the blackness away and said she was his walking guide.

His boots had been removed and he was naked and washed. His chin was rough with new beard and his scalp itched. He was thirsty enough to drink a lake and hungry enough to devour an ox. The tips of his fingers felt tender, as if they had been plunged into hot coals, and he thought the paper might cut his skin when he raised a stained faxed message that said: hold the Mayo—a reprieve, surely. And he understood that the mystery worked both ways, in the offering of faith and in the receipt of its blessings—ineffable, but never completely unconditional: if he had not called, he would not have been answered.

It was the angel who had brought him back here, and, clearly, had made a mistake, bringing him back to this world from the cusp of the next, but to a location he did not quite recognize: where was Eva who had been there when the stretcher bumped the final feet over the bridge, who had helped him clamber into the warm, safe bed? He had returned to life from death's frontier, but life had changed as if someone had rewritten his drama, without reason or explanation. He felt woozy and reached for support from a bedpost, as if he was caught up in one of those dreams where a swimmer struggles for the surface but cannot reach it.

Then he saw his tapes, neatly stacked, and the notebook that contained only a one-line message in her handwriting. Part of the puzzle fell into place. He had not meant the tapes as a testimony, as evidence. She had misunderstood. She had not heard the full account. She had not heard that, high on the mountain, when he did not know whether he would live or die, he had pledged himself to her, forswearing the dark other who would always stalk his dreams. When he found her, having lunch, perhaps, or taking a stroll, or drinking coffee, he would tell her, set matters straight. But, when he called down to reception to inquire about her whereabouts, he was told by a clerk that Ms. Kimberly and the gentleman had both checked out.

Both?

Yes, both.

Epilogue

She stood behind him, holding the handles to his wheelchair. His face was lopsided from the stroke he had suffered shortly before she returned home, but Neville Kimberly had not for one moment considered postponing or canceling his annual garden party. And so they were a reception line of two, stricken father and only child, back from what he had taken to referring to as her gap year, her year away. She was wearing a long-sleeved dress and brimmed straw hat to protect her pale skin from the unfamiliar sunlight. Her legs were bitten from a trip to the Rift Valley, to her schools and clinics where the young children lined up and clapped their small hands to welcome her home. Her father had insisted on his usual, tailored safari suit, refusing the blanket the nurse thought to throw over his weakened legs. Together, they surveyed the motley crowd, picking out the familiar guests, the cabinet ministers and business personalities, the doddery hunters and leather-skinned ranchers, the true bloods, as he called them.

"No gate crashers this year, Evie." His speech was slightly slurred but she caught the ironic, forgiving intonation.

"Not this year, Pops. No surprises."

Neither of them made mention of the fact that, for the first time ever, the Davenports, their dynastic neighbors, were absent. The gossips, of course, knew why: Jeremy had, it was said, been wronged and spurned, not once, but twice—not simply when she left him but when he flew to England to be at her side after the humiliation of that television broadcast. So how on earth could anyone expect the Davenports to behave as if nothing had happened? How could the Davenports do anything but return their embossed invitation card?

The reality was different, but Eva Kimberly had no energy or inclination to try to set the record straight. The Davenports were absent because there had been a conclave of the two families' elders. Testimony had been given, facts established and it was deemed inappropriate that there should be further embarrassment, or—worse still—public recrimination. Jeremy Davenport, in any event, was considering his options. It was said he was somehow involved in a newly established and somewhat shady diamond trading venture in the Congo and Zimbabwe. But she made no further inquiries. She had been a foolish wife for two men— but spouse to neither—and she deserved better than that. Much better. And if she could not have better from a partner, a love, then, well, perhaps it was preferable to have no one at all.

⬧

Faria Duclos accompanied Joe Shelby from the Lake District to the private clinic where Nigel Lampton, the neurologist, oversaw a treatment that would restore some of his strength but leave him dependent on regular infusions of medication for his mobility and vigor. A Faustian pact, Joe Shelby called it, with no clear term but one evident victory: three years tops was now extended indefinitely. He might even make it to a riper age.

Together Faria and Joe witnessed the efficacy of the medication that made his dead left arm begin to move again—as mysterious a process as a snake charmer summoning a serpent from a wicker basket. He flexed his arm like Tarzan. He made the biceps jump. He felt strength ease back into his legs so that the limp became less pronounced. Strolling in a park, he tossed away his remaining walking pole from the mountains with his revived left arm. He laughed. He cried. He knew, again, that if he had not asked, he would not have been delivered. And she knew that her mission had been accomplished: she had brought him this far after his ordeal; she had been at his side to discover whether the treatment would succeed or fail. She had been available for the worst of tidings and rejoiced at the best of news that made her vigil redundant.

Joe Shelby had spoken to Eva once directly and several times through lawyers who arranged an amicable division of their goods and chattels. She had been stunningly, graphically honest about events while he was on the hills. Her disclosures helped him understand her conclusion that their relationship was torn beyond repair.

Sitting in his room at the clinic in London, he and Faria Duclos watched the television news bulletins offering the familiar diet of blood and cordite. He felt no great hankering to be there, in the thick of it, but sensed her restlessness. He said that, if the comic did not call, he would not call either and was far more interested in perhaps returning to the hills, to thank the rescuers, to spy out a cottage that might be purchased for half the revenue from the enforced sale of an apartment in Primrose Hill. He knew Faria Duclos would bend idiom to say she wanted to trot the last paddock once more. But he would need time before he heard that call so clearly again.

ALAN S. COWELL, born in England, has been a foreign correspondent for Reuters and *The New York Times* for three decades. He has covered conflicts in the Middle East and Africa and, in 1985, was awarded the George Polk Award for his reportage from South Africa, whence he was expelled by the apartheid regime in 1987. He lives in London.